THE
VIKING SANDS

Thomas Torrens

The Viking Sands

Copyright © 2011 by Thomas Torrens

Please contact the author with your feedback at:

thomastorrens@aol.com

Dedicated with great appreciation to my principal Muse,

Rebecca.

CONTENTS

PROLOGUE

"My lot in life is that of a grain of sand."

July 14th, 2011, Chryse Planitia, Mars

Today NASA's Viking 3 spacecraft would be heading home. Three months earlier it had flawlessly completed its 270 day voyage from Earth, landing, without incident, on rock-strewn Chryse Planitia, not 500 meters away from where its predecessor, Viking 1, had set down 31 years before. The spacecraft had successfully completed all but one of its myriad scientific tasks and was now within the launch window for its 9 month return journey back to Earth.

The ultimate goal of Viking 3's mission was to be markedly different from those of the previous two Viking missions. While this spacecraft had also conducted sophisticated tests of the Martian soil, searching for any clues of microbiological life, it would attempt to do what no other Mars lander had yet done – return a sample of the rich, red Martian soil to Earth for comprehensive testing at NASA's sterile, secure Mars Soil Receiving Laboratory in Houston. Finally, perhaps, a long-standing scientific debate could be definitively resolved.

When the Viking 1 and 2 landers touched down on Mars in the summer of 1976, each carried an identical set of biological experiments to search for signs of life. Uncertainty and doubt then continued for 35 years thereafter, stemming from the enigmatic results of two of the experiments: the Labeled Release detection experiment and the Gas Exchange experiment, both of which produced tantalizing but inconclusive results.

In both cases, small samples of scooped Martian soil were exposed to a rich "nutrient soup" containing carbon-14. The experiments produced large quantities of radio-labeled gas and copious volumes of oxygen. Even under such cold, dark and hostile conditions, they also produced what appeared to be telltale fingerprints of combusted organics -- the same chemicals the Viking scientists had originally dismissed as contaminants from Earth. Only after a belated reassessment of the Viking results in 2010, using new technology, did they finally conclude that they were of Martian origin.

Most significantly, both experiments generated searing heat and radiant energy, totally unexpected by their designers. In almost an instant, the nutrient soup had been completely and violently consumed, leaving not the slightest residue. It was both highly dramatic and quite puzzling. No one could begin to explain these bizarre results. Perhaps there was a chemical practical joker in the soil? Some kind of super-oxidant, like a perchlorate? But such oxidants are thought to be incompatible with life, as they destroy carbon-based materials. Finding organics, after all, is not evidence of either present or past life –it's just evidence of organics. In any event, the question of life aside, it was clear that Martian soil possessed unique and tantalizing chemical proper-ties that could only be verified by controlled laboratory testing on Earth.

Viking 3 prepared to initiate its final task before launch, aimed at collecting and bringing its sample home. Responding to pre-programmed commands from the orbiting Pathfinder craft above, Viking 3 extended its collector boom, fitted with a metal scoop, one last time to gather a sample of Martian soil. Breaking through the lighter crust, it filled its blade with rich, deep red, sandy soil from below – about 200 grams. Then it carefully retracted the scoop back into its core and emptied its contents into a sterile self-sealing container. Viking 3's cameras continued to scan the horizon as, its last but most critical task now done, it initiated preliminary countdown to launch sequence.

Looking north from its landing site, Viking 3's cameras revealed the same familiar landscape of fine orange sand in gently rolling dunes, littered with pebbles and rocks. Dust lay in drifts behind rocks and mantled the tops of boulders. It hung in the air like a hazy smog, scattering the weakened sunlight into a diffuse, creamy orange-pink sky. Not too far away, across this rusty vista, the sun glistened on the hull of Viking 1, which had gone dormant many years before. While almost fully buried in flour-fine sand, the unmistakable red, white and blue insignia had survived the ravages of the thin Martian atmosphere. Above the far horizon, one of Mars' two small moons, Phobos, transited the sky. The midday temperature was a warmish –24 degrees Fahrenheit. All seemed quite tranquil.

Yet something was amiss. The anemometer atop Viking 3 had begun to turn. Wind speed began to accelerate quickly from a gentle 16 km/h SW breeze to readings of 32, 64, 96 km/h and greater. Panning its cameras around towards the equatorial south, Viking 3 saw a very different sight. Dust devils, wide and high as houses, whirled towards the spacecraft. They crackled with static electricity that could disrupt Viking's sensitive electronics. Behind them, the sky had turned a dark, blood red. The horizon was completely obscured by the beginnings of a horrific Martian sand storm that soon would cover the entire plain in a deep, impenetrable haze. Wind speeds quickly acceler-ated to hurricane force before the anemometer ceased to register. Nevertheless, the internal countdown to takeoff had begun and it was too late to stop it. The narrow launch window was *now*, and Viking 3 was already too far committed to turn back.

Immediately Viking 3 went into survival mode. Already shuddering from the growing tempest, it initiated steps to secure itself for blast off –

TEN: all external appendages were retracted into the core to trim the spacecraft for take off;

NINE: the light titanium alloy panels atop the ship slid into position to seal the nose cone into an aerodynamic bullet-shaped projectile;

EIGHT, SEVEN: racing against the approaching storm, pre-heating of the precious remaining fuel commenced;

SIX, FIVE: already shaking in the howling wind, Viking 3 com-menced ignition procedures for its main engine and navigational stability thrusters;

FOUR: bolts were blown to detach the ship from the base of its landing pad and from its lower extremities resting on the Mar-tian surface;

THREE: fuel pressure buildup peaked and fuel was pumped to the waiting engines;

TWO: ignition; and

ONE: *LIFT OFF!*

Struggling mightily against the shrieking tempest, Viking 3 slowly rose off its launch pad on a column of fire. The winds buffeted it mercilessly as it accelerated through the Martian troposphere, roiling with flying dust and debris. The angry blasts threatened to topple it and crush it like a discarded tin can. Yet, relentlessly, it gained altitude, and reached the boiling cloud tops as it entered the Martian mesosphere at 100 km, just above the tempestuous weather below. From there it would be smoother sailing, on through the deep blue of the outer fringes of the atmosphere and into the black, silent, stillness of outer space.

Course corrections received, Viking 3, now quickly escaping the last pull of the red planet's gravity, programmed itself into a Hohman transfer orbit to begin its 9-month journey back to Earth. As it left Martian airspace, it passed within 5 km of its twin backup craft, Viking 4, in a temporary parking orbit, waiting on the weather, for the descent to its assigned landing spot on Utopia Planitia.

Finally, after all of the years and many other unmanned missions, a spacecraft would return Martian soil to Earth for testing. The Viking sands were on their way to the faint blue star, 225 million kilometers distant, with both unknown and inconceivable future consequences.

PART 1
AWAKENING

"A single event can awaken within us a stranger totally unknown to us."

I

Tuesday, May 22nd, 2012, 17:00 CDT, Houston, Texas

Albert Stern was in big trouble. In less than a day NASA's Senior Mission Controller for the Viking missions had watched unbelievingly as his whole world crumbled around him. He was under investigation for being a criminal, even a terrorist. It was completely unnerving. And all of this had quite unexpectedly descended upon him with lightening speed because of the Viking sands – the seemingly harmless specimen of Martian soil that he was testing in NASA's laboratory in Houston.

Home early from work, Albert sat alone in his Houston townhouse, badly confused and agitated. Not usually a drinking man, he opened a bottle of Johnny Walker Green Pure Malt and poured himself a stiff one, drinking it down neat. Seeking distraction for his racing mind, he turned on his TV to the movie channels. On HBO was a re-run of "The Hunt for Red October". Captain Ramius, a Lithuanian-born Soviet submarine commander of the USSR's most advanced nuclear sub, was trying to defect to the US, taking the sub, the Red October, with him. He sought political asylum and a new life in America. In exchange he'd deliver the USSR's techno-miracle craft to the West. As Albert felt the warm glow from the Scotch broadening and relaxing his mind, he was drawn further into the plot.

What had his bright, young Assistant Director, Yoshi Tanaka, said to him about the Martian soil, the sands from the Viking spacecraft? "With its insatiable appetite for crude oil, it could be the most devastating weapon of the 21st century!" Like the Red October, perhaps? What incredible demon had he unwittingly stumbled upon? And what of his own life now in Houston; in America? He was soon to be out of the job he loved and, perhaps, even sooner, he would be in a jail. What was the sense in staying put to face the inevitable? Fight or flight: Albert had always chosen fight before. Now he realized that the odds were too heavily stacked against him to pursue that option. He had no choice this time but to flee. His inevitable midlife crisis had come quite suddenly and much too early.

Albert had an open Business Class ticket to London on United Airlines. It was meant to take him there in the week to come for his 15th class reunion at Jesus College, Cambridge, where he had done his graduate work in science and math. Now the authorities would forbid him from going anywhere. But he hadn't yet surrendered his passport. And the more he thought about it, he wouldn't. No, he would get the hell out of Houston, before the FBI inevitably linked the events of the last day together and pinned them all on him. The neocon bastards would impound the Viking sands and use them as their own weapon. He would be ground exceeding small by the wheels of justice; incarcerated; forgotten altogether in the turmoil. Not exactly what he had in mind for the rest of his life. No, he would not let that happen. "Life's a crap-shoot at best", he thought.

Albert dialed the 800 number for United Airlines reservations. The next flight for London was leaving at 11:46 AM the following morning. He would be on it with the Viking sands. What he would do with them when he got to London was still evolving in his head. But first, Albert knew, he needed to escape, and quickly. When the authorities came to search his flat the next morning he would already be gone.

Comforted by his decision, Albert fell into an ever deepening alcoholic haze. Involuntarily his racing mind played out the events of the last day and a half that had gotten him into his now desperate situation. How had this all happened so suddenly to him? Slowly, painfully, he began to remember....

Monday, May 21st, 2012, 07:00 CDT

At 7:00 AM, Albert Stern's Bose wave radio alarm began increasing in volume to awaken him from a deep sleep. The strains of Pachelbel's Canon in D Major soon filled both the room and Albert's growing consciousness. As he opened his eyes he could see through the window that the weather outside would be another hot, humid, late spring day in Houston. But no matter about the monotonous weather. Today, he reminded himself, was to be the most important of his career thus far with NASA.

After a quick shower and shave Albert sat down briefly before his HD TV. Sipping on a mug of dark roast coffee, he switched the channel to CNBC to hear the pre-opening stock market commentary. The crawler below the stoic faced commentator showed that both the Dow and NASDAQ futures were sharply down once again. There seemed little to suggest that the US economy would be emerging soon from its second, devastating, downward-spiraling recession in less than 5 years.

Basic commodity and food prices were surging worldwide causing acute shortages, but crude oil was the absolute king. Futures for it were up sharply again, placing the price above $200/barrel – more than ten times the price only nine years before. Supply was critically short and worldwide petro-politics ruled. Despite the environmental devastation that had been caused by the BP oil spill in the Gulf of Mexico, the US had reopened the area, as well as ANWAR in Alaska, to virtually unregulated drilling. All to no avail, however. The desperately needed petroleum reserves just weren't there. So once again, crude oil, and those who possessed it, was playing havoc with the world's biggest but stumbling economy.

Albert Stern was the Senior Mission Controller and Chief Scientist for the new generation of Viking missions to Mars. For Stern, the job marked the pinnacle of a very promising and rewarding career to date. He had grown up on the upper east side of New York City in a nominally Jewish, secular family. His father was a successful corporate lawyer; his mother a dilettante socialite who dabbled in charitable causes. So Albert came from some real money, albeit, *nouveau*. But he didn't come from much love. A dour Scottish nanny had raised him almost from birth. His parents had bought into the whole upwardly mobile social ethic and they had little time for a child's preoccupations. As soon as Albert was old enough, he started attending a full-time day school where he spent his afternoon hours mostly in solitary self-amusement, until his nanny came to collect him at day's end. If he saw his parents at all, it was for a perfunctory, approving chat before they went out for yet another evening on the town.

Instinctively, Albert sought to fill the large void in his life with imagination and growing self-sufficiency. He made few friends. He shunned social contact all through school. He was always the odd man out; the little Jewish boy who was somehow different from his primarily WASP classmates. He didn't truly appreciate the distinction, but he quickly learned that it was pejorative. He found himself the butt of cruel jokes and subtle discrimination that set him off hard against the world. Often he was deliberately pushed and shoved, causing him a barely suppressed rage that gnawed at him for several days after each incident. While he never retaliated, he began harboring elaborate fantasies of revenge, imagining the pain he would make these bullies feel one day. And he had no one to whom to turn. His parents offered neither real love nor understanding. Albert lived alone in a world of privilege, at the price of severe emotional deprivation and deep-seated, smoldering anger.

But he wasn't entirely alone. Albert's immigrant, merchant jeweler grandparents had been Holocaust survivors, and, despite the new world transformation of the next generation of Sterns to nominally Reformed, they remained Orthodox Jews. They were genuinely caring people who radiated some much needed warmth to their grandson, whenever they could find the time to see him, which was infrequent, at best. Albert grew fond of his grandparents and, thus, went through the motions of observing some of the more important rituals of their faith as a concession to their beliefs. They had told him of the atrocities of the Holocaust, their persecution, pain and narrow escape. But the elder Sterns had somehow managed to secret a cache of precious stones with them from the old world and had subsequently prospered in the diamond trade in lower Manhattan. In loving appreciation of their only grandson, they had established a modest trust for his education and subsistence. The *corpus* of the trust had devolved to Albert on his thirty-fifth birthday. He had invested it wisely, mostly offshore, through his Cayman Islands asset management account that he had set up years before, while he was a graduate student in England.

Recognized early as gifted, Albert progressed through prep school in Connecticut and then on to Columbia University. There he majored in science and math and graduated *magna cum laude*. He was awarded a Fulbright Grant to do his graduate studies at the University of Cambridge, in England, where he took his Masters degree in pure mathematics and quantum physics. While a graduate student at Jesus College, he found time informally to study astronomy as well – his great passion since childhood. He frequently attended lectures by the protégé of the legendary Fred Hoyle, Dr. Martin Rees, then Professor of Astronomy and a Fellow of King's College. Upon returning to America, he won a research position at Cornell University's Laboratory for Planetary Studies, where he wrote his PhD thesis under the supervision of Professor Carl Sagan. Eschewing a teaching career, he signed on with NASA, where he was recognized for his brilliance and rose quickly through the hierarchy.

Fifteen years into his NASA career, the agency announced the second generation Viking missions to Mars: twin spacecraft to be launched in 2011, to rendezvous with the red planet in 2012, and to return with soil samples for controlled testing on Earth. Albert already occupied a senior scientific position within the agency, but he saw this as his best chance and seized upon it. He applied for, and was selected, to head-up and oversee the mission and its staff.

All was not work for Albert, though. Tall, slim but muscular, handsome, with olive complexion, dark hair and eyes, he was a good athlete all through school. His interests never ran to team sports, preferring instead to compete with himself, whenever possible. He ran cross-country, hiked and rock-climbed. At Cambridge he accompanied his friends from the Cambridge University Mountaineering Club for long weekend scrambles in the English Peak District and the Scottish Cairngorms. In summer, during the Long Vacation Term, he headed for the French Alps, finding odd jobs in Chamonix to support his climbing passion. One Christmas break he had journeyed to Argentine Patagonia with a few of his CUMC colleagues for an idyllic, if Spartan, few weeks of southern hemisphere summer camping and climbing in the Andes. He had especially loved the vast Patagonian wilderness and he had promised himself to return to it one day. The irony of his settling professionally in Houston, where the terrain was so very flat that one could roll a tennis ball, unimpeded, all the way east to the Mississippi River, presented Albert with no satisfaction.

Perhaps the most telling example of the deep emotional void in Albert's early life occurred one late summer day, high in the French Alps, above Chamonix. He was climbing the treacherously difficult Bonatti Pillar on *Les Drus* with Desmond Price, one of his CUMC colleagues. Just two hundred feet below the summit, with Albert leading the pitch, the rope caught awkwardly on a protruding, razor-sharp granite chip. Albert had placed a piton in above him for protection when he had gained his stance on a narrow, exposed ledge. He had already signaled his friend to move up the rope, using his jumar ascenders. It was too late for Albert to try to free the rope with a pendulum motion from above. He couldn't see his rope mate below, but he could feel the tension on the rope increase as Price began to move up. The sixty feet of strong, nylon rope stretched under the stress, but failed to budge off the protrusion. As the rope flexed it repeatedly rubbed against the sharp granite flake. At the stress point, the taught rope began to fray. All of a sudden this pitch had become an unexpected race against death for his friend to surmount the obstacle and gain the security of the undamaged rope above the flake. Then, without warning, the piton belay above Albert popped out of its crack with a tremendous, destabilizing tug, leaving the full weight of Price in Albert's hands. Could he hold him against the abyss? Strangely, Albert didn't panic, nor did he feel any anxiety. He knew full well the likely consequences, but deep inside he was an emotionally empty well. The likely death of his colleague - his friend - stirred no strong feelings within him whatsoever. But the precariousness of his own position spurred Albert into cold, calculated action. He would have to let go of the rope to save himself. Remorselessly, he did so, at the exact same moment that the rope snapped in two at the frayed stress point. As Price fell 3,000 feet to his death on the glacier below, the remnants of the rope tumbled to Albert's feet on the narrow ledge. Without emotion, he picked it up and put it into his rucksack. There would be hard questions asked of him down below in the valley and back in England. Setting a new secure belay, Albert rappelled successively down the huge rock wall and walked reflectively back into town to the local *gendarmarie.* The eventual outcome of the inquiry was a finding of death by misadventure. Albert was fully exonerated and strangely un-scarred by the fatal incident. As with many things in his life so far, he had felt nothing: only a familiar empty void.

Unmarried at age 40, Albert was attractive to and attracted by women, but, somehow, he had never found the time to fit one into his life on a long-term basis. Great sex was always stimulating for him, but never on an enduring relationship basis. Perhaps it was the pressure of work; perhaps diffidence; or perhaps both. He tended to be a perfectionist. He liked order in all things around him; predictable patterns, with everything under control. He was heartily convinced of the importance of the work he was doing for NASA, almost to the exclusion of all else. This fostered a feeling of self-importance, which often grated noticeably on his colleagues. He lived in his own private world of supreme self-confidence, certain that life's real misfortunes were never meant to touch him. True, he had known some adversity, but he had sealed himself off from it, having become hardened and indifferent to the sufferings of others. Deep down, underneath, though, he sometimes wondered how he would react if he ever had to face serious personal hardship. But then he would quickly reassure himself that he would handle it easily, with the same cool confidence with which he did everything else.

Albert refilled his coffee mug and then switched the channel over to CNN. The news wasn't any better there. There were still over 50,000 US "advisory" troops in Iraq, desperately shoring up a civil war torn State that had been through three new governments and four national elections since 2005. Despite what the neo-conservative hawks at the Department of Defense had said in 2003, Iraqi oil production had never climbed back anywhere near to its all time peak of 3.7 million barrels/day. No funds were forthcoming from there to pay the costs of war and insurgency, running to over two trillion dollars so far. Worse than that, US-led NATO forces was still mired in a Vietnam-type counter insurgency with the Taliban in Afghanistan. The war there had dragged on for over a decade with neither measurable results and nor a plausible end in sight.

Next door to Iraq, in Iran, hard line President Mahmoud Ahmadinejad had severed all dialogue with the EU and the IEA over nuclear fuel enrichment and boasted that he now had batteries of nuclear-tipped Shihab-4 missiles aimed at Israel, ready for deployment at anytime. The hands of both the North Koreans and the Russians aiding the Iranians were plain for all to see. The "surge" in US troops in Iraq in 2007 had severely heightened tensions with Iran, as well as with Syria, and no dialogue was possible with these intransigent, hard line regimes. The Saudis, angered by the slaughter of the Sunni minority in Iraq, had cut back on its oil shipments to the West and had also ceased to act as OPEC's swing producer to balance out the world's dwindling crude oil supply.

The recent toppling of entrenched dictatorial regimes in Tunisia, Egypt, Libya and Syria had vastly exacerbated the situation. A wave of civilian rage was sweeping through the Middle East and North Africa, adding a strong fear factor to the already precarious world crude oil supply situation. The combination was driving prices ever higher, with no foreseeable end in sight. No one dared even think about the unthinkable possibility that the octogenarian Saudi monarchy could fall next. That would be Armageddon for world oil supplies and utter bankruptcy for the self-styled central banker of world oil.

Closer to home, in South America, Hugo Chavez in Venezuela, Evo Morales in Bolivia and other emerging leftist regimes in Chile, Argentina and Ecuador had chilled relations with the US to a new low. Mexico, overwhelmed by drug cartel violence and smarting with insult at the hard line INS policing of their US border, was turning sharply anti-American. Canada, awash in heavy oil sands and natural gas, was dragging its feet about building large, new pipelines across its environmentally sensitive arctic tundra just to feed the US market.

The net effect was the slowing to a trickle of oil to America from some of its historically biggest suppliers. It all added up to an ever-deepening economic crisis at home, brought on by the world's most lucrative but volatile commodity. As the US sank deeper into an energy-starved depression, the world's biggest institutional investors and sovereign wealth funds showed less and less inclination to continue to finance the already massive and growing federal deficit through purchases of Treasury bills and bonds. Liquidity had all but dried up and the international financial system teetered on the brink of collapse again, just as it had in 2008.

By 8:30 AM Albert had seen and heard enough of the world's troubles. He flicked off the TV, locked his apartment and headed down to the garage. There he started up his vintage British racing green 1979 MGB convertible, top down, and set off for NASA's Johnson Space Center headquarters through the morning rush of traffic. No air conditioning, but then, very good gas mileage. Which reminded him, he was very low on fuel, but he could stop to get some on the way home, after the evening's traffic had subsided. Did he have his gas ration smart card with him? A quick check in his wallet showed that he had it, with enough credits left for at least one fill-up.

II

Monday, May 21st, 2012, Johnson Space Center, Houston, 09:00 CDT

Albert's secretary, Laura Lincoln, greeted him with a forced smile.

"Is there anything wrong?" Albert asked.

"Don Carter was by earlier and said that he wanted to see you as soon as you came in. But everyone is waiting for you in the lab."

Annoyed, Albert headed down the corridor towards Carter's office.

Don Carter was a no-nonsense, neo-conservative ex-marine officer who had been appointed by the waining presidential administration in Washington as NASA Administrator. He had taken over an agency in dire straits. With US budgetary deficits running well over a trillion dollars annually, resisting all of the President's efforts to cut them, Congress was in no mood to spend additional monies on what it saw as discretionary or marginal programs. Thus former President Bush's new vision for space exploration, announced in 2004 as affordable, sustainable and giving NASA a new focus and clear objectives, had met the chopping block. Indeed, NASA itself seemed marginalized, drowning, as an incidental victim, in the red ink of the growing cost of crude oil imports.

"Come in, Albert. Coffee? There's a fresh pot brewing over there."

"No thanks, Don. I am wired enough over the prospects of beginning the Martian soil tests. But can you spare me ten gallons of gas from our motor pool stores?"

"Well you can still do the testing, I guess".

"Of course! I can't wait to get started". As if there was any doubt?

"Albert. I've had some bad news from Washington. Our budget has been cut back by seventy-five percent for fiscal 2012/13. I've been ordered to terminate all non-essential programs within a month's time and to mothball the rest. The entire Mars Exploration Program falls into the first category. They're shutting us down."

"But we're right on the verge of one of our biggest successes. Why?"

"Get serious, Albert. Why would you need ten gallons of gas from our motor pool? The economy is going straight to hell and we're amongst the first victims. Congress won't fund anything except essential social programs and infrastructure renewal. They all want to get re-elected."

"But you said we could carry out the tests?"

"Right. I have enough budget left for that. Then I'll have to lay off you and your entire lab staff. Those are my orders."

"And Viking 4? It's due back later this year. I've already programmed its re-entry sequence. Who's going to look after that?"

Carter shrugged. "That won't be my concern anymore. My term as Administrator will have ended by then."

In silence, Albert got up to leave. There really wasn't anything more to say. The shock rippled through him as he walked down the hall to the lab. Shut down? Laid off? It was more than he could comprehend. His whole career, which was supposed to be peaking today, was, in one fell swoop, shattered. It was impossible for him to grasp. The neat, precise order of his day had been irretrievably ruptured.

Yoshi Tanaka, Albert's bright, young, Japanese-American Assistant Director, greeted Albert when he entered the Martian Soil Receiving Lab. Albert had taken a shine early on to this bright and inquisitive young scientist who had graduated Cal Tech with highest honors and then gone on to do his doctorate at Berkeley. He was a liberal activist, an ardent environmentalist and a staunch opponent of the neo-conservative rhetoric and polemics of the Republican majority in Congress. Over a period of time, Albert had grown close to Yoshi, whom he treated like both a protégé and a son. Yoshi was one of the few people Albert had met professionally to whom he could reveal his private thoughts, fears and aspirations. They were always companionable, whether discussing some aspect of the project or sharing beers and hot dogs at an Astros baseball game. They tried never to miss a weekend game when the "Rocket" would be pitching.

Yoshi asked why Albert hadn't come to the lab sooner. "Don wanted to see me." Albert procrastinated. He guessed that none of them had heard the news. It wasn't like Carter to deal with subordinates.

III

The lab was set up according to the strictest rules of health and safety. It was a sealed "clean room", painstakingly assembled with aseptic technology. All areas were monitored with microscopic "coupon" slides distributed around the perimeters. They were cultured daily to see if any microbiological populations had gotten in and what countermeasures should be taken. Chemical cleansing was also performed on all testing surfaces. Everyone was required to wear a sterile over-garment and mask. No chances were being taken that any microbes could either get in to give false test readings or get out into Earth's population.

The experiments were set up and ready to begin. Multiple testing apparatuses stood ready to receive their samples of Martian soil. Nearby, arranged in rows of sealed test tubes and beakers, were numerous variations of the "nutrient soup" which had been tested on Mars. The theory was to try all sorts of organic, carbon-based substances to see if the potential Martian visitors had a particular appetite for any of them. If so, they would consume them and produce the telltale byproducts of the life cycle. Over fifty concoctions would be tried, even long shots like a long chain hydrocarbon, commonly known as crude oil.

The testing periods would be lengthy, to replicate those used on Mars. Every sample would be run through an eight-sol cycle; a "sol" being the length of a Martian day – just over 24 hours. Conditions would simulate those that the Viking landers had encountered on Mars to see if similar or comparable results could be produced. Then those results would be assessed in a sealed, well-equipped Earth lab.

By evening the first tests were running. The lab staff were leaving for home, still unaware of their impending fate. Albert couldn't bring himself to squelch their enthusiasm with the bad news. As the lab cleared out, Yoshi came over to see him.

"Anything wrong, boss?"

"Well, yes. Some bad news this morning. I'll explain tomorrow morning at the staff meeting. Go home and enjoy your evening. Don't worry, a bright young guy like you will be alright, one way or the other."

Yoshi left, quite perplexed. Albert looked around at the empty lab and wondered whether he should head home as well. But traffic was heavy outside during evening rush hour. He didn't want to waste any of his little remaining gas stuck in gridlock. Carter hadn't OK'd a fill-up from the motor pool. He'd have to find a tank full on the way home. So, it would be better to wait the traffic out in the lab.

Albert looked over the experiments in progress, towards the array of carbon-based samples still waiting to be tested. His eye was drawn to the vial of shiny yellow-black liquid labeled "Saudi Light Sweet Crude Oil". The irony of it was apparent. Here was the stuff that was holding the world to hostage and personally destroying his own. Maybe the Martian critters would like to eat it all and end the world's problems? He felt a powerful urge to test it immediately. He certainly had plenty of time to set it up.

Albert measured out less than a gram of the Martian soil and put it into a testing apparatus. He took the vial of crude oil and introduced into the feed tube. Soon it would begin to drip slowly onto the soil sample in a dark, humidified environment. Would it produce any reaction? It might take a week to find out. "Anyway, let's give it a try", Albert mused out loud.

Stepping away from the apparatus to a remote control panel across the room, he switched the experiment on. The drip commenced and....*FLASH!*

Albert was totally unprepared for the occurrence. It all seemed to have happened in slow motion. One moment he had been looking at the apparatus and in the next, the entire room had suddenly been engulfed in a blinding blue-white aura, accompanied by a rush of unbearable heat. The shock wave that emanated from the apparatus rolled across the room like a thunder clap, knocking him forcefully against the far wall and down onto the floor behind a lab table. It was all over in the slightest instant. Badly shaken and dazed, all that occurred to him was, "Holy shit! What the hell was that?"

Albert peered back over the top of the lab bench towards the apparatus. All that was left was a mangled, melted hulk of metal and wires. The entire setup was burnished blue-black from the searing heat that had been generated. But there hadn't been a fire or any serious collateral damage. Whatever had happened inside the apparatus had been total, complete and instantaneous. Not even the slightest residue appeared on the wreckage or on the marble lab surfaces. "Wow", he exclaimed, "those Martian buggers really like crude oil!" No other substance had shown any reaction as yet. But Albert certainly couldn't start to comprehend what had really happened, let alone, begin to realize its true significance.

The hour was growing late. Traffic had subsided outside. Albert wanted to leave, but he felt he had better cleanup the mess in front of him first. It would be awkward to explain to staff in the morning. Especially given that they had no futures with NASA. He picked up the shattered remains of the test apparatus and put it out of sight in a locked cupboard. He slipped out of his protective suit and then scoured all of the surrounding surfaces clean with hand-sized aseptic chemical wipes. A few grains of the Martian soil had tipped out onto the marble countertop. He blotted them up with a final damp wipe, and then absentmindedly stuck it into his pocket. One last look around, then Albert shut out the lab lights, locked the door behind him, and passed through the identity card reader, logging himself out of the restricted area of the building. He headed downstairs to where his car was parked, still dazed and confused as to what had transpired in the lab.

IV

It was 11:00 PM when Albert pulled out of the lab garage. He turned southwest onto NASA Boulevard, heading for the on ramp to I-45N. In about half an hour he would be back at his townhouse in the West University District of Houston, across from the gates of Rice University. He didn't want to push his luck with gas for his car, so he detoured towards an all-night Phillips 66 station on the corner of NASA Boulevard and Old Galveston Road.

At that hour there were none of the inevitable lines of cars waiting to purchase their weekly allotments of gas. The station was empty, but for a large tanker truck which was delivering gasoline. It blocked half of the forecourt with its bulk and its thick fuel hoses, pumping various grades of gasoline into the underground storage tanks. Albert maneuvered his MGB up to a far pump to fill-up.

After he swiped his credit card, the automated pump asked him to insert his ration smart card. He had to have the required credits to buy 10 gallons of premium at $9.99/gallon. Albert fumbled in his pocket. As he pulled out the card, a small, crumpled chemical wipe fell to the ground. Out of the corner of his eye he saw it blow gently across the forecourt, finally coming to rest where the nozzle of one the tanker's large hoses connected to the flange of one of the series of underground tanks. There was an almost imperceptible drip of fuel accumulating in a tiny puddle next to the hose. The slight scent of gasoline wafted through the heavy, humid air.

Albert got back into his MG and eased the old lady away from the pump and into the street leading to the Interstate on-ramp. A light breeze rippled through the otherwise still, stifling air. Back in the Phillips 66 station, the wind coaxed the crumpled wipe closer to the tanker's filling hose. The wipe came to rest right on the edge of the small accumulation of spilled gasoline. A block away from the station, Albert was ready to merge on to I-45N. Suddenly he was blinded by an immense blue-white flash bouncing off his rear view mirror. *WHOOOSH*, the whole sky lit up behind him, as if from errant streak of heat lightening. Before he could catch his breath, a strong shock wave shook the MG violently. An ear-splitting *CRASH* resounded mightily, bouncing off the nearby buildings to the accompaniment of shattering windowpanes. "What the hell? Twice in one day? What the fuck is going on?" he muttered to himself as he brought the MG to a stop along the curb.

Albert turned the car around and headed back towards the Phillips 66 station. The sight he saw there stunned him. The station was still intact but it looked like it had been cauterized by a searing heat wave. The tanker truck lay on its side with its top ripped open. The underground gasoline storage areas were gaping wide open, their tops blown away by the blast. The whole scene was both surreal and yet hauntingly familiar.... Dazed, confused and suddenly very tired, Albert headed home along the empty Interstate. As he undressed for bed, a few grains of red sand fell from his trouser pocket. He looked at them long and hard for a moment. Unconsciously he was trying to make some connection with the day's unsettling events. Then he fell into a shallow and fitful sleep.

V

Everything really began to unravel the next morning. On the way into work Albert heard a news report of a mysterious explosion in a gas station in the Webster neighborhood, near to the Johnson Space Center. Fortunately, no one had been killed, but the blast had done considerable damage to homes in the area and had awakened many people. With the advent of terrorist suicide bombings in the US in 2011, the Houston police were taking it very seriously. They had already called in both the FBI and Homeland Security to investigate.

Yoshi was waiting for Albert when he arrived at NASA headquarters.

"Hi, Yoshi. Is everybody in the conference room already?"

"Yeah, boss. Even the Administrator is there. He's got some other guys I don't know with him too.

"Probably some heavies from Washington." Albert wished that Carter wouldn't be so hard-ass about things. What was about to happen wasn't going to be easy.

As they entered the government-gray painted conference room the anxious murmuring stopped immediately and all eyes fell expectantly on Albert. He surveyed the room full of familiar faces. In the back, Don Carter stood aloof, as usual. But next to him were two men he had never seen before.

As kindly as possible, Albert delivered the news to his anxious staff. The project would have to be completed as quickly as possible. Testing had to be finished within a month and all final reports submitted. There would be layoffs commencing immediately. Only key personnel could be kept. He, too, would be leaving next month, when the work was done. It was beyond his control. There were a lot of bright, young, dedicated members of his team whom he appreciated immensely. He would do his best to find them new positions. Sorry, though, he could make no promises. Any questions?

The room was silent. Albert gestured with his hands in despair. Everyone started to file out. Don Carter caught Albert's eye from the back of the room. He beckoned for him to come over. Yoshi tried to intercept him.

"I really need to talk with you. Something strange happened in the lab last night. Were you still there? I found some badly damaged testing apparatus stuck in a cupboard. Can you come see?"

"Sure Yoshi. later. Don wants to see me first. He's being very insistent." Albert walked over to Don Carter and the two men with him.

"Come to my office. These gentlemen want to talk with you" Carter said, without expression.

The Administrator introduced the two men. "This is Sergeant Raul Garcia of the Greater Houston Police Department and Special Agent Brian Bretton of the FBI, Counter-Terrorism Unit. They have some questions for you. Use my office for as long as you need it, gentlemen." Without another word, Carter left the room.

"Good morning, Dr. Stern. We have a few questions" Bretton started.

Tall, solid, muscular Brian Bretton had seen a lot in his FBI career. His square jaw and uncomplicated visage belied his steely interior strength and resolve. He had been posted in New York City on 9/11, where he had witnessed the horror and death of the al-Queda attack on the twin towers. Then he had gone on to headquarters in Washington, DC, where, in late 2010, he had been called in to investigate the horrific suicide bomber attack on Union Station. Hundreds of people had been killed and maimed. Things had multiplied from there. Suicide bombings by "martyrs", car bombs, hand-held missile attacks on commercial aircraft, the whole horror of Middle Eastern *jihad* had become a terrifying part of American life. The enemy was furtive, cunning and almost impossible to stop. Thus every suspicious or unusual explosion was top priority for the FBI's Counter-Terrorism Unit. Bretton was now posted in Los Angeles, but he had been flown in early that morning, as soon as his Unit had learned of the gas station incident in Houston.

"Certainly". Albert was guarded. "What's this all about?"

"What can you tell us about the explosion at the Phillips 66 station on Old Galveston Road late last evening?"

"Nothing! What would I know about that, other than what we all heard on the news this morning?"

"It would be better for you if you told us the truth from the start. The smart chip in the gas pump recorded that you used your gas credit card to buy 10 gallons of premium unleaded last night at 11:12 PM. The explosion occurred less than five minutes later" Garcia intervened. "We have you on surveillance camera tape. No one else had been in the station for almost an hour before. Only the tank truck driver, who was inside talking to the all-night cashier when the explosion happened. They were both able to confirm our positive ID on your car."

Albert was completely overwhelmed. "Sure, I bought gas for my car there. That's all I did. I had nothing to do with the explosion!"

"The tape shows that something fell out of your left front pocket. It blew over to where the truck's filling hose connected to the underground tanks", Bretton continued. "Do you remember that? What was it?"

Blank, Albert's mind was blank. Then he began to piece it together. Was it a chemical wipe from his hasty lab cleanup? Had he stuck one unthinkingly in his pocket? It would be covered with grime, but did it also have some of the Martian soil on it? Didn't he find a trickle of red sand falling from his trouser pocket the next morning? In panic he wondered whether he could have been the cause of the explosion after all.

"No, I don't have any idea. Maybe a tissue? I really don't remember anything like that."

"And the explosion," Bretton continued methodically, "what do you remember? Have you ever seen anything like it before? It was very unusual."

"How so?" Albert asked in growing angst.

"There wasn't any fire. Whatever happened was sudden and devastating. We've never seen anything like it. The damage was huge, but very focused and confined. It looks like something consumed all of the gasoline in one big gulp. An instantaneous chain reaction. The heat was incredible. Everything that had any contact with the fuel was seared and ripped apart. There were strange heat marks too on the metal shards. But what was your recollection of the event?" Bretton was poised to take notes.

"I only saw it from a distance" Albert answered truthfully. "I was at least a block away. At first I thought it was a clap of lightening. But then I was blasted by the shock wave. Honestly, I didn't know what it was! I would have called the police, but I was already heading onto the I-45N ramp. Besides, I didn't have my cell phone with me. Anyway, someone was bound to call in after such a blast!"

"We ran your record, Dr. Stern, and we see that you are a good citizen", Garcia responded. "We take potential terrorist acts very seriously. Houston has been free of them so far. But we aren't taking any chances. We have to consider you as a 'person of interest' for now. You'll have to stay exclusively in the Houston area while we continue our investigation. Tomorrow we'll be interviewing your lab staff. We'll need a list of your key personnel."

"We're also getting a search warrant to have a look around your apartment", Bretton added.

"But I'm going to my graduate class reunion in England next week. I planned it a long time ago!"

"Sorry, Dr. Stern, you'll have to stay put for as long as takes. You can drop your passport off at the Houston Central Police Headquarters tomorrow", Garcia intervened. "Anyway, let's have that list by tomorrow morning. We need to talk with your people and have a look around the lab. Yeah, we know that it's federal government property. That's one of the reasons why the FBI is involved".

VI

Albert headed for the lab in a state of shock. In less than a day, his whole world was crumbling around him. He could inadvertently be taken for a criminal or even a terrorist. He was completely unnerved and depressed.

Yoshi was a few steps behind him. "Hey Albert, what's happening? Who were those guys? What did they want? We need to talk!"

"Come with me to my office and I'll explain."

Albert briefed Yoshi on the events of last evening and this morning. He trusted Yoshi and knew that he could rely on him. He came to the delicate subject of the burned and mangled GEX apparatus. "We've got to get rid of that thing fast. It was all beyond my control. I'm no criminal, but I'm in big trouble. It's gone way beyond just losing my job and yours."

"Even if we get rid of the physical evidence, Albert, they'll find it all on the security surveillance tape from last evening. They're coming tomorrow to interview us all. They'll secure the lab and the tapes for sure. But it's a lot bigger than that!"

"How so?" Albert quizzed Yoshi.

"Think, Albert. If this stuff can consistently do what it seems to have already done to crude oil and its products, it's the most devastating weapon of the 21st century! Can you imagine who would want it? The mind boggles. The Israelis could wipe out all of Iran's petroleum reserves with a few well-executed commando raids. Al-Qaeda could reap its vengeance on the house of Saud. Our government would hold a powerful trump card over Chavez and his cronies, knowing how much we have loved pre-emptive strikes in the past. The Chechens insurgency against the Russians would take on a whole new dimension. The possibilities are endless! No oil power nation would be secure from such a weapon. Besides, there's lots of money in it for whoever can sell the weapon to any of those guys."

"I hadn't thought of any of that" Albert replied thoughtfully. "We're scientists here, not politicians or generals. But maybe I'd better start thinking about the bigger picture, huh? The geopolitics are staggering. But this is US government property. It's not for sale."

"Maybe not, Albert, but maybe so. First you have to get the rest of the stuff out of here. If it gets into the hands of those neocon war birds at the Pentagon, we'll be responsible for world chaos. That's not what this was all about. It has to be put somewhere safe and out of reach. The Feds are coming tomorrow and they'll figure it out fast. You know I'll help you."

Albert's mind was racing. Sure, Yoshi was right. But what could be done?

"Come with me to Home Depot,", Yoshi suggested. "It's lunch time. I have a good idea".

Together they bought some small packets of fine sand, brick dust and clay. To that they added some iron rust. Before anyone had returned from lunch they had ground it all together in a mortar and pestle. "Looks like the stuff to me". Yoshi was triumphant. "Let's do the switch fast, before the cameras are back on." He knew the timing cycle of the surveillance tapes and when there would be convenient blind spots. "We'll keep cooking the real stuff in the set-up experiments. Maybe we'll get the positive scientific result we were looking for. But you'd better get out of here with the rest of it now. Remember, they are coming to search your apartment tomorrow."

Albert left Yoshi in charge and headed home mid-afternoon. By the next morning he would be gone forever from Houston, headed for London and into an uncertain future.

PART 2
RULES OF ENGAGEMENT

"We all boil at different degrees."

I

Thursday, May 24th, 2012, London, 06:00 GMT

United Airlines flight 958 touched down at London Heathrow Airport early in the morning after Albert had left Houston. He hadn't slept much since changing planes in Chicago. Nevertheless, he was both awake and alert and his mind was racing. He was comforted by the familiar sights of a gray English morning, to which he had become so accustomed in Cambridge, many years before.

At Customs and Immigration Albert entered the line marked "Fast Track". Nothing seemed amiss there, as he told the officer that he was visiting for a week to attend his college class reunion in Cambridge. His passport stamped, he headed downstairs to collect his luggage. Two small bags in hand, he passed through the green channel at Customs without incident and headed straight for the down ramp to the Heathrow Express. Every 15 minutes the train left for Paddington Station in London's West End. From there he would hail a cab to take him to the Millennium Knightsbridge Hotel on Sloane Street, where he had made a reservation.

Checked into a room on the Executive Floor, Albert paused momentarily to take in the familiar view of Sloane Street. It was busy with red double-decker buses, black London cabs and upscale cars, wending their way south towards Sloane Square. Big Ben was visible to the east, along with the great wheel of the London Eye. To the west he could see the famous emporium, Harrods. He took his Palm Pilot out of his jacket pocket and entered the name "Nigel Duckworth". He had been Albert's best climbing buddy in the Cambridge University Mountaineering Club. Although no one ever really got that close to Albert, Duckworth, uniquely, had created a real rapport of trust with him. They had both tried to stay in touch over the years. He dialed Duckworth's work number in the City of London.

"Good morning", said a rather prim and proper voice, "Mr. Duckworth's office".

"Oh, good morning. Is he in, please?"

"Whom shall I say is calling?"

"This is Dr. Albert Stern from Houston. We were climbing buddies years ago at Cambridge. I'm sure that he'll remember me."

A slight pause and a cheerful voice came on the line. "Good morning, Albert. What a nice surprise! What brings you here to London?"

"It's quite unexpected, Nigel. I need some help urgently. Could we meet tonight for dinner, perhaps? I'll explain everything then. I hope that Fiona and the kids won't mind this sudden intrusion."

"Always willing to help out an old climbing mate. You know that. Meet me at my club, the Atheneum, at 7:00 this evening. We can catch up then."

Albert put his passport and travel documents into the personal safe in the closet. He put the small jar of Viking sands in as well. Then he headed out on foot into the gray London morning to find a good, proper, cooked English breakfast.

II

It was 6:55 PM when Albert entered the Atheneum Club at 107 Pall Mall.

"Good evening, squire. Can I help you?", the doorman greeted him.

"I'm here to meet Nigel Duckworth at 7:00."

"Very good, sir. You must be Dr. Stern. Mr. Duckworth is waiting for you in the long bar. Right this way, please."

In the dark wood-paneled Victorian bar Albert was greeted warmly by his old friend. Duckworth looked his normal, prosperous self, nattily attired in a dark chalk-striped suit and silk foulard tie. He had put on a few pounds over the years, but he still looked reasonably fit. After Cambridge he had gone down to the City where he had fashioned a very successful career as an underwriter at Lloyds.

"What are you drinking?", Duckworth asked.

"Pink gin, straight up, please." The bartender mixed it and set it down on the bar in front of Albert.

"Strong stuff. Always was your favorite, though. Anyway, cheers! Good to see you again. And here's to old Desmond too, God rest him!" Albert raised his glass perfunctorily to the toast, devoid of any emotion. He certainly wasn't anxious to revisit that incident.

A few more drinks and then the two men were seated in the ornate dining room. The *maitre d'* had reserved Duckworth's favorite table looking out over lower Pall Mall and the lights of central London. Albert ordered native Colchester oysters as an appetizer and his favorite entrée, grilled Dover sole off the bone. A good bottle of sauvignon blanc was brought to the table and over a few more libations, Albert began to unburden himself to his old friend. He only went so far, though. He explained that he was in flight from the law, but that it was all a big misunderstanding. It would take quite some time to set it all right, though, and he was under immense pressure. Duckworth listened to it all reflectively.

"So, Nigel, I need some unusual help. Do you remember our old Pakistani friend, Iqbal Pasha, from Cambridge days? Do you know how I can contact him?"

"Old Iqy, sure. That wily rogue! Not much of a climber, but a hell of a cricketer! Got sent down eventually for doing too much of the latter. He's had a bit of a dodgy run since you last saw him. Been quite successful, though. Runs a posh escort service out of his club and casino in Mayfair for visiting businessmen and dignitaries. He's been in a few run-ins with the law too. Something about bringing in young Eastern European girls illegally and changing their identity so they could work for him. Never been convicted though. He must have a bloody good lawyer. Why would you want to contact him?"

"That's perfect. I need a new identity, fast"

"Sure Iqy can do that for you, if he's willing. But it will cost you." Nigel reached into his wallet and sorted through a few business cards. He handed Albert a well-worn one with a sly smile. "Here, give Iqy a call. Mum's the word about me to anyone else though."

Albert returned the smile and thanked his old friend profusely. "So, things haven't changed that much from our old graduate school days, eh? Still like the young ones, do you?" Smiles all around again and Albert left, promising to stay in touch. He walked up lower Regent Street to Piccadilly Circus and caught the Tube to Knightsbridge. There was still a lot on his mind.

III

Not far up Curzon Street from Shepherd's Market was Iqbal Pasha's Enigma Club. It was early the next morning. The club had not opened yet. But Iqbal had asked Albert to stop by then, so he rang the bell. A heavy answered the door. Albert explained that he had an appointment with Mr. Pasha. Inside the ornate, dark and empty club and casino, Albert was shown to Pasha's private office on the second floor.

"Albert, old man, it was good to hear from you again. A hell of a surprise though!" Pasha greeted him. "Nigel called too and said you needed some help from me. Some entertainment, perhaps, while you are in town? I can arrange something very special for you, my dear old friend."

"No Iqy, thanks anyway, but certainly not that. That's the last thing on my mind right now." Quickly Albert explained what he did need from Pasha.

Pasha bit his lip reflectively. "Bit of a sticky wicket, eh whot?" He clapped his hands, signaling his servant to bring them both tea. "So then, Albert, you are tired of being a Yank? Of course I can arrange it, but it won't be cheap."

"I figured as much, but I am willing to pay whatever it costs. I need it all fast."

"Mine is not to question why, dear old friend. I'll arrange it for you for old times' sake. But the risk is all yours. If they hit you for six, I don't want to know!"

Pasha gave Albert the address of Osman Ali, who owned an art and picture framing shop on the high street in Islington. "The framing is legit, but Osman does his best art work in the back room. Tell him that I sent you and to keep it very confidential, as always. I'll see what I can do to get you a good price. Take good care old friend!"

By 3:00 that afternoon, Albert Stern was no more. Out of the dingy shop on the high street next to a Boots chemist stepped Peter Shaw, with a British passport and driver's license to prove it. Born in Wimbledon in 1968 of an English father and an American mother; raised in California; and now residing in London, of no fixed address for the moment. He would see to that small detail at once. As added insurance, and for an additional GB Pounds 500, Albert had yet another new identity package tucked into his pocket. Intuitively, he sensed that he might need that one too as things moved along.

IV

Thursday, May 24th, 2012, Houston, 08:00 CDT

Brian Bretton was livid when he heard the news from Raul Garcia. Stern had failed to surrender his passport as directed. Two officers from the Greater Houston PD had gone around to his apartment at 7:00 AM that morning with a search warrant. When no one answered their insistent knocking, they had forced the lock. All they found was an empty apartment. No sign of Stern anywhere; no indication that he had slept there the night before. Some clothes tossed randomly around in the bedroom indicated hasty packing. The 800 number for United Airlines reservations was scribbled on a note pad next to the phone. He was gone, damn it! Right from under their noses. Where to though, and with what?

"I'll bet he's in England", Bretton said angrily. "Shit, Raul, I thought you said that he wasn't a flight risk."

"We both thought he wasn't, right?" Garcia attempted to share out the blame equally.

"Anyway, let's get busy finding him. Have your men contact United Airlines and see where he went. If he's in London we can get a federal bench warrant quickly and have it sent off to Scotland Yard and Interpol, with a request for urgent assistance. Did his passport have an RFDI chip embedded in it? Can we track him that way, by GPS?"

"No, he had an old passport without the new technology. By the way, we did a quick swab of the lab yesterday and talked with Stern's top assistant, Yoshi Tanaka. He tried to steer us away from the testing equipment but we found something incriminating locked away in a cupboard. It's a charred and mangled piece of apparatus. It's in forensics now, but at first look, the scorch marks on it seemed identically to match those that we found at the gas station. We'll see what really happened once we view the surveillance tapes, which Special Ops is doing right now."

Five minutes later United Airlines confirmed Stern's overnight flight to London. He had arrived that morning at 6:00 AM, six hours ahead of Houston time. They had no further information about his whereabouts after that. He hadn't booked a hotel through their overseas travel service.

Bretton dialed a direct line into Scotland Yard's Counter-Terrorism Squad. His friend and counterpart, Captain Ian Llewelyn, answered in a clipped British accent. The acquired, posh accent belied Llewelyn's tough upbringing. Born in a dreary

Welsh coal town, he had gone on to university in Liverpool and joined the police force there, patrolling its mean streets. His rise through the ranks to a position of high responsibility in national security was the direct outcome of his dogged persistence and unflagging work ethic.

"Hello, Ian, it's Brian Bretton in Houston. Sorry to spring this on you so suddenly, but we need your assistance urgently. We're trying to apprehend a suspected terrorist we think has fled to London. He's one of ours and he's carrying a lethal substance that's US government property. He's potentially very dangerous and a flight risk as well. We want him in custody fast! I'll fax you all the details immediately. Can your guys get on to this as quickly as possible?"

"I say, Brian, that's quite a jolt. But, right you are. We'll mobilize immediately and do our best to help. I'll be waiting for your fax. Will you be coming over to collect the goods if we secure them?"

"If you get him, I'll be there fast."

V

Friday, May 25th, 2012, London, 16:00 GMT

Albert returned to the Millennium Knightsbridge and quickly threw his few belongings together. He took the jar of Viking sands out of the personal safe, wrapped it in a washcloth, and placed it into his hand luggage. It was high time for Albert Stern quietly to disappear.

Albert placed his express checkout form in the slot at the counter in the lobby and exited the back entrance to the hotel, out onto Pavilion Road. Crossing quickly over, he headed into

Stackhouse Street. It was a shortcut he knew to Basil Street and the Brompton Road entrance to the Knightsbridge Tube stop of the Piccadilly Line. He first heard the sirens as he came abreast of the multi-story car park. Racing north up Pavilion Road were two police cruisers, lights flashing and sirens blaring. More shrill noises told him that at least a few more were at the front entrance of the hotel. Officers piled out into the hotel lobby. Albert picked up his pace, trying not to be too obvious. He headed quickly towards the tube entrance, his heart pounding.

Somehow Albert knew that they were after him already. In the station, he hastily pushed his day travelcard through the automatic gate slot and headed down the escalator for the westbound platform. The first incoming train was bound for Rayners Lane, but he wouldn't be going anywhere near that far. Three stops later he disembarked at the Earl's Court station.

It didn't take long to find the numerous estate agents on the high street listing rental flats in this seedy, transition-fusion neighborhood of mostly bed-sitters. It was an area that gave Albert exactly what he needed: anonymity. He rented an efficiency unit on a weekly basis for cash under the name of Peter Shaw. It was located in a *cul de sac* not far from the underground station. It was evening already and Albert was hungry and tired. The Star of India restaurant down the street looked as good as any. A nice hot chicken vindaloo curry with a pint of lager and lime and a restful night's sleep was what he needed most now. Next Monday morning would be time enough for Peter Shaw to start his new and risky life. For now Albert would lie low for the weekend and reflect on his options.

VI

Monday, May 28th, 2012, London, 09:00 GMT

The Israeli Embassy is tucked away on Old Court Place, across from the grounds of Kensington Palace and gardens. Heavy gates and concrete blocks bar the curious and potentially malevolent from approaching too closely. One has to make an appointment, bring one's passport and pass through heavy security to get inside the compound. Albert dialed the Consular Section of the embassy. After a prolonged wait, he finally got through to the Appointment's Scheduling Secretary. He explained that he was a British-American Jew who wished to visit Israel and possibly to emigrate there. Could he have an appointment to see someone today, please? After further delay, Albert was told to bring his passport and any travel plans and to present himself at the security gate at 2:00 PM.

Wearing a neatly-trimmed phony beard and moustache, Albert got off the Tube at Kensington High Street and walked a few blocks past the House of Fraser building to the beginning of Old Court Place. At 1:55 PM he was at the embassy gate, new passport in hand. After a computer check of his passport and an uncomfortable pat down, he was allowed entry into the grounds. Time to do his version of "The Falcon and The Snowman", he thought.

Albert was shown into the office of a Consular Officer, Ms. Layla Edelman.

"Good afternoon Mr. Shaw. You would like a visa to visit Israel? Will it be for business or personal purposes? A new passport, I see. Will this be your first trip out of Britain?"

"No, my passport was recently renewed. I would like to visit Israel to see if I would like to emigrate there. 'Right of return', you know. My grandparents were Holocaust survivors."

"I understand. We encourage such immigration. And when would you like to go?"

"That depends. I feel that I might be able to be of great help to Israel."

"How so?" Edelman reacted with surprise.

"Maybe I am not talking to the right person. What I have to say is quite sensitive. Could I see the head of the Section? Perhaps someone from the Mossad?"

"This is an embassy, Mr. Shaw. We have no Mossad people here", Edelman replied defensively.

"Sorry. I would still like to see the Section Head though. I need to explain this to the right person."

"If you insist. Please wait here." Edelman left, closing the door behind her. Several minutes later Albert was shown into the office of Mr. Ira Melman, the head of the Consular Section.

"So, you have something sensitive to tell us about how you can help the Israeli state? Do you mind if I record this discussion?" Naively, Albert didn't know that Melman would have him on videotape, no matter what he said.

"I'd rather you not. Hear me out first. Suppose I could help Israel deal forever with the Iranian nuclear threat, as well as with Saudi and Syrian bankrolling of anti-Israeli terrorist organizations. Would that be of interest? Am I talking to the right person now?"

Melman smiled. "Of course it would be most interesting and intriguing. Tell me more."

Melman was more than just the right person. Like many senior staffers at Israeli embassies worldwide, he had a solid background in both military and intelligence operations. He had been in the Israeli army, rising to the rank of colonel. He had seen lethal action in the Yom Kippur War as part of the Aman, the Israeli Army Intelligence branch. He had also worked with Shin Beth, Israeli Domestic Security, in Jerusalem during the prolonged *Intafadeh*. Melman had contacts deep into the Mossad as well.

Albert sketched out what he had, with several important exceptions. He didn't identify the origin of the Viking sands. It would be too risky and quite unbelievable anyway. Rather, he said that he had invented the substance and that he could assure them that it worked perfectly. In the hands of the Israeli military-security complex, it would give the Jewish State a weapon of unimaginable power. With it they could destroy the Iranian oil wealth, which fueled its imminent threat to Israel. Equally, the Saudis' covert financing of anti-Israeli organizations could be brought to an abrupt halt, along with its entire petrodollar fueled economy. He laid it all out for Melman, just as Yoshi had first imagined it in Houston.

"And assuming that all of what you have told me is true, what would you want for yourself in return?" Melman asked engagingly.

"I would want a very large sum of money. At least a hundred million dollars. And asylum in Israel. Even more than just asylum. I would want a completely new identity and protection for life. A small price for what I am offering to do for Israel, no?" Albert was subconsciously formulating his demands as he went along.

"Perhaps. Do you have the substance with you? Can you give us some to test? Naturally, we'd have to verify what you are telling me first." Melman was now quite sure that he was dealing with at least a crank, if not a madman.

"Hell no! I wouldn't bring it here. It wouldn't be practical for you to test it anyway. You'll just have to believe me. It works very well."

"Certainly. Of course we would like to believe you, but we would need some solid proof first. Maybe you could do a demonstration for us?" Melman countered, a note of sarcasm creeping into his tone. "You said you had inadvertently blown up a petrol station somewhere. Could you do that again, perhaps? Or, better yet, something even larger, like an oil depot, or a pipeline? You'd have to let us know in advance, of course. Maybe something really big like a North Sea oil-producing platform? That would certainly catch our attention."

Albert sensed that Melman was humiliating and toying with him. He certainly hadn't believed a word that he had said, and he didn't like it at all. "Damn it, can't you see that I'm offering you something that will solve your biggest problems forever? You want proof? I can give that. You will regret it, though", Albert went on, his anger growing.

"Calm down", Melman replied. "We wouldn't want you to do anything that would harm the national interests of our host country here. But you understand that what you have told me is quite unbelievable. We appreciate your interest in helping Israel, but we simply cannot take it all on faith". His smile was obsequious.

That was enough for Albert. He was frustrated and angry. He had taken great risks to come to the embassy and was furious with the cold, dismissive reception he was receiving. Deep down, though, he had almost expected it. Now he would have to make them see the light.

"I have nothing more to say for now. But I assure you that you will have your proof. When you hear of it, it will be unmistakable. Then you'll want to contact me urgently. That won't be easy." Albert reached in his pocket and took out a folded sheet of paper. "Here, take this and follow the instructions on it. It's an innocuous advertisement that you will run in *The Times* for two consecutive weeks, starting on a Monday. Wherever I am, when I see it, I will contact you." He handed Melman the paper and got up to leave. He didn't reach out to shake his hand.

Melman showed Albert out of his office. Ms. Edelman walked with him out to the lobby in silence. She asked, as an afterthought, if he still wanted a tourist visa.

"No, not yet." He walked quickly through the grounds of the compound to the street gate. Nervously eying the heavily present police security forces, he continued as confidently as possible by them, back up to Kensington High Street. There he boarded a District Line train to Earl's Court, back to the safety of his bed-sitter.

Back at the embassy, Layla Edelman asked Ira Melman what he made of Peter Shaw. "A crazy man, quite deluded", Melman replied. "Said he could solve all of our problems with some doomsday substance he claims to have invented. Would that it were true!"

"But is he dangerous? Should we report him to the police?"

"No. He's just another crank. I'll write up a brief note for the files though." With that, Melman tucked his scant notes on the meeting into a fresh manila folder, along with the paper that Albert had given him. Then he pushed it aside to attend to more pressing business waiting on his desk.

VII

Albert knew that he had to get out of London fast. There was no further reason to stay anyway. The narrow escape at the Millennium Hotel had really spooked him. Bretton had undoubtedly linked the explosion at the gas station to the one in the lab. He was sure that the London police knew who he was and what he looked like. There would be more close calls, even with his new identity and his feeble attempt to alter his appearance. Air travel would be too risky. They'd be looking for him at Heathrow, Gatwick and all of the other area airports. Besides, he had business to do elsewhere in Britain. He needed to prove the truth of what he had said to the Israelis if he was to have any chance of succeeding in his evolving plan for real wealth, security and a new life. Those were, apparently, to be the rules of engagement.

What had Melman said? They needed convincing proof. Only then could they talk meaningfully. He had suggested some dire things. Was he serious? Were there really any alternatives? No, and Albert knew it in his gut. He would have to do something drastic to convince them. Was he up to it? All of the repressed anxiety and confusion that had haunted Albert this last chaotic week came welling up like an explosive fountain into his conscious mind. Could he really commit an act of unvarnished sabotage; terrorism? These were thoughts alien to Albert's consciousness, but apparently not to the deeper reaches of his calculating mind. He had to weigh the final greater good against the lesser immediate evil. He knew that he had the ultimate weapon which could dramatically alter the balance of power in the world. It could also assure him of comfort and security for the rest of his life. It would be very risky business, but it was too late to turn back. He was already in play. There was really no choice. He was irretrievably beyond the point of no return. Whatever it took, now was the time to prove that he was a real force to be reckoned with.

Packing just a small piece of hand luggage, Albert locked up his rented flat and took the Tube to King's Cross Station. There he bought himself a ticket to Edinburgh on the overnight sleeper, with an ongoing ticket to Aberdeen, the headquarters of the British North Sea oil industry.

VIII

Friday, June 1st, 2012, Aberdeen, Scotland, 09:00 GMT

The giant Sterling oilfield was the largest undeveloped resource left in the UK sector of the North Sea. Discovered in 2005, it began its first oil production in January, 2010. It was hoped to be the salvation of the British energy sector, which had fallen into severe decline. The older British offshore oilfields, discovered in the 1960s, were approaching depletion. Located approximately 50 miles west of the Shetland Islands in 200 meters of water, the classic Jurassic sandstone reservoir of the Sterling oilfield had been conservatively estimated to contain over 5 billion barrels of recoverable oil in place. This was vastly larger than any of the other North Sea oilfields. By oil industry standards, it was an "elephant". Owned by a consortium of international oil companies, it was operated for the group by Anglo Petroleum Limited, its largest stakeholder.

The huge steel production platform sitting atop the Sterling offshore oilfield was built at Loch Kishorn, in western Scotland. It had been laboriously towed out to its location and set in place. It rose over 300 meters from seabed to the top of its production, living and maintenance modules, in the deep, inhospitable and often stormy expanse of the North Sea. On most days, fierce gales created mountainous, foaming gray-green to black seas, with huge, rolling, white wave tops. The investment to reach production phase had run into many millions of pounds sterling. At its peak the Sterling field would produce 750,000 barrels of oil per day from 60 wells located on the platform. The field was a water drive reservoir, with the producing strata sitting on top of the oil/water contact. Thus continuous water flooding through injection wells, to force the oil into the well bores, was the primary means of production.

Anglo needed an immense crew of specialists and other workers to produce the field. The latter are less skilled, being "roughnecks", "roustabouts" and tool pushers. Any able-bodied man could be taught the limited skills needed. Albert knew this when he applied for a job. The normal routine was two weeks on the platform and then two weeks onshore, in Aberdeen. There the well-paid crews spent their downtime squandering a fair portion of their pay packets in the gin mills, pubs and brothels of the old Scottish town. Albert was hired as a new crewmember without much hesitation. His identity as Peter Shaw was British and he looked strong enough to do the physically demanding work required. After a brief physical and some routine paper work, he was on a large transport helicopter with a crowd of others, *en route* over the stormy northern seas to the isolated Sterling platform.

It was still early morning. The gray, mist-shrouded sea looked like a churning cauldron below. The ride was bumpy as the helicopter fought its way through a strong westerly headwind. For most of the journey nothing was visible except the monochromatic panorama of sea and leaden skies. Then, after an hour, out of the starboard windows, a beacon of light finally penetrated the gloom. There on the horizon was the mammoth Sterling platform. It rose out of the sea like some enormous antipodal creature rearing its head. It was ablaze with lights and roaring fire like a dragon from its huge gas-flaring boom. It was a truly awesome sight.

The helicopter maneuvered towards the helipad on the platform's top deck. The winds had subsided and the giant Sikorsky set down like a great dragonfly settling over its prey. When the engines had stopped and the doors were opened, Albert and sixty others descended a ramp leading down to the platform.

"This way laddies", said Jock McLaughlin, the rig floor superintendent. "Step lively, now. There's hot tea and breakfast waiting for ya' in the mess module. Mind your steps on the wet deck."

Jock was a seasoned veteran of offshore oil operations. Short, stout and muscular, he sported a bushy white beard framing his tan, weathered face. He had seen many come and go over the years. This crew would be nothing new to him. He'd have to form them up into teams and get them all working together at peak efficiency, as he had always done.

Albert followed along down the long interior gangway towards the mess hall. The smell of bacon, eggs and toast was very welcoming. After stowing his gear in his cabin, he sat down to a generous Scottish breakfast, which included hearty oat porridge and black pudding sausages. He was on his second cup of tea when Jock came in to summon everyone to his morning briefing and duty roster assignments.

"You there, laddie, you're a new one here. What's your name then?"

"Peter Shaw", Albert replied.

"Any experience in the oil patch before? Been on an offshore rig or platform then?"

"No, but I'm a fast learner. I really want to learn about servicing production and water injection wells." Albert wasn't planning to spend more than one two-week shift on the Sterling platform.

"Good, there's a lot to learn! This is very dangerous work. Are you up to it then? Never mind, we'll soon find out. Let's start you off first with something a wee bit easier. You'll be working on the deck around the moonpools for Number 4 and 5 wells, as a roustabout. Get your life jacket and hard hat on and follow me."

Roustabouts frequently assist skilled workers, such as welders, mechanics, electricians and drillers. The work is very strenuous, requiring frequent bending, stooping, climbing and heavy lifting. Hazards include the risk of falls from derricks and other platforms, injuries from falling objects, cuts, abrasions, strains and death, if one falls from the platform into the deadly, frigid waters 100 meters below. Albert understood all of this, but he had come to do it. He had to learn fast how to access the well bores into the rich oil-bearing formations, 5,000 meters below the seabed.

His chance came sooner than he expected. After five exhausting days of working twelve hour shifts on deck, Jock McLaughlin shifted him to a training position with Bo Connery, the head of the water flood injection program. Bo's regular assistant had been injured in an accident the day before.

"It's what you wanted, no? You're smart enough to learn fast. We need you to, now", Jock said. Albert would finally learn the skills he needed to service, maintain and run the platform's 10 water injection wells.

He picked up the new skills quickly. The injection wells recycled formation water back into the reservoir. Along with other large volumes of water, they provided a full horizontal sweep of the oil sands, which were the producing horizons. The wells ran in series, not all together. They needed regular maintenance against corrosion and contamination. So they were periodically shut down in pairs for servicing. Albert learned the maintenance schedule and did some quick calculations. His shift would end on Friday, June 15th. On that morning injection wells 9 and 10 would have undergone routine maintenance and be scheduled for restarting. Timing would be everything. The outgoing transport helicopter would leave to take his crew shift back to the mainland at 8:30 AM. The new crew would be arriving in the incoming one about the same time. For a very brief period, though, the platform would be virtually devoid of any personnel.

Albert had carefully tucked away the container of Viking sands in his locked kit bag. He was alone most of the time as his cabin mate worked the opposite 12-hour shifts. There had been one scare though. The day he arrived Albert's cabin mate had noticed the jar of Viking sands. He had asked Albert why he was carrying red sand around with him. A flustered, Albert had quickly replied, "Its cherry-flavored Metamucil. I need it to stay regular."

IX

Friday, June 15th, 2012, Sterling Platform, North Sea, 05:30 GMT

Albert awoke as usual at 5:30 AM. He had been working the 12-hour shift from 6:00 AM to 6:00 PM daily. On this morning he still had an hour's work backlog to finish before he would board the outgoing crew helicopter back to Aberdeen. His most important work involved water injection wells 9 and 10. In the morning gloom, in his wet weather gear, he headed for the well deck. He had two generous teaspoonfuls of the Viking sands in his zippered pocket wrapped in tin foil. The deck was empty as he began his maintenance work on the two shut down water injection wells. First he checked to be sure that all valves were properly closed. Then he used a large wrench to open the flange through which water from the recycling tanks entered the well bores. He deposited the Viking sands into the small space between the top of the pipes coming in from the water reservoirs and the double closed valves connected to the two well bores. Satisfied, he closed it all back up tightly. Now there was nothing left to do but to set the timers for re-starting of the two wells. That would be at 9:00 AM. Albert wasn't really sure what to expect, but he knew that the die had now been irrevocably cast.

From behind him Albert heard Bo approaching. "Morning, Albert, there's a good lad. Did you finish the maintenance work on those two injection wells?"

"Yes, I was just double checking. Want to have a look?"

"No, I know you know what you are doing. After all, I taught you. And the timers are set for re-starting at 9:00?"

"All done, Bo. Let's go grab some breakfast before the 'copter comes to get us". The two men headed off together to the mess hall.

At 7:45 AM Albert could hear the first incoming chopper as it maneuvered to land topsides on the helipad. It would take at least half an hour to unload its cargo of stores and provisions. At 8:25 all hands going ashore were to assemble at the helipad with their gear to leave for Aberdeen. The weather was really rotten that morning. Gusting winds were blowing horizontal rain in from the northwest. Albert was edgy about getting off on time. He checked his watch again as he joined the boarding queue. Some inevitable last minute delays seemed interminable. But finally, at 8:45 AM, the engines were started. A bead of cold sweat rolled down Albert's back as the Sikorsky freighter lifted off and slowly began its southeastward journey back towards Aberdeen.

The going was rough. The helicopter struggled in the strong west winds and squalls blowing in from the North Atlantic. It wasn't making much headway. Five minutes aloft and the platform still seemed to be right below. The helicopter hovered without making any real progress. Albert was getting quietly frantic. Then he noticed the incoming chopper abreast of them, about 500 meters away. The two old chum pilots had stopped to have a radio chat!

8:55 AM. The chopper bucked the winds to leave the platform behind in the dark pall of a North Sea morning. Finally, it began to recede behind them. Albert pressed his nose to the porthole with a sense of anticipation and dread. The minutes dragged interminably on as the platform continued to disappear in the mist and gloom. Soon it would be nothing but a small beacon of light on the indistinct horizon.

9:00 AM. The timer switch on 9 and 10 injection wells snapped into the "on" position. The great pumps roared to life and began sucking water from the recycling reservoirs up through the piping and gauges and down into the well bores. In a miscible solution about 50 grams of Viking sands were being forcefully driven 5,000 meters below the seabed, into the churning foam of the water flood. Forced downwards under great pressure, they would quickly reach the oil/water contact line of the giant Sterling oil reservoir.

9:05 AM. Albert looked out at the last glimmer of light on the dark horizon. It barely marked the position of the platform that he had just left for good. Had it all failed? He turned away in resignation and, surprisingly, in relief, when suddenly, *the entire sky to the northwest was instantaneously illuminated!* This was not just a sudden, brilliant flash, as Albert had seen before. This was on a scale that defied the imagination. Erupting miles into the air was a continuous jet of blue-white aura, crackling with heat and static electricity, like a monstrous thunderstorm.

It continued, unabated, for almost a full five minutes. Unbeknownst to any observers, the Viking sands were entirely consuming the billions of barrels of oil reserves in the Sterling oilfield. The crew in the helicopter stood transfixed in terror at the incredible sight until *whoomph*, the craft was hit by a rolling shock wave spreading across the cold dark waters at a speed in excess of 200 miles per hour. Blasted miles off course and almost flipped over, the chopper dropped vertically at least 500 feet before the pilot was able to regain control. Looking back towards the Sterling platform there was nothing more to see. No smoke, fire nor flames. The hulk of the platform was still there, but enveloped now in a dark shroud of mist and fog. All the lights had blinked out.

There was no sense in even trying to help. The supply and rescue boat anchored a mile away from the platform, if it had survived, would be looking for survivors. There was nothing for it but to continue on to Aberdeen, before precious fuel ran out.

X

When the helicopter reached Aberdeen a full complement of company representatives were waiting along with the police and, of course, the press. Word had raced back ahead of them of the disaster at the Sterling platform. Details had been very sketchy. Reporters rushed the crew as it somberly disembarked.

Albert hung back, avoiding both the police and the press. He knew that he had to make a fast exit. Not just from the crowded scene, but from the country as well. When the full nature of the Sterling platform incident was revealed, both Scotland Yard and the FBI would surely link it to him. And they would know, too, where he was. He was right under their noses at that very moment.

Albert pushed his way through probing reporters into the company office on the dockside. All he wanted was his pay packet and a taxi to the airport. He would have to risk a flight to leave. But where to go? On the helicopter ride back he had already made up his mind. He needed to go somewhere safe, neutral and off the beaten path. Somewhere comfortably familiar, where he could collect his racing and jumbled thoughts.

"Peter Shaw" he said to the paymaster.

"Aye, then, here's your pay packet. That will be 1,080 Pounds. Would ya' like it transferred to ya' bank or in a cashier's check ?"

"No, I need it all in cash".

"Aye, laddie, ya' all do. Don't go spending all of it on women and booze during your downtime", the paymaster said with a wry smile. "And be sure ya' hang about now for the company debriefing"

Albert took the large wad of cash and slipped quietly out the back door. He certainly didn't want to talk with anyone, especially the police. He wasn't interested in the company debriefing either. The others could tell the whole horrible story of what they had seen. He hailed down a cab to take him straight to the airport. There he bought a ticket on Easy Jet to Stansted, with an ongoing connection to Geneva, Switzerland. By noon he was well on his way.

XI

Friday, June 15ᵗʰ, 2012, Geneva, Switzerland, 17:00 GMT +1

Albert passed through Swiss immigration at Cointrin airport without a problem. His British passport was looked at in cursory fashion. Breathing a sigh of relief, he hailed a cab to take him to the quiet little residence Hotel Mon-Repos on Rue de Lausanne, fronting the north shore of Lac Leman, across from the Parc Mon-Repos and the *quai*.

It was a glorious summer late afternoon. The lake was full of sailboats catching the westerly breezes. Across the inner port in *Eaux-Vives*, the famous fountain, the *Jet d'Eaux*, spewed a perfect column of water 140 meters into the air, creating a rainbow in its descending mist. Behind it all, floating above a cloudbank like a ghostly mirage, the *massif* of Mont Blanc shimmered in the distance, 50 kilometers away to the south in Chamonix, France. Albert knew that that was where he would be headed soon, back to the calm solitude of the Haute Savoie. He remembered the famous alpine routes that he had climbed years ago – Mont Blanc via the Gouter route; The Walker Buttress on the Grandes Jorasses; the Whymper Couloir on the Aiguille Verte. Those had been idyllic days, climbing on the good, solid Chamonix granite. But then he remembered that he had some business to attend to first in Geneva before he could leave for the mountains.

PART 3
TALES OF THE HUNT

"The patience of the hunter is always greater than that of the prey."

I

Saturday, June 16th, 2012, London, 08:00 GMT

The London morning newspapers shrieked the news. Atypically, the staid *Times* of London carried a big, banner front-page headline: "North Sea Disaster Cripples British Energy Sector". The Sun, the Daily Mail and the other tabloids followed suit, with lurid details of mayhem and death. Prime Minister David Cameron was to address the nation on television that evening. An emergency order was put into effect banning all private vehicles in central London and a dozen other major cities. Price gouging at the pump was soon evident. The already outrageous price of petrol in Britain had doubled overnight. The nation had gone into crisis mode over losing its last chance to maintain its energy independence.

At Scotland Yard, Inspector Ian Llewelyn was in conference early that morning with Chief Superintendent, Straun Utley. They were treating the Sterling platform disaster as a terrorist act, even though no one had stepped forward yet to claim responsibility. Llewelyn had been in touch with Brian Bretton though, and both felt that Albert Stern was the leading suspect. Scotland Yard had also brought MI6 rapidly into the picture. Amongst its remits, it was charged with combating terrorism. Agent Gavin Lorimer had come over from Thames House in Millbank to join the meeting.

"So who is this Stern villain anyway?" Utley demanded.

"A fugitive from American justice, sir. The FBI asked us to try to apprehend him a few weeks ago here in London. It sounded like a very unlikely story. Seems that he was a leading NASA scientist who took off with some valuable US government property. They are treating it as a very high level issue of national security. They've asked us to render all possible assistance to apprehend and return him. We almost had him a fortnight ago in London, but he slipped away. We don't know where he went. Looks like he's gone underground", Llewleyn replied.

"What the Hades does he have? How could it have anything to do with the Sterling disaster?"

"We're trying to piece that together now, Superintendent. The FBI tells us that he is carrying an explosive substance that can do cataclysmic damage. It's already done so in Houston. So we are trying to place him on the Sterling platform early yesterday morning. We have the roster sheets in from Anglo. No Albert Stern, but a few people of possible interest", Lorimer added.

"An unlikely terrorist, eh? What would be his motives? Why us? Why such a wanton act of destruction? You had better get this man fast before anything else happens. The PM was on to me at home last night with a demand for swift action. Do whatever is necessary to get the bastard! Interrogate him thoroughly. Don't be too gentle. And don't be in any hurry to return him to the Americans. If he's the culprit, he's a major criminal here now too. Got it, you two?"

"Yes sir, we're on it already!"

"Keep me fully posted. I assume that you already have an APB out on Stern at all airports? He's sure to try to flee the country."

"Yes, it went out yesterday evening. No one has seen him yet, though. We'll keep after it, sir", Llewelyn concluded.

Llewelyn saw Lorimer out of the building. When he returned to his office, he found that he had had several urgent telephone calls from Brian Bretton. The last said that Bretton was on his way to Washington and would be in touch again from there. No use trying his cell phone now. He was on a late night flight that was already in the air.

II

Monday, June 18th, 2012, Washington, DC, FBI Headquarters, 07:30 EDT

Brian Bretton had arrived on the red eye from Houston. Shaking off bone weary fatigue early on a Monday morning, he now waited to see the FBI Director. He had been summoned to Washington as soon as news of the Sterling platform disaster had reached the US. The entangled threads of recent events had made it plain that they were no coincidence. There was a clear pattern emerging in light of Bretton's investigations in Houston. He had moved quickly to impound any remaining samples of the Viking sands. Yet, enigmatically, controlled testing against minute samples of both gasoline and crude oil had produced no results whatsoever. It just didn't add up. The surveillance videotape had plainly shown an explosion in the lab that had all of the telltale earmarks of the subsequent one at the Phillips 66 station. And now there had been a cataclysmic one on a North Sea oil platform. Bretton was quite perplexed.

"Please come with me, Mr. Bretton. The Director will see you now", the secretary said. As she opened a large, wood-paneled door, Director Calvin Morse rose to greet Bretton.

"Good to see you, Brian. Come in and sit down". Morse's well-appointed office was on the top floor of the J. Edgar Hoover federal building at 935 Pennsylvania Avenue, NW. Out the window was a stunning view of the US Capitol. Already seated in the room was another man whom Bretton didn't recognize.

"This is Chris Wytham from Langley. He heads the CIA's Counter-Terrorism Unit. This matter calls for interagency cooperation at the highest levels. You two will be working closely under the joint directions of DOI Tim Baker and myself. I spoke with Tim this morning and he is fully on board. The office of the Vice-President has also told me that the Veep will be following this matter closely for the President."

Chris Wytham was in his early 50s. Tall and wiry, he looked younger than his age. He had handsomely chiseled facial features and dark, curly hair, not yet showing any signs of gray. His penetrating blue eyes were softened only by an incongruous pair of rimless wire glasses. He had been with the Agency for over 25 years. His postings had included Chief of Station positions in US embassies in Aman, Jakarta, Moscow and Nairobi. Wytham had been involved in covert operations for most of his career. He was the CIA's acknowledged specialist in profiling the minds of terrorists. He radiated a simmering intensity that Brian Bretton could feel immediately.

Wytham was also amongst the best of the Agency's senior operatives who specialized in remorselessly hunting down and eliminating terrorists. If anyone could track down and deal decisively with Stern, it was certainly Chris Wytham. He was the veteran of many clandestine rendition missions in far off places in the world. He had successfully caught, brutally interrogated and permanently incarcerated terrorists on behalf of the US government and its allies over the many years. He was certainly ready and eager once again to rise to this newest challenge.

Bretton shook hands cursorily with Wytham. He wasn't happy with the news. Despite the spirit of interagency cooperation in intelligence matters post-9/11, Bretton harbored a deep suspicion, if not a dislike, for the Central Intelligence Agency, the "Company", as they called themselves. He didn't care for either their methods or for their tendency to try to act as top dog in terrorism investigations. But he knew that he had no choice but to cooperate with Wytham.

"Give us your take on what Stern is up to, Chris", Morse continued.

"He's probably trying to move the stuff. Sell it I mean. He knows what he has, but he would have had to prove it to potential buyers. This is much too big for petty crime. He would try to deal with countries that could gain from having such a weapon. Both Israel and North Korea come first to mind. Then there's always al-Qaeda. His clients would have to be either countries without petroleum resources who are threatened by those who have them, or petroleum-producing rogue States who would like to eliminate their competition in one fell swoop. I wouldn't hesitate to put Russia in the latter category. Stern's not a terrorist, although he certainly has committed a terrorist act. The real terrorists are whoever put him up to it."

"Damn it", Bretton thought to himself, "he's probably right." Although he didn't like the CIA, Bretton still had to admire their analytical acumen. "Why Britain, then? Why take out a North Sea oil platform?"

"I think the Brits are just incidental victims of the bigger game. Stern needed to provide proof to someone and the Brits were an easy target. He could move freely there, especially if he had acquired a new, British identity. I expect that that was the first thing he did."

Wytham obviously knew what he was talking about. He had handled numerous assets as a case officer. He understood the psychology of the terrorist and he didn't see Albert as being one. Rather, he saw him as a person who could be easily manipulated by both circumstances and skilled foreign operatives.

"I tend to agree", Morse replied. "Stern may not be a terrorist *per se*, but he is certainly confused, desperate and definitely very dangerous. You two get in touch immediately with Scotland Yard and have them comb the last crew manifests from the Sterling platform, if they haven't already done so. They need to track where each crewmember went after leaving their Aberdeen offices. Something will turn up if Stern was one of them. He's bound to have fled the country. Try also to get some identification from the rest of the crew. Even if Stern has altered his appearance, he couldn't have done that good of a job."

Bretton and Wytham got up to leave. They would be partners now and the Director had made it very plain what he expected from such cooperation. Wytham would take the lead, given his long experience and the Agency's remit to conduct its covert operations exclusively outside of the US. Given that Stern had already fled to Britain, their next step would be to have a conference call with Ian Llewelyn in London.

III

Monday, June 18th, 2012, London, Israeli Embassy, 11:00 GMT

When Ira Melman heard the news about the Sterling platform explosion he was stunned. Not just at what had happened, but by the details that were now coming out in the press. An accident on a North Sea platform could happen at any time, but this didn't appear to be an accident. By all accounts it was clearly either sabotage or terrorism. Someone had caused it to happen. But what really caught his attention was what had actually happened. From descriptions in the press, and through diplomatic releases, it appeared that the entire giant Sterling oil reserve had been consumed in a towering column of heat and blinding light. No fires or mass destruction. The platform was still standing, albeit badly seared. But now it stood atop of nothing. There appeared to be no oil left in the deep seabed below it.

Melman took out his scribbled notes of his meeting with Peter Shaw. What had happened at the Sterling platform uncannily tracked Shaw's description of the effects his mystery substance would have on crude oil. "My God", Melman wondered, "did I unwittingly put Shaw up to causing such a horrific disaster?" He had facetiously demanded proof. It looked like he had gotten it in spades. Melman could no longer dismiss Shaw as a deluded crank. The man was serious, dangerous and potentially quite an asset in their hands. But how could they get to him now? Melman studied the handwritten note that Shaw had given him as a text of an ad to be run in the *The Times*. He could do that, but first, he thought, he had better check with Jamal Safir in Herzliya. He needed to bring his superiors up to date immediately.

IV

Monday, June 18, 2012, Herzliya, Israel, Mossad HQ, 13:30 GMT+2

Jamal Safir was the Director of the Mossad, the Israeli intelligence agency. Short and stubby, he was built like a fireplug. His round, engaging face, set off by prominent dark eyebrows, was a disarming veil for the sharp, incisive, calculating mind within. He was an Iraqi Jew whose family had fled Baghdad for France in the 1930s. They had been in flight again during most of the Second World War. Finally, they had immigrated to Israel upon the founding of the new Jewish State. Safir was ruthless in defense of his adopted country. It had given him needed shelter as a youth, after the savage excesses of the Nazi pogroms and the Holocaust. He had seen action in the several Israeli-Arab wars and had made his way up through the Aman into the top levels of the Mossad with steel nerves and unflinching loyalty. He was a great person to have on one's side, but a dreaded adversary to his enemies. Amongst his comrades in arms in the Aman had been Ira Melman. So he wasn't surprised when Melman called him on the secure line from London that afternoon.

"Jamal, Ira here in London."

"What's on your mind, Ira? Something about the Sterling platform disaster, perhaps?" Safir had seen all the news reports and had followed the secret, internal government dispatches on the matter.

"Yes, I have a lot to tell you about that." Melman went on to recount the details of his meeting at the embassy with Peter Shaw several weeks before. He would send Safir the videotape immediately by pouch. Now he needed to know whether and how to try to re-establish contact with Peter Shaw.

Safir listened intently. He knew more than he would disclose. The Americans had already been in touch about a fugitive named Albert Stern, who was carrying a lethal substance and who might well have been in touch with Israeli security. This they had gotten from Yoshi Tanaka, under heavy interrogation. It was obvious to Safir that Peter Shaw was Albert Stern. He didn't need to see the surveillance video to confirm it. The question was how to make the best use of this potential asset for Israel.

"Run the ad in *The Times* exactly as Shaw told you to do, Ira, and see what response you get. I expect that you will hear from him quickly, probably electronically.

Then we'll find a way to reel him in."

"OK. If and when he contacts us, what shall we tell him?"

"You'll have to locate him first. I doubt that he'd still be in Britain. I'd have gotten the hell out of there fast if I were him. Then you must make him comfortable with the means and goals of our communication. He needs to be encouraged and led to believe that we'll accommodate his demands fully. He also needs to believe that he would be safe with us. Understood? Let me know immediately when you hear from him and we'll dope out a careful reply to bring him along quickly."

"Right. As soon as we hear from Shaw, I'll let you know."

Safir was quietly hatching his own plan. The Israeli government had already been contacted through top diplomatic channels about apprehending and returning Stern to US custody, as a matter of highest priority. The joint FBI-CIA team had provided information and identification details. They were expecting full cooperation from America's staunchest ally.

But Safir had other ideas. He had a healthy disdain for American paternalism towards Israel. Hadn't they stuck them with the useless "roadmap" for peace? Wasn't it the Americans who tried to deny Israel any possibility of nuclear defense capabilities, while they were all the time surrounded by ever growing hostile threats? He couldn't stomach their attempted role as honest broker between Israel and the Palestinians. No, he completely agreed with Prime Minister Netanyahu's unilateral solution to fence in and to secure Israel's borders. Equally, he knew that the bristling aggression of a nuclear-armed Iran had to be dealt with decisively. So why even consider helping the Americans recover a weapon that could be devastating in the hands of the Jewish State? Not a chance! But it all must be done very carefully, so as not to arouse the suspicions of Big Brother.

Safir picked up the intercom and buzzed his secretary. "Contact Leah Shalev, please, at the Metsada Department. Tell her it's urgent. I have to see her as quickly as possible. If she's in Tel Aviv, have her brought here by helicopter." Shalev, he thought, would be perfect for the assignment he had in mind.

V

Tuesday, June 19th, 2012, Geneva, 10:00 GMT +1

Albert awoke late from his first deep sleep in weeks. The sun was shining brightly into his window. He could both feel the cool breezes blowing in from the lake. He dressed at leisure and went out for a walk. His first stop was a nearby *patisserie* to buy several croissants and a cup of French roast coffee. Then he stopped next door at the *journaux-tabac* shop and bought a copy of the *The Times* of London. He found a comfortable bench in the little park across from his hotel along the Quai Wilson, munched on his croissants and coffee, and scanned the newspaper.

The Sterling platform disaster was still front-page news. But it had been supplanted in part by accounts of the British government's emergency measures to deal with the national energy crisis brought on by the loss of its vast Sterling oil reserves. Britain was already rationing gasoline, like the US and most other Western countries. But now it had to deal with the immediate and long-term effects of becoming a net importer of crude oil and refined products for the first time since the late 1960s. All hopes of maintaining its energy independence had been dashed by one horrific, wanton act.

Albert whisked past all of this to the classified ads. He was anxious to see if there was anything there yet for him. As his eyes read down the center of the page, he spotted a terse, innocuous ad that leapt out at him:

"Rocket: Please contact us immediately.
We need you to bring the heat!"

Albert smiled with satisfaction. He understood the message perfectly. After all, he had written it himself. "So" he thought, "now we will play by my rules."

How to contact the Israeli embassy in London? He couldn't risk calling them or using any other method that would prematurely disclose his current location. If things went well, though, he'd think of a safe way for them to *rendez vous* with him in Geneva. The only option would be electronic communication. He would have to send them an email. For this he had created a hotmail account. Using one of the plentiful internet cafés in the city center, he could contact Melman in London.

But first Albert had to decide what to do with the Viking sands. It was too risky to travel around with them. He had had several uncomfortable moments during airport searches, creatively explaining why he had them. They had almost been confiscated when he was leaving Britain as a "suspicious substance". Fortunately, they didn't react to explosive swabbing tests. But he couldn't afford to lose them. Besides, naive as Albert was in matters of international intrigue, he was not so naive that he didn't know that the Viking sands were his only leverage. They could apprehend him, but unless they got the sands too, they would have nothing.

So he needed to put them in a safe place that only he knew and could access. His first thought was a safe deposit box in the vaults of a Swiss bank, like UBS. After all, he was in Geneva. But quickly he realized that that wouldn't be safe at all. The myth of Swiss banking secrecy had been exposed years ago. Under heavy pressure from the US in particular, the Swiss would open their vaults to police authorities from other countries with proper warrants in felony cases, such as alleged terrorism. Their records and secure storage were no longer inviolable. It would be easy for the FBI to impound the Viking sands if Albert attempted to store them in Switzerland.

No, there was another intriguing answer. He would go to Chamonix and hide them there in a unique place, known only to him. Then he would contact the Israelis, safe in the knowledge that although they could reach him, neither they, nor anyone else, could reach the prize, unless and until he decided that they had earned it.

Albert packed a small handbag with the Viking sands stowed inside and set off for the Gare des Eaux-Vives to catch the SNCF train to Chamonix. The familiar route went through Roche-sur-Foron where Albert changed for a train to LeFayet/St. Gervais Les Bains. There, with his excitement mounting, he boarded the Mont Blanc Express for the panoramic ride to Chamonix.

In just over 3 hours he was there. He walked from the central station a few short blocks to the Hotel Le Morgane and checked in. The hotel was conveniently located only a few blocks away from the base station of the *telepherique* of the Aiguille du Midi, the cable car system that runs 2,807 meters straight up from Chamonix to the observation deck on the Piton Central at 3,842 meters. Tomorrow Albert would be going half way up, to Plan de l'Aiguille, at 2,317 meters There he would hike the Grand Balcon Nord, with a purpose. But tonight he walked leisurely into the center of the charming mountain village and found one of his favorite restaurants from years past, Le Serac. There he sat down to enjoy a bubbling cheese fondue *Savoyard*, washed down with a demi-liter of good white wine.

VI

Wednesday, June 20th, 2012, Chamonix, France, 09:00 GMT +1

It was a beautiful summer morning. The sky was a clear, azure blue. The great snow covered peaks of the Mont Blanc *massif* towered over the deep glacial valley like giant sentinels. Albert walked down to the ticket booth at the base station of the Aiguille du Midi cable car and bought a ticket to Plan de l'Aiguille.

While most summer tourists would be going all the way up to take in the splendid views across the Vallee Blanche, Albert had a very different purpose in mind. Equipped with backpack, boots and a Leki walking stick that he had picked up in town, he left the cable car at the 2,317 meter mid-station and began the 5 kilometer traverse of the Grand Balcon Nord. Wending beneath the many granite spires above, this classic traverse eventually ended at Montenvers, overlooking the great glacier, the Mer de Glace.

The turn off the well trodden path between Plan de l'Aiguille and Montenvers that Albert was looking for was not posted, but he knew it well. He diverted on to a narrow side trail that weaved its way up steep slopes of boulders and scree to the start of the ascent route for the Aiguille de L'M by its NNE ridge. This was a classic alpine training peak, with only a 200 meter vertical ascent to an airily exposed summit. Looking down from there, the surface of the glacier was a sheer drop of 1,000 meters. Scrambling easily over solid granite, Albert reached the summit in just under an hour. There he paused for a nostalgic view, up the line of granite needles to the north, and across the Mer de Glace to the mighty Drus and Aiguille Vertes to the west.

But Albert wasn't there to sightsee. Descending slightly from the summit, he traversed 10 meters across, off the classic climbing route. There he found what he was looking for - a fissure or pothole in the rock on a level stance. It was about a foot deep and half again as wide. "Perfect!" he thought. He recovered a small plastic bowl, his rock hammer and a one pound sack of Quikcrete, ready mix concrete, from his backpack. Then he carefully removed the Viking sands in their non-reactive aluminum, screw-top Nalgene bottle.

Before he laid the bottle into the hole, he filled a small metal vial with a few grams of the sands and put it back into his pack. This would be his insurance policy, if put to his proof again before his expected big payoff. He lined the natural fissure with loose pebbles and then placed the bottle securely at its bottom. He mixed the concrete with water from one of his liter water bottles. Placing a flat lid rock over the bottle, he then applied a thin layer of concrete. He was very careful not to drip any so that it would be seen when he had finished. He also wanted to be sure that it was thin enough to shatter easily with a rock hammer, when the time came.

Satisfied, he set several other rocks into the concrete completely to mask the hole. When he had finished it all looked perfectly natural. "There", he thought to himself, "now I have my own safe deposit box in a place where no one would ever suspect."

He wasn't at all concerned about the oncoming winter's cold damaging the Viking sands. The coldest day in the Alps was well above a normal evening's temperature on Mars. Nor was he too concerned about the eventual onset of winter snow conditions. A seasoned alpine climber like Albert could always get back to the secret cache that he had just created.

Now Albert could return to Geneva and contact Melman in London, confident in the knowledge that he had hidden his trump card safely away. He descended quickly back to the trail and continued on to Montenvers. There he caught the mountain rack railway tourist train back down to Chamonix village.

VII

Friday, June 22nd, 2012, Langley, Virginia, CIA Headquarters, 08:30 EDT

Unbeknownst as yet to Albert, the destruction of the Sterling oilfield had reverberated like a giant shock wave through the world's oil-producing nations. All of them were very edgy. They felt particularly threatened. The fact that no one had yet stepped forward to claim responsibility had fueled wild speculation and deep dread amongst them. In Saudi Arabia, Russia, Nigeria, Venezuela, Indonesia, Kazakhstan and, notably, Iran, security at all oil producing, transporting and processing facilities was put on highest alert.

Had this been an al-Qaida strike of a terrifying new sort? What terrible doomsday weapon had they developed and when would they use it again? Why was Britain the victim? And why was there no boastful claim or new video tape delivered to al-Jazeera?

As both nations and international oil companies scrambled to secure their precious resource facilities from further attack, supply dropped precipitously and the price of crude oil shot up again. This time it passed rapidly through the $250/barrel mark. Oil giant, Anglo Petroleum Limited, had been driven to the brink of bankruptcy in less than a month, after the loss of its crown jewel asset. Angst was exceptionally high, worldwide.

Against this background both Brian Bretton and Chris Wytham were working separate but cooperative paths to locate Albert Stern. Bretton had been in frequent touch with Ian Llewelyn in London. Wytham with Inspector Jaap van Noort, a bi-lingual Flemish Belgian, at Interpol headquarters in Lyon, France. Bretton had learned from Llewelyn that no one matching Stern's photo had been positively identified as part of the last Sterling platform crew. But that one such crewmember, a British subject named Peter Shaw, had left hurriedly for Geneva after arriving back in Aberdeen. Wytham had asked Interpol to check on this with Swiss authorities, which van Noort was doing in Geneva at that very moment. But that wasn't nearly enough for the relentless CIA agent.

Brian Bretton had never been to the sprawling campus in Langley, Virginia, that hid the Company's Headquarters from prying eyes behind screens of mature trees. He and Chris Wytham drove in through the triple security barriers and parked in the lot reserved for senior staff. As they entered the original headquarters building, Bretton was impressed by the great CIA seal inlaid in granite on the floor and the Memorial Wall, on the right of the main entrance hall. It bore the simple inscription, "In Honor Of Those Members Of The Central Intelligence Agency Who Gave Their Lives In The Service Of Their Country". The wall bore 83 silver stars, 48 identified as officers who could be revealed and 35 who would always remain secret, even in death. Once through the last security card reader, however, it all looked just like any other government building to Bretton.

Wytham showed Bretton to his office on the second floor. Quite airy, it looked out over a verdant courtyard, surrounded by large oaks and a variety of maples in full summer leaf. Bretton had grudgingly warmed to Wytham as they worked together. Now they were developing an excellent rapport.

"Brian, let's assume as a working hypothesis that Stern is in Switzerland. If he has acquired a new identity as "Peter Shaw", we can check on that immediately. Sound good to you?"

"Sure, how do you plan to do that?"

"I've asked my secretary to put a call in to our Chief of Station at the US embassy in Bern. Bill Churchill, is an old friend and a damn good agent. He should be on the line in a few moments". When the phone rang, Wytham put it down on the speakerphone cradle. Churchill came on the line and Wytham told him that he was on a three party call with Brian Bretton as well, from the FBI.

"Bill, we need your help on an urgent matter. The DOI is personally overseeing this." Wytham then explained the situation to Churchill in succinct detail and asked him to send an agent to Geneva immediately to look for a Peter Shaw. Checking with Swiss Immigration at Cointrin airport would be a good starting point and then with the cantonal police who, by law, kept a record of foreign guests registered at all hotels.

Churchill replied that he would send one of his best people to Geneva. He had seen the top-secret intra-agency dispatches and was well aware of the seriousness of the matter.

"I'll put Bob MacLean on it today. He'll be in Geneva before evening. We'll talk again tomorrow, after Bob has made his initial inquiries. If Shaw is there, don't worry, we'll find him."

Satisfied, Wytham hung up. He then rang Llewelyn in London. Llewelyn confirmed that there had been no further sightings of Albert Stern since the day he had slipped out of the Millennium Knightsbridge Hotel over a month ago. But of great interest was the fact that a Peter Shaw had rented a bed-sitter in Earl's Court later that very day. He had paid a week's rent in advance in cash and then never returned to the small flat. British Rail records from King's Cross Station showed that this Peter Shaw had bought a single to Edinburgh and Aberdeen three days later. Where he had been in the interim, no one knew. But what was becoming increasingly clear to all concerned was that Peter Shaw was their fugitive, Albert Stern.

"Why would a seemingly mild-mannered, reputable senior scientist at NASA suddenly become a terrorist?" Bretton asked rhetorically. "Sure, his world was turned upside down in a very short time, but hardly a level of stress to turn him into a desperate killer. What do you think could have triggered such a complete turnaround?"

"As I said before, I think that he was put up to it by circumstances. He knew he had a formidable weapon if he could put it into the right hands. He must have tried to sell it in exchange for wealth and security. His only clients would have to be countries that could use it to settle scores with long time adversaries who had petroleum based-economies. Like Israel and Iran right now. I'm betting that he went to see a country like that, but was rebuffed as some kind of lunatic. They must have put him to his proof, not believing that he could deliver. It was probably a hell of a setback, even though he should have expected it. Desperate people do desperate things. Underneath he's clearly some kind of deep-seated sociopath, as mass destruction came just too easily for him."

"So it's key for us to know whom he went to see in London before he left for Aberdeen", Bretton concluded. "He only had the Monday to do it. Embassies are closed over the weekends. We need to have Llewelyn and Lorimer do a quick swab of the diplomatic circuit to see where Peter Shaw may have turned up".

"Do you really think that any embassy he went to would now be willing to share that information with us and the Brits? Certainly not. Perhaps they got a lot more than they bargained for, but now you would think that they'd want to have Stern and his weapon all to themselves. I doubt that we'll get much cooperation."

Agreed, but not optimistic, Bretton and Wytham called Llewelyn in London and asked for further help from both Scotland Yard and MI6.

VIII

Saturday, June 23rd, 2012, En Route to Geneva from Chamonix, 11:00 GMT +1

As the SNCF train approached the normally unmanned border crossing into Switzerland at Bardonnex-Saint-Julien, it came to a halt. Albert had been through this sleepy little outpost many times before. The train usually proceeded straight on through it without stopping. Since the creation of the EEC, frontier-crossing formalities between Switzerland and Community members had become quite relaxed, if not non-existent. So this struck him as very unusual. His level of awareness was immediately heightened.

On to the train came a Swiss frontier policeman in gray uniform, along with another man in a dark, double-breasted suit. The *gendarme* asked all passengers to take out their passports for inspection. In particular, they wanted to know who were carrying British passports. The man in the dark suit was wearing a badge that Albert could just make out down the aisle. It read "Interpol". As they moved down the aisle checking passports, they came to a stop in front of Albert. Inspector Jaap van Noort gave him a long, hard look of appraisal.

"*Bon jour, monsieur*, passport, please", he said. Albert had already figured it all out. They were obviously looking for him. They must have tracked Peter Shaw from Aberdeen to Geneva and then on to Chamonix. Trying not to look nervous, Albert handed a new British passport over to the inspector.

"*Monsieur* Philip Bloom? Please remove your sunglasses. May we look in your rucksack, please?" The Swiss gendarme had eased his right hand up to his belt, near to the holster of his Glock service revolver.

"Certainly", Albert said casually, offering it to them. They were looking for the mysterious weapon, of course. But all they would find were some dirty socks, hiking boots, clothing and his personal toiletries. Nothing suspicious. They didn't bother to look too closely at the contents of his travel kit, however. That's where he had hidden the small vial of Viking sands, inside of the cylindrical tube of an almost empty, push-up Polo deodorant stick.

Inspector van Noort once again studied Albert's face. If he were looking for Albert Stern, he wouldn't have easily recognized him. Now Albert sported his own well-trimmed beard and moustache with long, unkempt hair, dangling slightly over his ears. He looked like an average, later day hippy, returning from a hiking sojourn in the Alps.

"There are no entries in your passport, *monsieur*", the inspector said. "Where have you been prior to Chamonix? Geneve, perhaps?"

"No, I flew from London to Lyon and then I caught the train to Chamonix. Now I'm going to Geneva to stay with friends for a few days before going back to London. I have to work next week, you know"

"I see, *monsieur*, very well. *Merci*", the inspector said, handing Albert back his passport. With that, he and the gendarme moved on into the next car.

Albert watched them disappear. Then he broke into a belated, cold sweat. He knew that his cover as Peter Shaw was blown. They were getting uncomfortably close. He certainly couldn't return to the Hotel Mon Repos, nor could he continue to be Peter Shaw. He was down to his last new identity, with no real progress to show for it.

As the train pulled into the Gare des Eaux-Vives in Geneva, Albert got off and hailed a cab. He would have to find a small place quickly to set up his new base of operations as Philip Bloom.

IX

Monday, June 25th, 2012, Geneva, 10:00 GMT +1

Albert had spent Saturday and Sunday nights in a small, inexpensive hotel near the main railway station, the Gare de Cornavin. It was on the edge of the colorful but somewhat sleazy Les Paquis district. This was the liveliest part of the city. It was home to immigrants, ethnic restaurants and sex shops.

On Monday morning, however, Albert walked across the Pont du Mont-Blanc, spanning the River Rhone as it exits Lac Leman, and through into Place Molard. He was looking for an *agence immobiliere*, where he could rent a small, one bedroom efficiency flat in the Veille Ville, or old town, up the hill, overlooking the Place Bourg du Four. This location was key. He wanted a clear view out his window on to the plaza and the well-known watering hole there, La Clemence, or "La Cloche" to the locals. Aside from bringing back good memories of beers with his friends and hustling local women after his summer climbing trips while at Cambridge, he knew that he could use the picturesque, stone-cobbled plaza and café as a safe place to meet whomever was sent to him by Melman, after he had arranged it all.

Albert settled in to his rented studio apartment and then headed down the Rue de L'Hotel de Ville to find an internet café. For 5 francs an hour he could have a quiet cubicle and a computer all to himself. He logged in to his hotmail account and then typed in "lmelman@israel.org.uk."

His message was short and succinct: "Rocket here, responding to your ad. When can we have an online chat by instant message? Reply ASAP. No names please."

In less than 5 minutes Albert had a reply from Melman in London. They immediately opened an electronic dialogue:

IMelman (IM): Where are you now? We are very anxious to meet with you again.

Rocket (R): How do you propose to arrange it? Who will you send?

IM: We will have to know where you are first.

R : Only if you first acknowledge that you are willing to meet all of my terms and conditions, as we earlier discussed.

IM: Yes, yes, we certainly will, if you can still deliver the goods.

R : No problem, they are quite safe. Now you also know how well they work.

IM: Where can we meet with you?

R : I am in Switzerland. Send details of your proposed intermediary and I will give you further instructions on where and when the meeting will take place.

IM: I will need some time to arrange it. A day, perhaps.

R : Fine. Until tomorrow at this time. I will be online then.

X

Wednesday, June 27th, 2012, Herzliya, Israel, Mossad HQ, 11:00, GMT+2

When Jamal Safir heard the news from Ira Melman , he was quite pleased. Not that he hadn't expected it, though. He had already devised a plan of action and cleared it personally with both the PM and the Defense Ministry. Over the course of the last few days, Melman had located Peter Shaw in Geneva and had agreed with him on a *rendez-vous* there with an agent. Now that agent was waiting outside of Safir's office to see him, as he had requested.

Safir opened the door personally and greeted Captain Leah Shalev of the Israeli army. Covertly, however, she was a skilled operative of the *Kidon*, a highly secret sub-unit of the Mossad's Metsada department. It dealt in foreign assassinations. Even an older man like Safir couldn't help liking what he saw. 32 years old, 5'2", 115 lbs., all bundled into a magnificently sculpted package. Long, dark, curly hair, flashing brown eyes and a glowingly sun-tanned, olive complexion. Clad casually in tight, faded jeans and a khaki shirt, Shalev was a real knockout. Safir would always joke with her that she was Israel's answer to Salma Hayek. But that was as far as it went. Beneath her striking exterior beauty was a battle-hardened agent who would kill without remorse in defense of the vital interests of her country.

Shalev was not your typical Israeli woman. She was the only child of a national hero. Her father was a highly decorated army brigadier general who had distinguished himself in Israel's 1967 and 1970 wars for its very survival. Her grandparents were Holocaust survivors who had immigrated to Israel, shortly after it had been founded. At her father's insistence, Shalev had been raised on a *kibbutz* on the West Bank. There she had seen, first hand, almost daily sabotage and murder during the long and bitter first Palestinian *intifadah*. These early experiences had started to harden her into the person she was ultimately to become. She did her mandatory national service, at which she excelled. Offered a commission in the army, she leapt at it. She graduated with highest honors from the General Staff College and saw fierce guerilla combat early on, along the Lebanese border against Hezbollah insurgents. She progressed quickly through the ranks and eventually drew the attention of the Aman, the army intelligence unit of the Israeli Defense Force. From there, an invitation to join the Mossad was almost inevitable.

On a personal level, the stunning Shalev was amused by men, but not very interested in creating any long-term relationships. Still, she certainly had had more than her share of "amusements" in her three plus decades. Known as sharp-witted, independent and deadly efficient, she was very much her father's child. In all, Leah Shalev was exactly whom Safir needed for this critical job.

"So, Leah, good news. The assignment we discussed the other day is on. You'll need to move quickly. You're going to Geneva tonight. Your cover will be that of a senior development economist, visiting our permanent mission to the UN Economic and Social Council".

Shalev laughed huskily. "Something I know a lot about, right, Jamal? But I certainly am ready. What are my orders?"

"You will meet this Peter Shaw. He has given us very specific details on how and where to contact him. Remember, Shaw has something we badly need. It's a matter of highest national security. You are to use any and all means to get it." Safir gave a wry smile.

"Don't worry about that. I'm well trained", Shalev smiled back knowingly.

"I know, but it might not be that easy. He's an amateur and very skittish. You will have to take the time to win his confidence and to assure him that you will look after him well. He'll need a lot of comforting and more than just hand holding. He will have to satisfy you first that he has this stuff and that it still works as he claims. You must see this with your own eyes. Then you have to convince him that he must deliver it to you before you can arrange safe passage for him to Israel. Tell him that he will be well taken care of here. He also wants a lot of money. He should believe that he will get it, wherever and however he wants it."

"And when I have succeeded in all of that? When I have this stuff in my hands?"

"You will kill him. Quietly, and in such a way as to make sure we are not implicated. We don't want the Americans to know that we have the stuff until we have used it to crush our enemies. You will think of a good way to do all of this, yes?"

"Of course."

With that Shalev got up to leave. Safir bid her a warm good-bye and reminded her again that her success could be the key to her country's very continued existence. "Do not fail us, Leah", were his parting words.

"I've never let you down, Jamal. You know that you can always count on me", Shalev replied, sinuously swinging her tight little *derriere* as she closed the door behind her.

XI

Friday, June 29th, 2012, Place Bourg du Four, Geneva, 14:00 GMT +1

Albert was nervous as he looked repeatedly out of his window down on to the open square below. He had given precise instructions on how the agent was to identify himself to him. He looked down at the tables full of tourists soaking up the sun over drinks and checked his watch again. No one down there looked to be the likely contact.

Albert didn't notice at first, but then saw that a small, attractive, well-dressed woman had seated herself at an outside table on the edge of the crowd. She called the waiter over and ordered two liter bottles of the local favorite, *Biere Cardinal*. She placed one bottle opposite her, as if waiting for a friend to come, and poured some of the other one out for herself. In her hand she had a folded copy of the *Tribune de Geneve*, with which she began to fan herself against the summer heat. This finally caught Albert's attention. Those were the opening signs he had specified to initiate a contact. Reacting to the afternoon's warm sun, Shalev casually opened her suit jacket to reveal perfect 36C breasts, neatly contained in a tight-fitting silk blouse. That definitely got Albert's attention.

"Could this really be?" he thought. "They sent a beautiful young woman to meet me? It must be a ruse!" She couldn't be down there alone, as he had insisted. Yet he was fascinated and wanted to take a closer look.

Albert left his flat and headed downstairs into the square. Trying to look as nonchalant as possible, he made his way around the crowded tables to a park bench along their edge. He sat down and pretended to be engrossed in a newspaper. All the time his attention was riveted on the woman sitting no more than a few feet away. With furtive glances he studied her carefully. Wow, he still couldn't believe it! But, at the same time, he scanned the rest of the square for any telltale signs of others who might have come with her.

Shalev looked at her watch. 2:15 PM and no one had yet approached her. But her well-trained eye had noticed a man enter the square and sit down on a nearby bench. Albert couldn't possibly know it, but she had already identified him. As part of her military security training, she had been well schooled in the ancient science of physiognomy, the study of the configuration of faces. Despite Albert's attempts to alter his appearance, his facial features perfectly matched the photographs she had been shown by Safir. So she knew he was there. Now she waited patiently for him to make the first move.

2:30, Shalev had been waiting now for half an hour. The man on the bench was still sitting there, feigning disinterest. Perhaps she could stir him into action? She picked up her purse and took out a ten franc note, which she left on the table. Finishing the last few drops of her beer, she got up and walked slowly away, right in front of Albert. In sultry fashion, she headed out of the square and started down the Rue du Puits-St.-Pierre, towards the old armaments square and its arched, romanesque colonnades. She was in no hurry.

Albert took a hasty look around and then got up to follow Shalev. There were a few others on the narrow, cobbled street, so he kept his distance at first. But as they both came abreast of the colonnades Albert had closed the distance to a foot or two. He was now ready to make his move. Without warning, he grabbed

Shalev from behind by her slim right wrist. He tugged her smartly under the arches, off the street and away from prying eyes.

Shalev's instinctive first reaction would normally have been to deliver a swift karate chop to the throat of her would be assailant. But she knew what was happening and so she suppressed her well-honed military training. "Mr. Shaw", she protested while freeing her hand from Albert's grasp, "this is not what had been arranged!"

"I know", Albert replied, quite flustered. "But I had to be sure that you were alone. You knew it was me all along?" In spite of all of his instincts to be extremely cautious, Albert was thoroughly transfixed by the lovely vision standing right in front of him. The waft of her Opium perfume filled his nostrils and threatened to seduce him on the spot.

"Let me introduce myself, Mr. Shaw", Shalev said, holding out her hand once again, enticingly. "I am Captain Leah Shalev of the Israeli Aman. I am here to bring you safely back to Tel Aviv. Shall we go somewhere quiet where we can talk?"

Directly through the colonnades was the Restaurant Les Armures. Dark beams, wrought iron, medieval arms, and a robust Swiss menu that had lured the likes of both Jimmy Carter and the Clintons over the years. The basement bar was full of old world charm and, most importantly, privacy. In a wood-paneled booth for two, over a liter of chilled, white Swiss Fendant, Albert and Leah fell to talking.

XII

Monday, July 2nd, 2012, Langley, Virginia, CIA Headquarters, 09:00 EDT

Chris Wytham was thoroughly frustrated. Bill Churchill had rung him that morning from Bern with bad news. Churchill's man, Jim MacLean, had been to Geneva. But he had not turned up any further useful information on the current whereabouts of Albert Stern. MacLean had tracked Stern - now as Peter Shaw – very thoroughly through Swiss immigration at Cointrin; to his registration at the Hotel Mon-Repos; and then to his purchase of a 5 day round-trip excursion railroad ticket to Chamonix at the Gare Cornavin. Swiss CFF/SBB records showed that Peter Shaw had boarded a SNCF train to Chamonix on the morning of Tuesday, June 19th. He had until Saturday, June 23rd, to return to Geneva. Urgent assistance had been requested from the French government to turn up any records of Stern's hotel stay in Chamonix and his return train journey to Geneva. But, as usual, the French were not in a hurry to cooperate. Most maddening was the fact that the border posts in and out of Switzerland to France were manned in a cursory, if not non-existent, fashion. Almost anyone could slip easily between the two countries without showing a passport or having an entry stamp affixed. This really shocked Wytham, who was now used to functioning in a post-9/11, high security environment.

Nevertheless, the Swiss had still been quite helpful. At the request of both the US and the UK, in cooperation with Interpol, they had monitored train traffic between Geneva and Chamonix during the period in question. They had boarded trains arriving at the Swiss border post and checked all passengers' passports.

But no trace had been found of a Peter Shaw returning to Geneva from Chamonix.

Brian Bretton had just arrived. "Where the hell is he now?" Bretton asked rhetorically, in obvious frustration. "Out there somewhere, like a ticking time bomb. Heaven alone knows what he'll do next."

"My guess is that he's back in Geneva, Brian. But why would he have gone to Chamonix? Perhaps to stash something there?"

"And how did he get back into Switzerland? The Swiss checked the trains carefully. He didn't enter by car or bus, either, through Thonex."

"No, at least not as Peter Shaw. I think he's getting pretty damn good at being a chameleon. Cunning bastard. He must have yet another new identity. They can be bought for a stiff price in London".

"What news do we have of Stern's embassy contacts while in London?" Bretton asked.

"Predictably, none. The Brits queried almost every relevant embassy at the highest levels. No one will own up to having ever heard of a Peter Shaw or Albert Stern. No country has issued an entry visa for any such persons. Whomever he talked with is playing their cards very close to the chest. Wouldn't you, given the events that followed?"

"It sure looks like we are at a dead end. No use you going to London, Chris. He's long gone from there. Our only hope is to look for him in Geneva. That's the most likely place for him to be in now", Bretton concluded. "Let's get moving before he makes his contact there and they spirit him and the stuff away to God knows where. I'm sure the Swiss will continue to help us."

I'll call Bill Churchill in Bern to alert them that I'm coming", Wytham said.

Chris Wytham's secretary made the necessary arrangements for him on a priority basis. He would take United's evening flight to Frankfort the next day and then connect to Bern the morning after on Lufthansa.

XIII

Tuesday, July 3rd, 2012, S. Waziristan, Pakistan/Afghanistan, Border, 08:00 GMT +4

The tall, gaunt, gray-bearded figure had called his _majlis al-shura_ - his advisory council - to meet him in his tent. Seated stiffly cross-legged on an oriental rug, his Kalichnikov propped against the tent pole behind him, he called the meeting to order.

"_Allah Ahkbar_! Ayman, tell us all what this Jew has and how we can use it to destroy our enemies". News of the Sterling oilfield's demise had reached to the farthest corners of the world. The unusual nature of the event had caught the attention of the terrorist leader. Such an awesome weapon had infinite possibilities for targeted havoc and mayhem. Most importantly, it could strike a dagger deep into the heart of his most sworn enemies.

"It is some substance which consumes crude oil. It is a wonder! It could cripple a country overnight" Ayman replied.

"How do we know that it is real?"

"Our sleeper cells in London have confirmed it, leader. You know that we have people inside their security services. They are frantic to find the man and the substance before he strikes with it again."

"Then it must be ours We must find him, take the substance for our own and destroy him. Then we shall enter into our final, victorious *jihad*!"

"Yes, leader, we can bring the great infidel devil finally to its knees. We can take from them their few remaining resources. The Americans will feel our wrath once again, *inshallah*!".

"No, Ayman" the leader contradicted him. "Not the Americans again. Not yet, anyway. Our biggest enemy is the hypocritical, corrupt regime that holds our most sacred religious sites hostage. They will feel our wrath first. We shall destroy the source of their filthy wealth entirely. It is time to bring down these tyrants! And we shall also punish the haughty Shiites in Iraq. Our brother, Abu Lahab, could finally bring them to their knees with such a weapon. When we are done, there will be no one left in our world to pander to the Americans' great thirst for oil."

The council was instructed by the leader to find Albert and the mystery weapon at all costs. Cells were to be mobilized where needed. Martyrdom operations were to be conducted, where necessary. Al-Queda's *mujuhadin* had to have this weapon.

As the council filed out of the tent, the leader gestured for Ayman to stay on. "Where is this Jew now, Ayman?"

"We think that he is in Switzerland. In Geneva. Our sources tell us that he fled there after the great explosion in Britain."

"Do we know what he looks like? How shall we find him there?"

"We have a copy of a computer-generated identisketch that one of our faithful stole from the British police. We also know that the Americans are very anxious to find a missing NASA scientist named Albert Stern. We have his vitals too. The photos of him match the identisketch very well. We are confident we could recognize him."

"Then send our best man to find him. Send Ahmed Samir, with whomever else he chooses. Alert our contacts in Switzerland and in Iraq. We must capture this man quickly, before anyone else gets to him."

"Yes, leader. We fear that the Israelis are already pursuing him for this weapon. But when Ahmed finds him first?"

"Have him kill the infidel dog. But he must be sure that we have the precious substance securely in our hands first."

"It shall be done as you command, leader, *inshallah!*"

XIV

Wednesday, July 4th, 2012, Tehran, Iran, 14:00 GMT +2 ½

It was clear to the Chief of the Iranian Secret Service, General Reza Houshmand, that the Israelis were up to something big. His contacts in Hezbollah had alerted him to movements of certain key personnel within the Israeli intelligence service. He already knew that the Israeli Mossad had sent a high-level Kidon operative to Geneva on a covert mission. It had something to do with the frantic hunt the Americans and the British were conducting for a missing NASA scientist. Information was vague, but clandestine sources embedded deep within the Israeli security structure had provided enough detail for Houshmand to be on full alert. He needed to know more, however, before he could act decisively to intercept whatever treacherous operations the Israelis were planning.

It wasn't unusual for secret information of this sort to find its way to Houshmand's ear. The Iranians and the Israelis had been spying on each other for decades. There had always been a deep suspicion and distrust between them. Intense surveillance by both sides had gone hi-tech in 2005/06 when the ever-accommodating Russians had launched spy satellites Sinah-1 for Iran, and Eros B for Israel. But now, with the hard-liner, Mahmoud Ahmadinejad, consolidating his grip on the Iranian presidency, the level of mutual fear and enmity had grown to a crescendo. Ahmadinejad had publicly threatened numerous times "to wipe Israel off the map". Now he had nuclear-tipped missiles aimed at Haifa, Tel Aviv and Jerusalem.

Houshmand summoned his deputy, Shaheen Ansari, into his office. "Shaheen, what is this Israeli bitch doing in Geneva? What or whom is Shalev seeking?"

Ansari had read all of the week's intercepts from both the British Security Service and the coded US diplomatic traffic to Bern. He was very adept at both cryptography and the psyche of covert operatives. "It seems that this is all connected with the great explosion last month in the British sector of the North Sea, General" he replied. "There is talk of a new doomsday weapon which can destroy crude oil deposits in place. It seems that a rogue US scientist from NASA has taken it and he is now in Geneva, trying to sell it to the highest bidder. The Israelis want it badly. We think that this Israeli agent has gone to Geneva to make a deal with him. If she succeeds, the Israelis will surely try to use it against us."

"Then she must be stopped, Shaheen" Houshmand replied. "We must get this Jewish bitch before she seduces her prey and steals the weapon. We have had run-ins with her in the past. She's cunning and ruthless. This time she must not escape our vengeance. We shall send our lion, Abbas, to devour her."

Houshmand's orders from the top were clear and unambiguous. Kill Leah Shalev before she could complete her mission. Any means were acceptable. Get the doomsday substance from the American traitor, after extracting from him all relevant information on its use. If he wouldn't cooperate, even under torture, kill him and destroy the substance forever.

"The Lion", Captain Abbas Sorushian, of the Revolutionary Guards Qods Force, would head immediately for Geneva to do the job. All Qods were highly trained professionals, specializing in assassinations and bombings. The Lion was a very effective, seasoned, cold-blooded killer. As if he needed any more incentive to kill Shalev, he also carried a permanent reminder of his last meeting with her in Lebanon. In his right leg there was still a deeply embedded piece of shrapnel that had come from a hand grenade that she had thrown in amongst his troops.

XV

Friday, July 6th, 2012, Geneva, 20:00, GMT +1

As the week progressed, Albert became increasingly captivated with Leah Shalev, just as she had planned it. Dazzled, in a way he hadn't experienced in many years. He felt some very long-suppressed primal instincts stirring within him. But at the same time, he knew that he had to be extremely cautious. She hadn't come to Geneva just to make him feel good. He had no real experience of such an enigmatic woman. Dripping with feminine charm, she had also already shown that she had some very hard edges to complement her ample 36C-24-35 curves. He fantasized over her at night, but he tried hard to keep her at bay during his waking hours. It certainly wasn't easy. Could she be trusted, though? Could he believe her?

It was an evening of the weekend of the Fourth of July. It meant nothing to the Genevoise, but Leah had thoughtfully suggested that they go out to dine to celebrate the occasion. Albert had very mixed emotions. Celebrate the Fourth of July when he was a fugitive from the very country that they would be feting? Still, he couldn't resist the chance to spend a soft summer evening with Leah along the shores of the gently rippling lake. Besides, they had a lot more to talk about before he could even start to be convinced of her *bone fides*.

Out of an abundance of caution, they had carefully been avoiding *centre ville*, Geneva, for their various *rendez-vous*. It was too dangerous to be seen together and, for Albert, to be seen at all. Of necessity, he had become a night owl. This evening they had chosen to meet at the charming little Restaurant Le Leman, on the northern side of the lake in Nyon, some 10 or so kilometers out of Geneva. The inviting interior was a wood-paneled, candle-lit brasserie-style room, set out handsomely with crystal, silver and fine earthenware. The menu was fairly extensive, but the house specialty was *Filets de Perche* from the lake, served in two variations, *Limon* and *Meuniere*. Between them they opted for both, accompanied by *pommes frites, salade verte,* and crusty French bread. It was all to be washed down with a well-chilled bottle of Mont sur Rolle, a refreshing Vaudoise white wine. But the conversation, not the repast, would be far more important to Albert.

Leah looked across the table at Albert with an alluring smile. She was stunning that evening, neatly packaged in a short, clinging, black silk dress. Her hair was up in a French twist, and her big, brown, limpid eyes seductively reflected the candlelight.

She had dressed to impress. With luck and the full use of her skills, she thought to herself, she might accomplish her mission before the dawn of the next day. "Peter" she inquired sympathetically, "tell me more about how you got to this point in life".

"You can call me Albert, Leah. You know who I really am. How this all happened is still a big confusion in my mind. Less than two months ago I was a senior scientist at NASA, in Houston. Then my entire world turned upside down. In a few days my comfortable, meaningful life was shattered. I was a victim of circumstances way beyond my control."

Albert then went on slowly to recount to Leah all that had happened since he had fled Houston. Perhaps it was the wine and the intimate atmosphere, but now, for the first time, he felt comfortable doing so. He had to admit that he was beginning to like her very much, although he still heard the warning sirens in his head cautioning him to beware of this Israeli enchantress.

Leah feigned to be listening in rapt attention. She knew that she was finally penetrating Albert's initial, hard, resistance. Now she would try to steer the conversation in the direction that she wanted it to go. "So, you have this substance, these Viking sands, in a safe place, yes?"

"Of course. They are very safe."

"With you? Hidden in your flat? Are you sure that's safe enough? Perhaps in a safe deposit box here in Geneva?"

"No, not in a bank vault. There is no more inviolable banking secrecy in Switzerland. The US authorities could reach it easily with a felony warrant for me. I'm even worse than a felon now, a terrorist, they claim! They would have no trouble persuading the Swiss authorities to demand that one of their banks turn over anything I might have put away for safe-keeping."

"So you have still have it personally under your control?"

"Yes, as I said. It is very safely concealed", Albert replied, the slightest suggestion of irritation creeping into his voice.

Leah knew to back off at that point. She had heard enough anyway. The evening had passed pleasantly and she didn't want to spoil the growing atmosphere of trust and intimacy. They each ordered a dessert and espressos to linger over. Albert had drunk a lot and he needed to excuse himself. All Leah needed was that moment. As he left the table she reached into her purse and took out a small capsule full of the equivalent of time-release, maximum strength Ambien. She opened it up and slipped its contents into Albert's espresso, stirring it lightly, not to disturb the thin layer of *crema* on the top.

Albert returned and Leah suggested that he order a cab back to Geneva. When the cab arrived they got into the back seat together. Albert gave the driver his address in the Old Town. Riding along the lakeside back to Geneva, Albert felt Leah snuggle towards him. He could feel the exciting closeness of her warm hips and legs against his own. As he moved a bit nearer, he suddenly began to feel very tired. He slipped his arm around Leah's shoulder and felt his head nodding down involuntarily towards her full, generous breasts.

"All of a sudden I'm feeling tired, Leah, so very tired", Albert mumbled. "Just my luck" he thought wearily to himself. He had to snap out of it!

"Try to relax, Albert", Leah said comfortingly. "It's probably just the strain of all of the unrelenting stress that you've been through, finally catching up to you." But Albert's thoughts began to muddle as Leah's heady perfume filled his senses and lulled him further into his growing stupor.

By the time the cab reached the Place Bourg du Four, Albert was semi-conscious. It was after midnight and the crowds of revelers at La Cloche were filtering slowly away into the warm night air. Leah paid the cab driver and helped Albert out of the back seat. With Albert leaning heavily on her, Leah made their way to Albert's second floor apartment, overlooking the square. He fumbled badly with the keys. She took them gently from him and opened the door. Together they stumbled into the one room efficiency apartment and fell together on to the bed. Leah comforted Albert, stroking his head tenderly. She rose from the bed and stood in front of Albert unzipping her little black dress. He wanted so badly to touch her, but he was barely awake! The last thing Albert remembered before he fell into a very deep sleep was the sight of a voluptuous Leah standing in front of him in only lace thong panties, her delicious body backlit by the warm glow of the filtered streetlight coming up from below.

Leah smiled to herself as she put her dress back on. Albert was out cold for at least the next 7 hours. This would give her all the time she needed to search the apartment thoroughly. She reached into her little black, sequined purse and took out a Beretta 86F .380 caliber pistol that had been supplied to her through the Chief Information Officer of the Israeli embassy in Bern. Carefully she screwed the silencer on to the front of its short, stubby barrel. Done, she put it down on the dresser near to the bed. If she found what she was looking for, she could complete her mission that evening. A single, muffled bullet shot in Albert's temple and she'd be gone forever, unseen into the night. By the next evening she'd have been whisked back to Tel Aviv. The Viking sands would be with her. Safir would be both pleased and proud.

But it wasn't going to be that easy. An hour's meticulous search of the tiny apartment turned up nothing. Leah had methodically gone through everything there, every nook and cranny, as she had been trained to do. The place was essentially bare. Certainly no Viking sands were hidden anywhere. All she could find were Albert's small wardrobe, his toiletries and some basic food staples. She had found his American passport, however, along with two others, both British. One was for Peter Shaw, whom she knew, and a new one for a Philip Bloom. She made a mental note of this as she checked her watch. It was now 2:30 AM. She looked over one more time at Albert, sprawled out on the bed and snoring lightly. She covered him over with the duvet. Then she jotted down the number of her new disposable cell phone on a note pad on the night stand, tucked her pistol into her handbag and slipped quietly out into the night. She walked pensively down the hill to her "safe house" studio apartment that the Mossad had arranged for her in Eaux-Vives. Or at least she thought it was safe.

XVI

Monday, July 9th, 2012, Geneva, 18:00 GMT +1

The Lion had arrived in Geneva from Tehran a few hours earlier on Iran Air. He was immediately uncomfortable with being in such a decadent, consumer-oriented environment. But he had been well trained to resist the satanic allures of blatant capitalism. He also felt an immediate ambivalence towards the chic and lightly clothed women parading around the streets in plain view. It was shocking to him, but certainly fascinating as well.

He had been met at the airport by an attaché from the Iranian Permanent Mission to the UN in Geneva. They had been briefed as to his arrival and instructed to find him a safe room, somewhere on the edge of the city center, for a short stay. They were to render him all possible assistance, but to ask no further questions. The head of security was to provide him with firearms of his choosing.

The Lion knew Captain Leah Shalev from unpleasant past encounters. He had been an unofficial military advisor to Hezbollah in one of its training camps in southern Lebanon. There had been numerous skirmishes with the Israeli army on the border. Shalev had commanded several commando raids against the training facilities. They had exchanged fire a few times already. He was sure he would recognize her, if he could only find her. Then he would finally settle all of their old scores. He relished the opportunity.

Intelligence from Tehran indicated that Shalev was pursuing an American using the name of Peter Shaw, a British subject. Shaw had the doomsday substance. Find Shaw and Shalev would not be hard to find. The Lion intended to find them both, as quickly as possible. How would he do it, though?

The field communication device of choice for covert operations in the 21st century is the disposable cell phone. Cheap and plentiful, they can be programmed for local or international use, depending on what one is willing to pay. They were purposely limited in duration and not meant to be re-used. Rather, they were to be thrown away instead. GPS-enabled phones with location-based services had become the world standard, but they were almost impossible to track. Even when one was successful in doing so, the user was normally long gone. The Iranians knew all of this, but they had developed a hi-tech system to try to circumvent the problem. Their Sinah-1 orbital satellite could pick up cell phone signals. It couldn't monitor conversations, but it could track numbers and connections. With the aid of super-computer backup, it could seek to establish a pattern of usage.

The task would be daunting, however. There were cell phones in use everywhere in the greater Geneva area. Assuming Shalev was using one to communicate with Shaw, how could they zero in on hers? The answer was, once again, analyzing certain usage patterns. They were looking for a cell phone that communicated uniquely with only one other number in the area. Of course, that could be a mother and child, the former checking on the latter's location at school or at play. But the trump card the Iranians felt they held was that they knew both the direct access number into the Mossad headquarters in Herzaliya and the direct line for the Chief Intelligence Officer at the Israeli embassy in Bern. So, they could narrow their search criteria dramatically, if Shalev was behaving predictably. If they could pick up signals from a cell phone contacting these numbers uniquely as a pattern, they would know it was Shalev. Then they would have Shaw's cell phone number as well. If they both changed their numbers when their cell phones expired, the process could be repeated. Once the numbers were known, the satellite could pinpoint their use locations by using the world GPS system.

It would take awhile, but The Lion had the time to wait. He wanted to be sure that he fulfilled his orders to the letter. As soon as Shalev's cell phone could be identified and her location pinpointed, he would be ready to strike.

XVII

Wednesday, July11th, 2012, Bern Switzerland, 10:00 GMT +1

Chris Wytham had been in Bern for almost a week. He had worked closely with Bill Churchill and Jim MacLean seeking additional information from the Swiss authorities about the possible whereabouts of Albert Stern, aka Peter Shaw. But all leads had turned up cold so far. Stern seemed to have just vanished. Today Inspector van Noort was arriving from Geneva, where he had had no success either in locating Stern. It was all very frustrating. The DOI in Washington had been on to him every day for progress reports. The office of the Vice President had put him under very heavy pressure to have the fugitive found and returned home for swift justice.

Churchill's secretary interrupted the morning meeting to say that Inspector van Noort was waiting outside. "Show him in, please, Lori."

"Good morning, gentlemen", van Noort greeted the group.

"I wish it was", Wytham replied, wryly.

"I understand your frustrations. They are mine too. I personally inspected the passports of all passengers arriving to Geneve from Chamonix on June 23rd, the day that the suspect's rail excursion fare expired. We found nothing. Nor did my colleagues find anything on the preceding four days".

"Many thanks, Jaap, I really appreciate it. Today I'd like you to look at some more pictures. Our identification section in Langley has sent us a fresh set".

The technicians back in Langley had taken Albert Stern's basic facial features and computer-manipulated them in every way he might possibly have tried to alter his appearance, short of plastic surgery. Every permutation of facial hair and coiffure were contained in the photo set, along with other possible facial enhancements. Wytham laid them out on the conference table for van Noort to study.

Van Noort started to look over the several dozen new iden-tisketch pictures. More than half way through, he paused at one, picked it up and looked at it long and hard. It showed a possible version of Albert Stern with beard, moustache and long, straggly hair, looking like an aging hippy. He tried hard to jog his memory.

"Yes, this one looks a bit familiar. On the 23rd June, on the morning train from Chamonix, I believe I saw a man like this. But he was not Peter Shaw. He did have a British passport, but his name was something else. Hard to remember, Philip, perhaps?

I do recall that it was a new passport, with no entry stamps in it. His rucksack was full of dirty hiking gear. Nothing suspicious. We passed him on through."

"Damn it, you had him!" Wytham exclaimed, exasperated.

"Maybe not. I can't be absolutely sure. This looks something like that man, but not exactly", van Noort replied, rapidly trying to cover his ass.

"So he's back in Geneva", Wytham said, "or at least I think so. Then he's been there almost three weeks. Why? What is he up to?"

"He's got a contact there, I'm sure", Churchill suggested. "Whomever he contacted in London has arranged to have him met there. It's very convenient for him to sell the stuff for big money. Put the proceeds into a Swiss numbered account. Sure we can get access eventually, but it would take a long time to crack through the Swiss banking secrecy defenses."

"I just got some new info from Llwelyn in London that might help us", Churchill continued. "It seems that Albert Stern rented an international cell phone from a British Telcom kiosk at Heathrow airport on May 22nd. Scotland Yard has sent us copies of the phone records that they got from BT. Here they are. Needless to say, Stern never returned the cell phone."

Looking at the phone records it appeared that Stern had made only a few calls. The first was to a Nigel Utley at Lloyd's of London. The second was the Enigma Club in Mayfair. Then there were several to an art and framing shop on the high street in Islington. Most interestingly, though, there were also several calls to the Consular Section of the Israeli embassy in Kensington, made on Monday morning, May 28th. After that, even more intriguingly, there was a call later that day to the hiring office of Anglo Petroleum Limited in Aberdeen. That was it, but that was enough.

"But the Israelis have steadfastly denied that they ever heard of or saw either Albert Stern or Peter Shaw" Churchill said.

"Well they are lying!" Wytham retorted. "Stern obviously saw them before he headed off to Aberdeen. Could they have goaded him into some drastic proof of his wild claims?

Surely they must have been convinced after the Sterling disaster. I'll bet you that it is one of theirs he's arranged to meet in Geneva."

"But the Israelis are our friends and allies. They would have told us if they had seen him.", Churchill observed, suprised.

"Sure, Bill, but look at how much they would have to gain if they could get hold of this incredible weapon" Wytham replied. "All of their enemies are big oil producers. There are degrees of friendship, I guess. The Israelis are looking out for number one first."

"We need to know what Israelis have come recently to Geneva and for what ostensible purposes. There couldn't have been too many", MacLean ventured. "The cantonal authorities can tell us that. I'll get right to it." MacLean left the group to make the necessary phone call.

Ten minutes later MacLean returned with a small list of recent arrivals in Geneva from Tel Aviv. Mostly they were regular staffers at the Israeli UN mission, all of them well known to the Swiss authorities. The only exception was a "Dr. Leah Shalev, Senior Development Economist", on temporary visit to the mission.

"Dr. Leah Shalev", Wytham snorted with glee, "we know her well! A development economist, my ass! I'll bet you that's 'Lethal Leah', a real legend in the Aman. I wouldn't want to mess with her, even though she is one hell of a piece of ass! Some of my guys in Langley have her picture up on their walls. She's something to see dressed in desert shorts and a khaki T-shirt. I'd recognize her immediately if I saw her."

"So you think that if we can find this Israeli bombshell, we'd find Stern not far behind?" Churchill asked.

"Chances are very good", Wytham replied. "It's the best lead we've had yet. But Shalev doesn't mess around. She's deadly efficient. Stern may be initially dazzled by her, but he won't last long with her around."

"So I'd better go to Geneva and follow this up immediately, before she's finished her job", Wytham concluded. It was quickly agreed amongst all at the meeting that Wytham would set out early the next morning. Gavin Lorimer of the British Security Service was already on his way and would meet him there. The US Permanent Mission in Geneva would give Wytham both cover and office space under the auspices of the ubiquitous Chief Information Officer.

XVIII

Friday, July 20th, 2012, London, 11:00 GMT

Osman Ali had just attended Friday prayers at the North London Central Mosque in Finsbury Park. He had listened to some fiery oratory about the forthcoming, final *jihad*. Now he would do his small part to further that cause.

Ali was a Pakistani from Peshawar who had immigrated to London 6 years earlier. He had fled his native country right after the removal of the Taliban in neighboring Afghanistan by the US and its allies. From the very beginning, he had been a Taliban sympathizer and a radical *jihadist*. He had received terrorist training from al-Queda at their then biggest camp, just outside of Kandahar. When the Pakistani government moved to round up al-Queda fighter and sympathizers in the ill-defined Pakistan/Afghanistan border areas, Ali managed to secure safe passage to Britain, where he settled in Islington. But part of the price of his extraction was to become part of an active al-Queda sleeper cell. Ali was more than happy to accept the condition.

The cell met on even numbered Fridays, after prayers. For secrecy and security, the meetings were held in revolving locations. Today it would meet in Ali's small flat, above his art and picture framing shop in Islington. Iqbal Pasha never attended, but his two bodyguards, Aziz and Mostafa were both there. Everyone was sitting around the small room, drinking sweet mint tea and chatting, when the cell leader, Abu Zar, entered the room and called the meeting to order.

"In the Name of Allah, the Merciful, welcome my brothers", he intoned. "Today we have some important business. The leadership is seeking urgent information on the whereabouts of the

American Jew scientist who has the doomsday weapon that destroyed the great oil platform in the North Sea. They believe that he had acquired new identity documents here in London before he fled the country. We are to ask our brothers here if any one of them sold him new identity papers. His name is Albert Stern, but he known to the British police as Peter Shaw."

Osman Ali spoke up immediately. "Yes, leader, I know of this man. Iqbal Pasha sent him to me in late May to buy new identity documents. I made him two sets of British identities. Peter Shaw was one of them. I did it only because our brother, Iqbal, had asked me to do so. I asked no questions of the man. I followed my instructions faithfully. I was paid very well for the job."

"And what was the name on the second set of new documents, brother?", Abu Zar asked.

"I have it right here, in my records", Ali fumbled with some papers. "It was 'Philip Bloom'"

"Excellent, brother! I will send this to our leadership. They will be pleased. They know from their sources inside of Scotland Yard that this 'Peter Shaw' fled to Switzerland in mid-June. No one has been able to find him since. But if he is still there under this new name, we shall find him for ourselves. A team of holy warriors is assembled and ready. Now they can leave for Geneva with this vital new information. Well done, my brother."

"Why does the leadership want this weapon so badly, *imam*?" Aziz asked from over in the corner.

"To crush our enemies, the infidels who exploit us and the hypocrites who pollute our holy places. They both shall feel our holy wrath again. With this weapon we can bring both the satanic Americans and the hated house of Saud to their knees, *inshallah*! Ours is not to ask why or how, though. Ours is to obey."

All present agreed heartily and praised the noble cause. Then they turned to the other business at hand of planning their next terrorist attack on the London mass transit system.

XIX

Monday, July 23rd, 2012, Al Anbar Province, Iraq, GMT +3

Ahmed Samir had been summoned to Anbar Province from the al-Queda stronghold in Baqouba. All that he had been told was that the leader had a special assignment for him. As he waited patiently outside the traditional little wattle and daub safe house in which the leader sometimes spent his nights, he sweated profusely in the 114 degree heat of a blistering Iraqi summer. "Good", he had thought to himself, "something different, perhaps, from plotting regular martyrdom missions." A Saudi-born fighter, Samir had come to Iraq as a dedicated *mujahadin*. He was trained to kill, mercilessly and efficiently.

Samir was escorted inside by an armed guard. Seated at a small table in the inner courtyard was Abu Lahab, the head of al-Queda in Iraq.

"*As-salaam alaykum*, brother, how goes the struggle in Baqouba?"

"*Alaykum saalam*, leader, very well indeed."

"We have a special assignment for you. It comes from our top leadership. You will have to travel abroad at once", the leader said, handing Samir a plane ticket from Aman, Jordan to Geneva. "We will transport you to Aman tomorrow, from where you will set off."

"What is the nature of this assignment, leader?"

"You will like it, brother. It calls for all of your skill and training". Abu Lahab then went on to explain to an almost incredulous Samir.

"This weapon, leader, how will we use it?"

"We will strike with it at the heart of the corrupt regime of the country of your birth. It will be the instrument to bring down its decadent leadership. We will destroy their obnoxious wealth and trigger an uprising of the faithful against the self-indulgent ways of the privileged royals. We will restore adherence to the true beliefs. And we will also choke off the evil Americans' access to unlimited crude oil. It will be a great day of triumph for our righteous cause, *inshallah!*"

When he arrived in Geneva, Samir was instructed to contact a sleeper cell in the Les Paquis district. They would be expecting him and they would provide him with all necessary assistance. His mission was clear and succinct: locate Stern/Shaw, now Philip Bloom; get the weapon from him by any means; and then silence him forever.

A mutual embrace, an exchange of *masalaamas*, and Samir was on his way.

XX

Friday, July 27th, 2012, The Lubyanka, Moscow, Russia, 20:00, GMT + 3

Deep in the bowels of the former KGB headquarters on Dzhersinsky - now Svobody - Square, great interest had been aroused. Word had come down from the Kremlin that a strategic new weapon was potentially up for the taking. The Russian Federal Security Service, or FSB, had taken over the KGB portfolio years before, but the new agency was still mainly staffed with lethally trained, old guard of the KGB. Nothing had changed so far as they were concerned.

Colonel Ivan Chestnoy opened the file on his desk marked **COBEOWEHHO** - "TOP SECRET". In it was all available information to date on the events in Britain at the Sterling offshore oil platform. Covert FSB agents operating in the UK had gathered together an impressive collection of detail on, and leading up to, the massive oilfield disaster. It definitely stirred Chestnoy's interest.

"Misha", Chestnoy said to his colleague, Major Mikhail Kutusov, "this weapon that the American has stolen, our leadership thinks that it could be of immense use to us."

"*Da*, Vanya, we must get hold of it. With it we could become the last and only great oil producer left. We could hold the world to ransom. No more pandering to the West."

"Quite correct, but also we can't afford to let anyone else have it. Our enemies could wreck us with it. The Chechens, the Dagastanis, the Georgians, even our dear American friends. With it, any of them could wreck our main oil production and transport facilities. It is a very high stakes game."

"Just like the old days". Kutusov obviously relished the prospect.

"Have you read through this *dossier* yet, Misha? There are some incredible things in it. It seems that this substance, this terrible weapon, came from Mars. The Jew, Stern, stole it from right under the Americans' noses. He fled to London and went to the Israelis, trying to sell it. Here's our intercept of a secret report that the Mossad correspondant in their London embassy sent to our old nemesis, Jamal Safir, in Herzliya." Chestnoy smiled. "It seems that the Israelis unwittingly caused the Sterling disaster by putting Stern to his proof."

"*Bolshi moi*! Where is Stern now? Do we know?"

"The British Security Services think he fled to Switzerland." Chestnoy continued to read from the file. "They believe that he acquired a British alias in London, which he used to sign on to the offshore platform crew. They have a 'Peter Shaw' leaving Aberdeen on Friday, June 15th for Geneva. This Shaw was a rig hand on the Sterling platform. So if Shaw is Stern, he's been in Switzerland for almost five weeks now."

"We must get to him before anyone else does. We can mobilize our agents at our Permanent Mission in Geneva. There's one old comrade in particular there who can handle a job like this. You know who I mean - Boris Sergeivich."

"Ah yes, Boris Sergeivich Korsakov." Chestnoy referred to Commander Korsakov, an old cold war warrior, who was acting as Chief Information Officer for the Geneva mission. "Perhaps we can get him to find Stern, if he is still there. But that may not be the best course for us."

"Why not? What else can we do?"

"If you read further in the *dossier*, you'll see that this substance arrived in the hold of the Americans' Viking 3 landing craft from Mars. The Americans always do things with redundant back up systems. So they sent a second craft to Mars as a fail-safe option. Viking 4 trailed Viking 3 by a few months and executed a duplicate mission. It is returning now with its hold full of the same lethal substance."

"So the Americans will have the weapon no matter what becomes of this Stern person, *pravilna*?"

"Not if we can hijack Viking 4 as it is returning to Earth", Chestnoy smiled impishly, with great self-satisfaction at his clever idea.

"Hijack it?" Kutusov replied with amazement. "How could we do that? We have never been able to crack the Americans' computer security. Their degree of encryption is too high."

"*Da*, but with some inside help, *nyet problema!*"

" Some inside help?"

"There is this young Japanese-American Deputy Mission Controller at NASA in Houston who was Stern's protégé. He will be losing both his job and his promising career at the end of August. He desperately needed money - don't they all? So we purchased the access codes from him that control the Viking 4's navigation and re-entry sequences."

"If the Americans find that out, they'll force the truth out of him and then change everything before we can use his intelligence."

"That's true, but he will meet with an unfortunate automobile accident after we use his information", Chestnoy concluded wryly.

PART 4
LES JEUX SONT FAITS

"It's choice, not chance, that determines one's destiny."

I

All of the players had now converged on Geneva. All bets were down; *rien ne va plus*. The wheel of chance would finally spin its deadly game.

The beginning of August is the time of the annual summer festival in Geneva, *Les Fetes de Geneve*. It all starts with the evening techno *Parade de Lac* around *la rade*, the inner harbor, as a kind of moving rave party on 10 or 15 semi-trailer floats. The floats then park along the lakeshore and the revelers party all night. There are carnival rides, games and exotic food concessions all around *la rade.* The mood is festive. The streets and lakeshore are crowded with the populace of the canton. The wealthy, the young, hippies and internationals, all flock to Geneva in August to play, shop and relax in the heady summer air. It's not uncommon to see security guards with wires dangling from their ears patrolling the lakeside, as young Saudi princes enjoy themselves among the carnival rides and game booths. And on the avenues running by the lake the luxury hotels are full. Rented E class Mercedes crowd the side streets, or pass by in convoys. For all who come, life in Geneva is easy with its banks, its expensive stores and its safe and secure environment. Against this festive background Albert and Leah were trying to finalize their deal, and then flee.

Meanwhile, 15 million kilometers away, in deep space, Viking 4 was beginning its final approach to Earth. It had successfully completed its backup mission in the deeply riven canyons of Utopia Planitia. Except for a pre-programmed course correction and a slight re-orientation of its solar panels, nothing new had been communicated to the approaching spacecraft since it had left Mars in mid-December, 2011. It seemed to have been completely forgotten in the wake of the virtual closedown of NASA's Mars Exploration Program.

Forgotten by most, but not by all, however. Albert, for one, was keenly aware that tightly secured in Viking 4's inner hold, shielded from the damaging radiation of interstellar space, was at least another 200 grams of the Viking sands. But, apparently, this had not yet dawned on the FBI, the CIA and the rest of the frantic US security complex, obsessed with hunting him down. Albert knew that he would have to deal with Viking 4's arrival on Earth, and he would have to do it soon.

II

Saturday, August 4th, 2012, Geneva, 20:00 GMT +1

Leah was becoming very frustrated. Time was passing and she still had not struck a deal. Nor had she seen any hard evidence that Albert still had the Viking sands. Pressure was building on her to deliver. She had spoken several times by cell phone to Jamal Safir in Herzaliya. He was feeling the heat from above as well. It was getting very uncomfortable for all concerned. As Leah dressed in her apartment in Eaux Vives for the opening evening of the *Fetes de Geneve*, she resolved to bring matters to a head.

It was dark and the bright neon lights of Geneva sparkled on the shimmering waters of the lake. They were visible from the window facing the balcony of her second floor flat. She looked out pensively, framed as a silhouette in the French doors leading to the small balcony. The Rue Merle d'Aubigne, below, on which she lived, was unlit and deeply enveloped in shadows. She felt quite alone and safe, but she was not.

In the Rue E. Dupont, the short street which connects Rue du 1er-Juin to Rue Merle d'Aubigne, the Lion was waiting in the shadows. The Iranians had located Shalev through her pattern of cell phone usage. Although she was already on her third disposable cell phone, the pattern had been clear and predictable enough to pinpoint her location by GPS. They also had a fix on Stern's location. First things first, though, for the Lion. He had been stalking Shalev for days, looking for the ideal opportunity for a kill. Now he was poised to strike. The night was overcast and moonless. The neighbourhood was quiet, peaceful and poorly illuminated. The Lion was dressed all in black. He blended unobtrusively into the surrounding gloom.

The Lion opened his Nike gym bag and withdrew the dissassembled pieces of an AI AS50 semi-automatic .50 calibre sniper rifle. The entire lightweight rifle could be assembled from its three major components in just under three minutes, which included a night vision scope and a barrel-mounted silencer. Quietly he began putting the rifle together. He could see Shalev in her front room, still sitting with her glass of white wine and looking out at the night. As he finished assembly he looked through the scope and calibrated the rifle's sights. A single head shot was all he would need. Braced against the gray stone wall of the solid old Swiss building and shielded from sight by the row of parked cars, he fixed Shalev firmly in his cross hairs. But as he was about to squeeze the trigger, a sound startled him.

Walking down the other side of the street was an old lady and her small dog, heading for the lakefront park along the Quai Gustave-Ador. Had she seen him? The Swiss can be very inquisitive, indeed, quite nosey, people. The Lion pulled the rifle down along his leg like a walking stick and hung back into the shadows along the wall. The lady had stopped across the street as her little dog piddled. She seemed to be looking straight across the street in the direction of the Lion. Silently he reached behind his neck and withdrew a well-balanced throwing knife from its sling. One step towards him, one peep, and he would silence her with a single thrust of the razor sharp blade.

The dog finished its business and the lady pulled it away from the curb. The two of them continued up the street, around the corner and off towards the park, along the *quai.*

Still annoyed at the interruption, the Lion brought the rifle back up to his shoulder and looked through the night scope into Shalev's dimly lit apartment. Damn, she had been there only a moment ago! Now she was gone.

The Lion waited patiently for about five minutes. Then Shalev reappeared, stunningly dressed for the evening, holding her cell phone in her right hand. The Lion fixed her pretty face firmly in the crosshairs. What a pity, he thought fleetingly, to kill such a voluptuous specimen of semetic pulchritude. There were many other things he'd rather do to her. Then he gentley squeezed the trigger.

Leah was startled when her cell phone rang just as she finished dialing Albert's number. She pulled it away from her ear, moving her head sharply to the left, away from the piercing ring tone. At the same moment she saw a small window pane in the French doors shatter in front of her and she heard something whistle by her right ear, no more than a few millimeters away from her head. With a thud the bullet imbedded itself in the wall behind her. Reacting by instinct, she fell immediately to the floor, as if hit. She crawled across the room to the safety of the apartment's inner foyer.

Her mind was racing franticly. Who was it? How had they found her? No time to puzzle it out now. She had to deal with the threat decisively. She grabbed her Beretta and headed for the front door. Out into the hallway, she sent the old wrought iron lift down, as if someone was in it. At the same time she raced down the dimly lit stairwells to the ground floor, where she found the door into the cellar service area. There was a back door from there into the alley behind. Safely through it, she vaulted the small back wall into the alley.

Staying in the deep shadows, Leah made her way around the back of the building and then across the head of her street. She was heading for the Rue 1er-Juin, which paralled her own. From there she could reach the short, interconecting street from where her would be assassin had taken his shot.

On the side street the Lion was dissasembling his rifle in the dark. She had fallen like a sack of wet sand. He had seen that with his own eyes. Another job well done, he thought. So he didn't hear the slight rustling sound behind him as Leah approached him, Beretta drawn, with a full clip loaded.

"Who the hell are you?" Leah demanded, holding her pistol braced with two hands in front of her. "Hands on your head, now, or you're dead!"

The Lion whirled around to confront her. He immediately recognized his old nemesis. How could it be, though? He was sure he had hit her cleanly. But there she still was, ten paces in front of him. Not responding, he began to put his hands up. In the same motion he reached behind his neck to pull out his throwing knife. As his arm started forward to throw it at Leah, fired three quick shots into his chest, heart high. She had also recognized her old adversary and she knew all of his lethal moves.

The Lion staggered back on to the curb, still clutching his knife. "Damn it", Leah thought to herself, "he must be wearing body armour!" A head shot would take care of that. But before she could deliver it, the still stunned Lion rolled deftly into the street and crouched behind a parked Bentley.

"Israeli whore" the Lion gasped, "I'll cut your throat!"

"Sorushian, you pig, how did you know I was here? How did you find me?"

The Lion was in no mood to respond further. He remained singularly focussed on killing Shalev. But he needed a diversion to get at the handgun in his gym bag, still sitting against the wall near her. Providence provided him one. The old lady and her dog rounded the corner returning from the *quai*. Darting like a cat in the dark, the Lion grabbed her from behind to use her as a shield. The old lady tried to cry out, but the Lion muffled her with his big left hand. He kicked the yapping dog, which took off in fright down the street.

Leah needed a clean head shot at Sorushian. But he had the terrified old lady held firmly in front of him, knife at her throat. She had gone limp in his arms in a dead faint, but she still was an effective human shield. The Lion was maneuvering in the shadows towards the hand gun in his gym bag when the unexpected happened.

Racing out of the darkness, the enraged little dog reappeared and bit ferociously into Sorushian's left ankle. He winced visibly from the sudden pain and struggled to kick the dog away again. As he did so, he leaned awkwardly to the right, giving Leah a momentary clear shot at his head. That was all she needed. The muffled thud from her silencer registered a single shot through The Lion's left eye. He and the old woman fell to the ground in a tangled heap, with the little dog yapping and licking furiously at the dazed old woman's face. The Lion's mission was over. He had failed.

III

Leah was badly shaken. It wasn't the violence that was affecting her. She was well-trained for that. But now she knew that her cover was blown and that urgency was the essence her of continued survival. She had to act quickly to bring her mission to a conclusion. Still in the deep shadows of the darkened street, she slipped quietly back into the entrance foyer of her building.

Leah's cell phone indicated that Albert had called four times in the last hour. Calmly now, she dialed him back. "Hello, Albert, sorry to have missed your calls. Something came up unexpectedly", she said nonchalantly.

"It's 9:30, Leah, and we have business to finish tonight. Can you meet me in the *Jardin Anglais* in half an hour? I'll be sitting on a bench near the *Horloge Fleurie*".

Acting on increasingly insistent instructions from Safir, Leah had pressed Albert for some first hand proof that he still had the Viking sands and that they were as potent as he had said. Now he was ready to show her. Equally, Leah had promised Albert a wire transfer of a substantial advance on the $100 million dollars he was demanding. If he could deliver the Viking sands to her before they boarded an El Al jet together to take him to asylum in Tel Aviv, he would have it.

"OK, Albert. What do you have in mind? Remember, I need a credible demonstration before I can arrange any payment to you. Do you have a plan? We have little or no time left. I'll tell you more when we meet." Leah rung off, composed herself and walked quietly out of her building.

As she walked unobtrusively in the shadows along the wall, she saw flashing blue and white lights from the Swiss Securitie cars blocking the entrance to the Rue des Eaux Vives at its far end. Someone had already called the police. An ambulance had just arrived. A body wrapped in a tarp was being loaded into it. The Swiss in the old neighbourhood usually put their shutters down in the evenings, but tonight, the buildings were ablaze with light. A myriad of curious faces were peeking out of the windows. In the confusion, Leah headed in the opposite direction, unnoticed, towards the *quai*.

Ten minutes later she had walked the length of the Quai Gustav Ador and entered the picturesque park adjoining the Pont du Mont Blanc, which crosses the mouth of the Rhone as it exits Lac Leman. The opening night of the *Fetes de Geneve* was alight with festivities. All along the lakeshore a throng of pedestrians promenaded leisurely, taking in the sights and sounds. The fully-illuminated *Jet d'Eaux* spewed its great column of water high into the night sky. The row of tall, gray, stolid bank buildings on the southern shore were ablaze with neon lights. All of the streets adjoining the inner harbour were brightly lit with kiosks selling *crepes au Grande Marnier* and other local food treats. The floats had paraded by earlier, across the bridge and down the upscale Rue du Rhone.

The inner harbour was now crammed full with illuminated pleasure craft. Their noisey and celebrant crews and guests were jockeying for position to get the best view of the fireworks fussilade, scheduled to start at 10:30 PM. The atmosphere was that of a relaxed and festive city, enjoying the ambiance of a soft summer evening.

Albert was sitting in the shadows on a bench next to the Flower Clock as Leah approached. She looked a bit disheveled to him, but still as luscious as ever.

"Hi, Leah, everything OK?" Albert said with concern.

"Yes. I had some difficulties but I have dealt with them." Leah was noncommittal. "But things are getting really dangerous and we need to move quickly. What have you planned for this evening? I need to see your proof tonight."

Albert had spent some time before Leah came inspecting the marina along the *quai*, next to the park. There was a labyrinth of jetties with docking space for all sorts of pleasure craft, ranging from sailboats to cabin cruisers. Most of them were out in the harbour awaiting the fireworks display, so the marina was mostly dark and deserted.

At the end of one network of docks was a 24 foot Sea Ray Sundancer day cruiser with the name *"Jolie Mademoiselle"* painted in gold script on her stern. Her fuel capacity would be about 75 gallons of gasoline. She was to be Albert's demonstration tool.

"Let's go for a walk out of the park, over towards the marina." Albert slipped his hand into Leah's as they walked. "I will produce the proof you need, with a little help from you."

They tried to remain inconspicuous as the walked down the long, dimly-lit jetty, stopping seemingly to admire various boats as they went. No one seemed to notice them. The marina was almost deserted. The night watchman had been given the evening off to enjoy the opening night of the *Fetes*.

When they came to the *Jolie Mademoiselle* in its slip at the end, Albert drew Leah close to him and kissed her. He wanted them to appear as a pair of lovers having a romantic walk down the dock, under the mist floating downwind from the *Jet d'Eaux*. Understanding what was going on, Leah didn't resist.

"Here, hold this a second." Albert slipped something out of his pocket, wrapped in a handkerchief. It was a small glass vial containing about a fingernail size measure of the Viking sands. The top of the vial was sealed with a thin layer of white paraffin, which is soluble in gasoline. "We're going to give the *Jolie Mademoiselle* her last ride."

The plan was simple. Albert would drop the vial into the gas tank of the day cruiser after he and Leah had unfastened her mooring lines. A few good pushes and the boat would drift slowly away from the end of the pier and out into the inner harbour, riding the gentle evening swells. The paraffin would take about five minutes at most to dissolve, exposing the Viking sands to the cruiser's full gas reserves. The desired result was quite predictable by now to Albert. He assured Leah that she would finally have more than ample proof.

"Damn it, the gas cap is locked!" Albert exclaimed, sheltering them both in the shadow of a large sailboat, berthed in the adjoining slip.

Leah didn't see this as a problem, given her training. Her Israeli army knife was equipped with a special tool with which she deftly picked the simple lock in a few seconds. Then they both turned their attention to the boat's mooring lines. It was 10:25 PM.

"Wait a few moments for the fireworks to start. Then we'll have some of our own." With this Albert started quickly to unwind the boat from its mooring cleats fore and aft, motioning Leah to do the same amidships. In less than a minute they had the boat free. Then Albert dropped the small vial into the cruiser's gas tank. He and Leah nudged it smartly away from the dock and watched it begin to drift off, into the crowded and boisterous *rade*, riding the gentle evening chop.

"Let's go, Leah!" Grabbing her hand, Albert pulled her along, back down the deserted jetty. It was exactly 10:30 PM and from a barge anchored across the *rade*, near the Quai du Mont Blanc, the first fussilade of fireworks suddenly illuminated the dark night sky with extravagent, fiery explosions of red, green and blue pinwheels.

They headed back into the adjoining park, mingling nonchalantly with the jostling crowds of Genevoise ogling the dramatic fireworks display. Albert looked nervously at his watch: 10:40. "Surely", he thought, "the paraffin should have disolved by now." Leah looked on with both anticipation and skepticism.

The whistling roar and light from the barrages of rockets being launched from across the inner harbour almost blotted out the initial signs of the final demise of the *Jolie Mademoiselle*. Lost in the fantastic glowing patterns in the sky, the sudden eruption of a brilliant, blue-white column of light in the inner harbor went momentarily unnoticed. Some nearby boat celebrants were even heard to yell, "*formidable*", as if approving of the seemingly impromptu celebration. But when the terrible explosive clap and searing heat began to engulf them, followed by the sonic boom of a shock wave rolling across the water, the celebratory shouts quickly became those of absolute horror.

Boats rocked uncontrollably, like toy ships on a pond. Some of the smaller craft capsized. Urgent shouts of *"au secours!"* rose from all around, mostly being drowned out by the ongoing fireworks fusillade. It would take a few minutes before the roiling waters of the inner harbour were churned up further by harbour police cruisers, speeding to the chaotic scene.

Leah was dumb-struck by the force of the reaction. She had been told to expect something dramatic, but this was a lot more than she had anticipated. Albert knew better. He stood quietly alongside her in the shadows of the park, viewing the inevitable effects and the ensuing mass confusion. He knew that he didn't have to say anything more to convince her.

"Come on, let's get out of here", he said at last, tugging smartly on Leah's arm.

"OK, but I don't want to stay at my place tonight. It would be too dangerous."

That was just what Albert had wanted to hear. "Fine, I have just enough room for two at my place" he said with a smile. Hand in hand they walked away from the boisterous, growing crowd along the lakeshore, through the Place Molard and into the narrow cobbled streets that led up the hill to Albert's apartment in the Vielle Ville.

Lying together intertwined in bed later that evening, Leah began to unburden herself to Albert. She told Albert of her almost fatal encounter earlier in the evening with the Iranian agent, Sorushian. She told him that she was frightened for both of them. Clearly their enemies had tracked them down. They were only a few footsteps away. It was obvious that they would use any means to get at him. Both of their lives were in imminent danger.

As Albert listened, he tried to comfort Leah, but she very definitely was getting through to him, as she intended. She needed to instill in Albert a sense of urgency to go together to get the Viking sands immediately. Then Leah could finally conclude her mission, as she had been directed.

IV

Sunday, August 5th, 2012, Geneva, 07:30 GMT +1

The news of the incident in the inner harbour the night before shone like a beacon of clarity to Chris Wytham. It was obviously the work of Albert Stern. All of the telltale fingerprints of his *modus operandi* were there. He was still in Geneva and still as dangerous and unpredictable as ever. His capture was now a matter of prime urgency.

Seated in the coffee bar of the Geneva Noga Hilton, Wytham impatiently ordered his second round *of café au lait* and *brioches*. Gavin Lorimer then came in to join him. It was a glorious Sunday morning, but it was a working day for both of them under the circumstances.

"I can't believe that he is right here under our noses and we still can't find him!" Lorimer said in frustration.

"But at least we know now that he's still here. It must be taking him longer than he expected to close his deal", Wytham replied.

"So you think that last night's incident was the final proof?"

"Clearly so. Stern had to do something to show that he still had the Viking sands and that they worked as he has claimed. Someone had to see it, to verify it, with his own eyes - or should I say with

125

her own eyes? She must be under instructions from Safir to get absolute confirmation before any money changes hands."

"Shalev, you mean?"

"Sure, Gavin, I'm convinced that she was sent here to make a deal for the Israelis. If we can find Lethal Leah, we'll certainly find Stern."

"The Israeli mission is being as tight-lipped and uncoopera- tive as ever", Lorimer observed. "We've used diplomatic channels and the Swiss authorities to try to get them to tell us where to find Dr. Shalev. She's never at the Israeli mission nor does she attend any of the ECOSOC sessions at the UN. They insist that she's very busy doing work in the field during her short stay."

Wytham's cell phone rang. It was Chief Inspector Jean- Christophe Malbec of the Swiss Securite. Had Wytham heard about the murder last evening on the Rue Merle d'Aubigne? The police had been investigating it into the dawn hours. The victim was an Iranian named Sorushian. He had entered Switzerland on a diplomatic passport. There had been a shootout, witnessed by a very traumatized old lady who lived nearby. The shooter was a strikingly attractive woman whom the old lady described as being of middle-eastern or semitic appearance. No one had seen her since the incident. The police had found a gym bag on the street with a dissassembled sniper's rifle in it. A flat on the second floor of 3 Rue Merle d'Aubigne had a bullet hole in the french doors leading out to the balcony. Forensics had already confirmed that the .50 caliber slug dug out of the wall in the front sitting room had come from the sniper's rifle. The police had an all points alert out to find the shooter.

"That's her!" Wytham exclaimed. "That's Shalev. She must have been staying in that flat. I'll bet you it's an Israeli embassy rental. They've staked it out, right? But she sure as hell won't return there now."

"I agree, but what do you make of the rest of the story?"

"We knew Sorushian" Lorimer continued. "He was a very bad actor. He was in charge of Iranian Revolutionary Guards Qods force which conducted numerous commando raids on Israeli positions fortifying the Lebanese border. He must have come here to stop Shalev."

"Let's try to piece this all together." Wytham took over the analysis. "Stern was in touch with the Israelis in London. After the Sterling disaster, they decided to take him seriously. He came to Geneva and they sent Shalev to meet him. He must want a lot of money and anonymous asylum in Israel. Shalev needed further proof and she got it last night in the inner harbor. But perhaps she hadn't bargained for being a target herself? It's in the Iranian's vital interests to stop her. I wonder who else is targeting the two of them?"

"Like al-Queda, perhaps?" Lorimer conjectured.

"Very likely. They've had to have heard all about this potent weapon. It would suit their *jihad* purposes perfectly. I wouldn't be surprised if they're here already, looking for Stern. It's time to play hardball with our Israeli friends. We have to find Shalev now, before anyone knocks her off. She's the key to finding Stern. I'll ask the DOI to lean heavily on the Israelis from the top. He and Safir go back a long way. The Veep is pressing him hard for a result anyway".

"Well, Chris, Shalev's cover is now blown. She and Stern will be on the move soon. Where do you think they will they go next?"

"Clearly to get the rest of the stuff. Stern couldn't have it with him. Shalev would have gotten it by now and been long gone.

Now she knows first hand what it can do. She can vouch for it to Samir. She'll want to secure it and get it off to Israel as fast as possible, with or without Stern. Knowing Lethal Leah, she's led him on as far as necessary. She won't need him anymore, after she's got the prize. Besides, it would be inconvenient as hell for the Israelis to give Stern asylum in Israel. I think that Stern's days are numbered. If we have any chance to get him and to break all of this up, we'll have to move quickly."

"Where the hell do you think that he stashed the stuff then?"

"I guess we need to know why he went off to Chamonix. He's a climber of some note, but I doubt that he went there just for a romp in the Alps. It's down there I'm sure. Watch, now, they'll be going back there to get it. But the damn French won't cooperate with us. So we'll have to use some of our own hi-tech surveillance."

"You mean a drone?"

"Right. I'll call our friends at Ramstein to put them on the alert. Meanwhile, Inspector Malbec wants some more information about what we know of Sorushian and Shalev. Let's head over there and be helpful. We are going to need a hell of a lot more cooperation from the Swiss before this is over."

"Before we leave, Chris, let's get one thing straight " Lorimer hastened to add.

"What's that, Gavin?"

"When we get this villain, he's coming back to Britain with me."

"Not likely, he's our fugitive."

"He may be your national, Chris, but he's committed a major felony in Britain. He's a terrorist under our law. I'm here to bring him back for trial. Your charges against him pale in comparison to what he did to us!"

"Maybe so, but let's decide all of that once we have Stern in custody", Wytham countered. "In the meanwhile, let's cooperate to get him first."

V

Sunday, August 5th, 2012, Geneva, 08:00 GMT +1

Albert awoke to the pleasant sight of Leah's sensuous nude body lying beside him. It had been quite a night, one of which he had always dreamed. But as he reached over fondly to caress her, Leah recoiled and awoke immediately. It seemed like the morning after would be all business. Draping the sheet over herself, she sat up in bed and composed herself.

"Good morning, Albert. Time to get down to final arrangements. We need to get the Viking sands and then both get on to the El Al direct flight to Tel Aviv as soon as possible. The mission here will arrange the flight for us as soon as I tell them that we're ready. It really has to be immediately. After last evening's events, the Swiss will be breathing down our backs too. So where are they and how do we get them?"

"Wait a minute, Leah." Albert was visibly annoyed at her sudden switch of *persona* from the night before. "I need an advance on my fee first, before I'll deliver anything at all. You know what the sands can do now. I'm sure you've already told your superiors. I'm not giving them anything unless I first see some money in my numbered account here at UBS. At least a twenty percent advance on the $100 million I asked Melman for in London. Better tell them that right away!"

"They already know, and it will be arranged. But I must know where the sands are so that we can go to get them quickly."

"After you've arranged the wire transfer to my satisfaction" Albert replied, testily.

Without another word, Leah reached into her purse and took out her Blackberry. She typed in an encrypted text message to Safir in Herzaliya, while Albert watched. She pressed "send", requesting an immediate reply. In a few minutes a response came back asking for account details and a bank Swift code for an overnight wire transfer.

Albert smiled with satisfaction. "Tell them to wire the $20 million to Account Number 13261756889 at UBS SA, Main Branch, Geneva. The Swift Code is UBSWCHZH12A. Instructions with the wire transfer should describe it as an 'advance on real estate purchase'. Got it all, Leah? I want a tested cable to confirm the wire transfer, with a value date of tomorrow, Monday, August 6th. When I see that, we'll go get the sands."

"Fine. I'll have a copy of the cable faxed to the mission here early tomorrow morning. I can go pick it up then."

"Good. When you go up there, you'd better get us a car from them too. A non-descript, common one, that won't attract any attention. Maybe a silver Ford Mondeo? We'll have a ways to go to get the sands and we certainly can't use any form of public transport. Then there's the tricky question of my current identity. Neither the Swiss nor the French usually check IDs crossing the border by car, but given what's happened lately, I bet they will. I'll need some kind of identity card with yet another new name on it to travel freely within the EU.

"Oh, and where in the EU will we be going?"

"I'll tell you tomorrow, after I've seen the cable, Leah. So get dressed and get going, while I attend to some business of my own".

"Fine. But I need to take your picture first, Albert." Leah took her Blackberry out again and framed a full face photo of him. "This will be for your new identity card." She didn't ask him to smile. Satisfied with the image, she tucked the Blackberry back into her bag and left immediately for her embassy, to start to organize things for the next day.

While Leah was gone, Albert wrote out some ongoing wire transfer instructions for the $20 million which he expected to receive. He would log-in to his secure account and email them to UBS from an anonymous internet café before they left for Chamonix. The money was ultimately destined for Albert's offshore numbered account in the Cayman Islands.

VI

Monday, August 6th, 2012, Geneva, 11:00 GMT +1

By late morning Leah had arrived with a copy of the wire transfer confirmation cable and a non-descript motor pool car. She also had a Belgian Identity Card for Albert that had been made for him by Aly Elbaz, a skilled Moroccan-born craftsman at the Israeli mission. Albert was now about to assume his third new identity, this time as a Belgian national. Forged Belgian identity cards and passports were amongst the most "available" in Europe. Satisfied with everything, Albert left to send his banking instructions to UBS from a nearby internet café.

"Come on, Leah" he said when he returned, "we're off to Chamonix".

It was dusk when Albert and Leah finally drove down the hill from the Veille Ville and onto the Route de Malagnou. They were heading towards the border crossing to France, at Thonex. As they approached the Swiss border post, Albert broke into a cold sweat. His hands were clammy and damp gripping the wheel. Would the Swiss gendarme stop them and ask for their papers? Would he be recognized this time? And if they made it safely out of Switzerland, what might happen at the French border post, 100 meters further down the road?

"Try to relax, Albert" Leah said. "This car has diplomatic plates on it. Didn't you see the "CD" before the "GE" on the license plates? Normally, they will just waive us through". But as they approached the border post, the gray uniformed Swiss *gendarme* gestured for them to pull over and stop.

Albert rolled down the window, trying to be calm. Leah immediately seized the initiative. "*Bon jour*", she said, handing over her *carte de legitimation*, while Albert added his EU idenity card. "I'm Dr. Leah Shalev of the Israeli mission. This is my colleague, Herbert Moran. We are on our way to Chamonix for a short break. The weather has been so fine lately!"

The *gendarme* looked decidedly unamused. After a brief perusal of their documentation and a notation of the diplomatic license plate on the car, he waived them through with a curt "*salut*". The French border guards couldn't be bothered. They saw so many diplomats pass through the border each day that didn't even get up from their seats. Albert eased the car away from the border crossing and breathed a deep sigh of relief.

"Whew, we're through. Good work, Leah! We'll be in Chamonix in less than a few hours. But we dare not stay at the same place as I did last time, so I've booked us in at a small bed and breakfast up the valley, in Argentiere. It'll be just a short drive from there tomorrow morning to where we need to go."

"So you put the sands in a safe deposit box in Chamonix?"

"Not exactly, Leah. They are safe alright, but we'll have to do some hiking and scrambling to get to them".

As they emerged from a short tunnel a way down the autoroute, a sign proclaimed, *"Vous etes en face de L'Aiguille du Midi, une de les plus grandes montagnes du monde!"*

Hardly. The entire Mt. Blanc chain at 14,000+ feet would only be foothills in the Himalayas or Karakoram ranges of Asia.

"Up there, Leah," Albert said with a smile, "that's where we are going early tomorrow morning."

A short ride further down into the valley and they arrived at La Chapelle d'Elisa, a beautifully restored old coaching inn, dating back to the late 18th century. As Albert went inside to check in, Leah took a new set of license plates out of her overnight bag and fitted them on to the car in place of the Genevoise CD plates. They were now driving a very common silver Ford Mondeo, with ordinary plates from the neighboring Canton of Vaud. Hidden away in Argentiere, Leah was satisfied that they could remain anonymous and unnoticed for a short time at least. That was all she needed anyway. Her Beretta 86F pistol was tucked safely away in her purse.

VII

Monday, August 6th, 2012, Geneva, 21:00 GMT +1

Philip Alan Bloom, an international arms dealer from Akron, Ohio, had checked into the Mandarin Oriental Hotel du Rhone on Saturday evening. He had just spent a busy day visiting with the local sales representative of EADS NV, Europe's second largest arms manufacturers. The company developed and marketed civil and military aircraft, as well as missiles, space rockets, and related systems. Bloom had a long shopping list on behalf of anonymous clients, worldwide. Geneva was a very convenient place to transact such business.

Tired from the day's haggling, wining and dining, Bloom walked through the lobby and headed for the bank of lifts to his Business Suite on the Executive Floor. He got out on the top floor and fished his electronic key out of his jacket pocket. A click in the slot and he entered the tastefully darkened, nicely appointed suite, with views out over the Rhone River.

"Philip Bloom? We've been waiting for you", an unexpected voice said from out of the darkness.

"What? Who's there?" Bloom couldn't see where the voice was coming from in the subdued light.

"Get him and sit him down over here!" Ahmed Samir ordered his two henchmen. Without much of a struggle, Bloom was thrust roughly into an armchair and held forcibly down by two burly, middle-eastern looking men, dressed in black and packing handguns. Suddenly he was totally confused and terrified.

"Bind his hands and feet, quickly!" Samir said.

"Who are you? For chrissakes, what do you want of me?" Bloom blurted out frantically. A hard slap in the face quickly silenced him.

"I ask the questions, understand?" Samir said. Bloom nodded weakly in response.

"So, Philip Bloom, or is it Peter Shaw, or Albert Stern? Whatever you call yourself, you are a Jewish dog! But one who has something we want. You know what I am talking about, don't you?" Another hard slap in the face focussed Bloom's attention keenly on his inquisitor.

"No, I don't know what you want! I don't know any of those other names! You have the wrong person! This is a big mistake!"

While Samir continued to question Bloom, his two associates began tearing the suite apart, obviously looking for something specific.

Samir took his .38 caliber Glock 25 from his belt and put the muzzle up against Bloom's right temple. "We have come for the weapon. You have it with you here, don't you? You were going to sell it to that Israeli bitch, weren't you? Now you will give it to us immediately or you will be slaughtered." Samir cocked his handgun.

Bloom was very frightened and confused. "Weapon, what weapon?" he thought frantically. Yes, he dealt in weapons, but no one had ever tried forcibly to get one from him. "I have no weapons here! Only catalogs and specifications. Have a look over there and see. My merchandise doesn't fit in hotel rooms!", he said, trembling with fear. "I don't deal with any Israelis either!"

"Leader", an associate called out, "we can't find anything here. He must have put it somewhere else for safe-keeping. Let's take him with us and make him talk. Or shall we just behead him now and get it over with?"

"Wait", another called out from the bedroom next door, which he had thoroughly tossed. "I found this receipt from the main UBS office on Rue du Rhone. It shows that Bloom was there earlier today to transact some safe-deposit box business. That's where he put it, eh?"

"Probably", Samir replied. He slapped Bloom hard across the face again with the butt of his pistol. "That's where it is, isn't it?"

Samir knew that he couldn't fail in his mission. If Bloom wouldn't talk now, there were many intricate tortures he knew with which to coax him. He would be begging to take them to the right place when they were finished with him.

"No, no", Bloom pleaded. "I just put some cash away for safe keeping. There's no weapon in that safe deposit box."

But Samir didn't believe him. He would have to find out first if the way was clear for an abduction. He took his cell phone out of his pocket and speed dialed a number.

Sitting down in the spacious lobby facing the Rhone river, an associate, dressed as an affluent business man, had spread his papers out on an ornate coffee table in front of his comfortable wing back chair. This was a common sight at the Mandarin Oriental. A lot of business gets done informally in the lobby. Nothing to arouse the suspicions of hotel security.

After a brief cell phone conversation, the middle-eastern business man lit a Dunhill cigarette, perched it on the ashtry, and got up, heading for the men's room. It looked like he would return very shortly. At the foot of the chair, obscured by the coffee table, was a locked attache case in fine grain leather. Samir's fail-safe mechanism was now in place.

Samir untied Bloom and told him to stand up. Frightened badly, Bloom meekly complied. "You are coming with us. We will take very good care of you. I'm sure we can do a lot to improve your memory of where you put what we want. I will lead you out through the lobby into a waiting car outside. Do anything to call attention to yourself and you will be killed instantly, understand?"

With that, Samir reached into his pocket for his silencer and screwed it contemplatively into the end of the barrel of his Glock 25. He made another cell phone call to be sure that the Mercedes was waiting at the ready, in the hotel's forecourt. A healthy tip to the doorman had assured that it wouldn't be disturbed from its parking place. Then they were all on their way out.

136

One of Samir's two associates went down and secured an empty elevator for them. He had persuaded an indignant old couple to exit abruptly, a few floors below. Down the empty corridor at a trot, Bloom was hustled into the lift. Its doors were promptly shut behind him, away from prying eyes. Samir pushed the Lobby button, keeping Bloom ahead of him all the time. Samir's two henchman stood on either side of their quarry. Through the pocket of his sports coat, Samir kept the muzzle of his gun jammed against the base of Bloom's spine.

The elevator door opened on a bustling lobby scene. "Surely in this crowd we can move unnoticed out the door and into the waiting car" Samir thought. But as they started as a group across the lobby, the clerk at the main desk spotted Bloom. He tried frantically to get his attention.

" M. Bloom! M. Bloom! I was just calling your room. There are some gentleman waiting here to see you."

Bloom had arranged a nightcap with some perspective arms purchasers from Brunei. They were now waiting impatiently to see him. Surrounded by their own armed security people, they headed straight across the lobby towards Bloom. Fearing some kind of imminent confrontation, the hotel's own private, uniformed security people also moved briskly towards the growing group.

That was all that Samir needed to see. He just could not fail. He nodded affirmatively towards the middle-eastern business man, now positioned near the main door, cell phone in hand. One touch of a speed dialed number and instant chaos ensued.

The far end of the lobby by the bar was completely engulfed in a ball of searing flames. The percussion from the blast blew out the plate glass windows fronting the river with immense force. It hurled daggers of jagged glass at innocent pedestrians promenading along the river *quai*, across the narrow street. Inside, the bar area was completely obliterated. Injured and dazed patrons staggered around in pools of their own blood. The carnage was horrendous. It bore the clear signature of an al-Queda operation.

In the mass confusion, Samir and his henchman, in a tight wedge, plowed through the stunned crowd ahead of them with their hostage. They pushed Bloom out of the main door and into the waiting Mercedes. Then they were gone in a moment.

Two days later the headless body of Philip Alan Bloom was found dumped in a back alley in the Les Paquis district. Samir had obviously failed in his mission.

VIII

Tuesday,, US Permanent Mission, Geneva, 07:30 GMT +1

The staid old city of Geneva was in a state of shock. Never before had any terrorist incidents occurred within its limits. Now there had been an explosion in the inner harbor, an abduction and a devastating blast in the heart of the city, all within a few days. Dozens had been killed and many more had been injured. The cantonal authorities were searching desperately for explanations and for the perpetrators. But Inspector Jean-Christophe Malbec knew with whom he wanted to talk urgently.

Chris Wytham answered the phone in the guest office he had been temporarily allocated at the US Permanent Mission in Chambesy, Geneva. It was Inspector Malbec. He was coming over to see him immediately. Ten minutes later, Malbec was shown into the little office, hidden discreetly away from the main diplomatic concourse. He didn't waste any time getting straight to the point.

"*Monsieur*, we believe that your fugitive, Stern, is the cause of all of the catastrophes of the last few days. Nothing like this has ever happened here in Geneve! We must find him and arrest him immediately. He is now a criminal accessory in Switzerland."

"Please calm down, Jean-Christophe" Wytham replied. 'I agree with you completely. My government has been trying to apprehend Stern for some time now. He keeps slipping out of our grasp. Do you have any current leads on him?"

"*Oui, bien sur*. We think we know where he may be headed now. He and the Israeli woman. She checked a silver Ford Mondeo staff car out of the motor pool of their Permanent Mission on Monday. It crossed the border at Thonex later that evening. A border guard noted the license plates as being Geneve diplomatic, allocated to the Israeli mission. He remembers her and a companion, whom he said had a Belgian EU Identity Card. They drove off towards the Autoroute Blanche, to Chamonix."

"Exactly what we expected", Wytham observeded. "They're going to get the stuff. Can your French colleagues apprehend them?"

Malbec looked at Wytham with a wry smile. "The French never help us, especially not with diplomatic affairs. We will have to pursue them ourselves, covertly."

"No time really", Wytham said. "We'll have to use some covert technology of our own – with the permission of the Swiss authorities, of course."

"Of course, but what technology is that, *monsieur*?"

Earlier Wytham had been in touch with the US Air Force Base at Ramstein, in southern Germany. On the highest priority basis, he had asked to have a Predator drone readied and waiting to undertake a very sensitive mission of interdiction. He had made it very plain to USAF top brass at the base that he was backed to the hilt by both the DOI and the Pentagon. The "go" order would come down directly from the Vice President's office. The targets would be very high value. Now he explained it all quickly to Malbec.

Wytham had to take some educated guesses to try to track Stern. "Remember, he's a skilled mountain climber. He put up some impressive new alpine routes during his summer climbing sessions, while a graduate student in England. So I doubt that he went to Chamonix to put the sands in a bank's safe-deposit vault. No, he must have put them in a place only accessible to a good mountaineer, somewhere high up in the Alps."

"Very possible, *monsieur*," Malbec replied. "The French securite has only now belatedly confirmed to us that Stern spent a night at the Hotel Le Morgane back in July, under the name of Peter Shaw. That hotel is only a few hundred meters away from the base station of the *telepherique de l'Aiguille du Midi.*"

"So let's assume that he took the cable lift up to hiking trails, which he knew well. He wouldn't have gone all the way to the top with the stuff. It's all snow and ice up there and thronged with tourists. No, he had to have disembarked at the half way station, at Plan de l'Aiguille. So we need to track him and Shalev from there. I doubt that they'll waste any time. They must be up there already, along....."

"Along the Grand Balcon Nord", Malbec completed the thought. "The trail that leads to Montenvers".

"Right, now let's give our friends in Ramstein some specific guidance, fast."

"And if they fail to find them? If the drone fails to make the hit?" Malbec asked.

"Unlikely, but I've already provided for that too. I had Bill Churchill assemble a small extraction squad the other day, just in case. In France we'll have no authority or cooperation. If we can catch Stern there, we'll have to take him to a safe place out of country before can we ship him off to the US. A quick snatch and transport job. Jim MacLean is heading up the group. They're leaving for Chamonix in a few minutes.

We flew in Brian Bretton of the FBI as well. He's the only one amongst us whose ever seen Stern in person. He interviewed him early on in Houston. I'm sure that he will be able to recognize him, no matter what he's done to alter his appearance. It's 50 km to Chamonix from here, so they should all get there just before the cable car starts operating for the day. They'll be on the lookout for the Israeli mission staff car – a silver Ford Mondeo with Geneva diplomatic plates."

IX

Tuesday, August 7th, 2012, Ramstein AFB, Kaiserslauten, Germany, 08:30 GMT +1

The MQ-1 Predator drone had been rolled out of its storage hangar and readied for takeoff. This medium-altitude, long-endurance, remotely piloted aircraft was used primarily for armed reconnaisance. However, it was also a very accurate firing platform for surgically-precise interdiction operations against high value targets. At longer ranges, the aircraft was flown by a ground-based pilot via a Ku-Band satellite data link for beyond line-of-sight flights.

The Predator was well equipped for its sensitive missions. It carried a color nose camera for flight control, a day variable-aperture TV camera, a variable-aperture infrared camera for low light or night operations and synthetic aperture radar for looking through smoke, clouds or haze. Most importantly, its Multi Targeting System was armed with two laser-guided Hellfire missles and a pair of .50 calibre M3M flexible machine guns for strafing ground targets.

Flight Lieutenant Joseph E. Rooney, Jr., was a skilled operator of the Predator drone. He had logged many hours at the controls on both training missions and covert operations for the CIA. He would be well challenged by today's mission, however. It would take the aircraft down through southern Germany, across Switzerland and into central France, in the Chamonix valley of the Haute Savoie. The latter would be the target area, but also the most risky part of the mission.

The French would certainly not permit any covert intrusion into their airspace. So Rooney would have to fly the Predator at very low altitude, through the deep glacial valleys, to avoid detection. This current model had state-of-the-art stealth technology built-in, so it was practically invisible to radar anyway. Its single engine was whisper quiet.

The distance to cover was just over 300 miles, which the Predator could do easily in a little more than 2 hours. It would be over the Chamonix valley by 10:45 AM, at latest. Rooney eased it off the runway and up into the towering cloud banks covering southern Germany. He made its heading south by southwest, straight towards its target area in east-central France.

Rooney was in constant touch with Chris Wytham on an encoded satellite line. Wytham reported to him the assumption that Stern and Shalev should be travelling east, on the south side of the River Arve. If they were indeed there, they would be somewhere along the 5 km mountain track hugging the granite ramparts of the Chamonix *aiguilles*, at about an altitude of 2,200 meters. It would be a clear violation of French airspace to track them there with the drone, but that was a risk they would have to take. Unfortunate navigation "errors" occasionally occurred on training flights, the French could later be told apologetically.

X

Tuesday, August 7th, 2012, Chamonix Valley, France, 09:00 GMT +1

The telepherique up to the Aiguille du Midi didn't start operating until 9:00 AM. It was the was height of the summer tourist season. The line of holiday makers, day trekkers and alpine climbers waiting to board already wound half way around the parking lot.

Annoyed at the wait and the exposure, Albert reluctantly joined the end of the queue with Leah. It wasn't until 9:40 that they reached the ticket kiosk. The ascent to Plan de l'Aiguille would take at least 20 minutes. That would put them at the beginning of the Grand Balcon Nord traverse by just after 10:00 AM.

Albert was greatly relieved when very few hikers disembarked along with him and Leah at Plan de l'Aiguille. The day was gray and overcast, with a low ceiling. Most of the tram riders preferred to continue on up the second phase to the Aiguille du Midi, which would be above the clouds, in dazzling sunlight. Only a few other hearty souls would attempt the Grand Balcon Nord crossing to Montenvers that morning.

As Albert and Leah set out along the rocky path, a bank of mist and fog shrouded the towering granite spires of the Chamonix *aiguilles*. Albert hadn't expected to be back so soon to recover the

Viking sands, but he was satisfied that they had been safely cached while he had successfully carried on his delicate negotiations.

After about 3 km of solitary hiking, Albert and Leah turned off the well-trodden path towards Montenvers and followed a narrow side trail that weaved its way up steep slopes of boulders and scree to the foot of the ascent route for the Aiguille de L'M.

"Are you up to this, Leah?" Albert asked, looking up at the 200 meter near vertical ascent to the summit.

"Of course I am! We Israeli army officers are tough. I climbed Mt. Sinai a few years ago in the desert heat just to see the early morning sunrise over the Red Sea. You lead and I'll follow."

Scrambling together over good, solid granite, they reached a ledge just below the summit in 45 minutes, at about 11:15 AM. It was an airily exposed perch, overlooking the Mer de Glace glacier, a sheer 1,000 meters below. Here Albert stopped and removed a geologist's hammer from his backpack. Kneeling down, he began to chip away at a small cairn of flat stones on the ledge. As they scattered under his blows, Leah saw an unexpected, round patch of concrete appear beneath where they had been. Albert used the pick end of his hammer carefully to puncture a hole in the center of the thin layer of concrete.

"Here, let me help you", Leah said, taking her Israeli army knife out of her pack. Bending over, she began to chip away at the remnants of the thin concrete veneer that still partially covered the gravel-lined, natural crevice in the rock. Working together they exposed a 500 ml Nalgene screw-top aluminum water bottle, almost half full of rich red sand. Albert reached down with satisfaction to retrieve it. He handed it to Leah, and, looking up, found himself quite unexpectedly starring into the business end of her Beretta 86F .380 caliber pistol.

XI

Gaston Rischard was the local commandant of the Chamonix Valley Territorial Air Defense Force. It was a part-time unit without much activity. In older times, during World War II, Chamonix was a very sensitive area, being right across the mountainous border with Fascist Italy, and not that far away from Nazi Germany. But in the 21st century, it was quite moribund. Serving in the TADF has merely become a convenient way for local youths to fulfill their national service requirement without having to leave home.

Like most great powers, the French had armed surface-to-air missile batteries protecting their major cities. Even provincial capitals and other strategic locations were similarly fortified. But Rischard was quite amazed when his sleepy tourist outpost had recently received a truck-mounted battery of state-of-the art Aster 30 –SAMP/T missiles to replace their antiquated Hawk SAMs.

In the midst of a routine morning radar scan, Rischard's assistant, Pierre Bourcier, reported an unusual, intermittent blip appearing on his screen. It seemed to be low over the Mt. Blanc *massif*, which is strategically interdicted airspace. Neither man could believe the initial reading as they worked frantically together to check and re-check it. But there it was again, a shadowy intruder with no definitive radar signature.

They couldn't get a visual fix on it with field glasses because of the low ceiling that morning. It certainly couldn't be a commercial airliner gone astray at that altitude, nor could it be a small, private aircraft. No one was permitted to over fly the Chamonix Valley corridor without first having filed an approved flight plan. And the unidentified object appeared to be moving in a repetitive, oval flight pattern, seemingly scanning the Grand Balcon Nord below it. Repeated radio attempts to reach the aircraft were to no avail. If it carried a transponder, it was either inoperative or purposely turned off. What then to do?

Rischard contacted the regional headquarters of the French Armee de l'Air in Lyon. Perhaps they should scramble several Dassault Rafale fighters to check the situation out? No, Lyon HQ replied, they could get a quicker fix on the supposed intruder using the newly orbited Helios 2B surveillance satellite.

Minutes later Lyon reported back that the unidentified intruder appeared to be a small, unmanned, single engine aircraft. Satellite pictures with up to a 10 meter resolution quickly identified it as an American drone aircraft, bristling with armament. As it circled at about 2800 meters, it passed repeatedly close to the cable system operating the Aiguille du Midi *telepherique.*

The French were acutely aware of the danger that this posed. There had been several fatal accidents in both France and Italy when US Air Force fighter planes on NATO training missions had severed the cables of *telepheriques* operating in both St. Etienne, France and Cavalese, in the Italian Dolomites. More to the point, the French military command was also quite incensed by repeated, "accidental" USAF incursions into their airspace.

"Commandant Rischard, hold the line", a voice in Lyon said. "Wing Commander Dupuy wants to speak with you."

"What are your orders, sir?", Rischard asked with trepidation.

XII

"Leah, what are you doing?", Albert said in shock, as he stared into the barrel of Leah's revolver.

"Sorry, but I'm just following my orders", Leah replied coldly.

"But I've kept my part of the bargain! You have the Viking sands. You're supposed to take me to Tel Aviv now, to asylum. That was the deal. Those were your orders, right?"

"That would be very inconvenient for Israel. We couldn't harbor a terrorist, a mass-murderer. Particularly not one wanted by our most important ally. No, my orders were quite different. I was to hunt you down and kill you, after I recovered what the Americans were so desperately looking for. Our dear friends will see us again as their most faithful allies, fully to be trusted, as always. Unfortunately, the Viking sands will have been lost in the struggle." Leah smiled cruelly.

Albert knew he was in a life or death situation. Leah was just out of reach on the small ledge, leveling her pistol for the kill. But he still had the geologist's hammer in his right hand. A quick blow at her shooting hand should send the pistol tumbling down onto the ledge. What did he have to lose?

He lunged forward and swung with all his might to deliver a sharp blow, just as Leah was squeezing the trigger. The pistol fired a round that ricocheted off the granite wall behind him. Leah's hand was seriously broken, but she somehow managed to hold on to the revolver. As Albert reached out to grab it from her mangled fingers, an unexpected visitor arrived.

Rearing up out of the mist and fog, a strange aircraft appeared quite suddenly. Like a giant bird of prey, it hovered 200 meters above them, peering at them through its cold electronic eyes. It was heavily armed and intent on killing.

Training its twin machine guns on the ledge, it let loose a lethal hail of bullets. Leah was mortally struck in the base of her skull. She fell over like a limp rag doll, dead. Another burst tore apart the aluminum bottle she had been clutching in her left hand. The greatest weapon of the 21st century was scattered hopelessly to the winds. Crouching behind a rock outcrop on the ledge, shielded only slightly by Leah's lifeless, bullet-riddled body, Albert was sure that the end had finally come. But maybe not quite yet.

From far below in the valley, a howling banshee shriek accompanied a rising column of flame. Traveling at an incredible 4.5 mach, the deadly accurate, laser-guided, hit-to-kill missle slammed into the hostile aircraft with terminal force. A billowing orange fireball engulfed the intruder drone, as it disintegrated into a fiery shower of searing debris. In a matter of seconds it was all over, leaving only an eerie stillness after the firestorm.

XIII

Tuesday, August 7th, 2012, US Permanent Mission, Geneva, 11:25 GMT +1

"I've lost contact, Chris!", Rooney's voice reported suddenly over the speaker phone.

"Repeat, Joe, repeat, what do you mean?"

"I mean that suddenly my screen has gone black. My controls have gone dead. The aircraft won't respond to any of my inputs. I've lost her!"

"How, Joe? How the hell did that happen?"

"I had them in my sights and I had commenced firing. I'm sure that we hit the woman. I saw her fall. Then there was a huge power surge and only blackness. Something hit the drone with immense force. Whatever it was, it destroyed it!"

"A missile, a French SAM missile?" Wytham almost cried in disbelief.

Rooney's voice crackled back, "That's all it could have been. I had complete control of the aircraft. It was executing the mission perfectly."

"The man, Stern, was he hit too?"

"I didn't see that for sure, but he must have been. We were firing 8 rounds a second. No one could have survived such an onslaught!"

"Was either one of them holding anything? Did you see?"

"The woman had an aluminum bottle in her hand, from what I could tell. It was shredded by one of our machine gun bursts. It fell with her in fragments,"

That was all that Wytham could learn from the thoroughly disconsolate Rooney. But it was chilling news. They had provoked an international incident between NATO allies. Forty million dollars worth of sensitive US government property had been lost. There would be hell to pay for all of that. But Shalev was gone, along with the Viking sands and, hopefully, Stern was too. Wytham picked up his secure link satellite phone and reported the events to Jim MacLean and the extraction team, now at their stakeout location in the base station parking lot of the Aiguille du Midi cable car system.

XIV

Tuesday, August 7th, 2012, Chamonix Valley, France, 11:30, GMT +1

Completely stunned, Albert tried desperately to collect his thoughts. It had all been too surreal. In a matter of seconds, his world had been turned completely upside down again. But, incredibly, he was still alive and unharmed. Teetering on the narrow ledge in front of him was Leah's .38 caliber Beretta revolver. Her Israeli army knife was still in the crevice. He picked them both up and tucked them into a pocket of his cargo pants. He had never fired a gun in his life, but, instinctively, he knew that he might need to do so soon.

The fiery events on high couldn't fail to have been noticed in the valley below. Albert had to get away from the scene quickly. Steeling himself, he raced back down the rock face to the main footpath. Then he detoured directly down, towards Chamonix, on a steep relief trail. He was heading back towards the car park at the cable car station. In his pocket he still had the keys to the Ford Mondeo. Once again, he was in complete flight mode. He would have to formulate his plans as he fled. But he knew that he was angry - really angry. Indeed, he was furious. He had suffered many unexpected betrayals, but this one was truly incredibly cruel. There would have to be serious payback soon.

Albert knew that he had to stay in the EU for the time being. Ultimately, he would have to flee from Europe altogether. There would be time enough to think that all out later, though. For now he wanted to seek shelter in an urban center which he both knew and which would afford him some desperately needed breathing space. Most importantly, he needed access to an anonymous computer network. He still had some final, but vital, business to transact with his adversaries.

Indelibly imprinted in Albert's mind were the cold electronic eyes of the killer drone that had assaulted them. It had seen Leah hit and fall to her death. It had also seen the Viking sands scattered hopelessly to the winds. But how well had it seen him surviving, before it disintegrated into a ball of flames? Would his pursuers assume that he could not have possibly lived through such a lethal onslaught? That would buy him some desperately needed time. But it wouldn't be long before the French authorities recovered Leah's shattered body from the Mer de Glace glacier and wondered why his wasn't there as well. No, it certainly wasn't over yet. Time to flee again and regroup for the final chapter.

XV

Reaching the car park on foot, Albert sensed further, imminent danger. There were at least a dozen silver Ford Mondeos in the lot. His was far in the back. Most of them had French plates, but a few were Swiss registered.

The parking lot was crowded with tourists and hikers heading disconsolately back from the cable car base station. The service had been suddenly suspended, to their great dismay. Yet something else seemed terribly amiss to Albert. A black Chevy Tahoe with tinted windows was parked towards the front of the lot.

Albert had seen these many times before in official motorcades in the US, when, for example, the Vice President had made his periodic oversight visits to NASA. In Europe, however, it was an unusual sight. Although no one was around the SUV, the telltale black half globe on top immediately told the trained eyes of a scientist that there was a TV camera inside. This was surely the "eye" vehicle of a surveillance operation over the immediate area.

Albert stopped at the edge of the parking lot and removed the red fleece vest he had been wearing. He pulled the visor of his hat down to shade his eyes, found a secluded vantage point and then sat down on a bench to observe.

He didn't have to wait long. As a hiker approached one of the silver Ford cars, two tall men emerged from behind the Chevy Tahoe. They started walking briskly towards him. One of the men looked familiar to Albert. Wracking his mind he wondered where he had seen him before. Tall, muscular and clean-cut, he was very American looking.

"Houston", Albert thought, "I saw him in Houston. He was the FBI agent who came to question me after the incident in the lab. They're here looking for me! It must be their fail-safe plan."

It was Brian Bretton and the extraction team. But he had just heard from Chris Wytham that both Albert and Leah had most probably been killed by the drone. So the continued surveillance was only an extra precaution. The agents didn't really expect to see either of them turn up to reclaim their car.

Albert knew that there was no sense in trying to reach the Ford Mondeo at the back of the lot. They had it all covered. He certainly couldn't try to get lost amongst the milling crowds of tourists in Chamonix, not even for just an evening. It was too small and simple a place. No, he had to leave as fast as possible, but how, without being seen?

Towards the near end of the lot Albert was surprised but pleased to see a 1977 vintage Mini Mk IV with French plates. "I'll have to steal it," he thought.

Why that car? While the new Mini was now a BMW product, this older one had been built in Cowley, England, by BMC, at the original MG and Rover works. He knew that it had the same quirky Lucas electronics as his own vintage MGB. No computer chips or smart key devices to stop him. If there was any car he could hot wire, that one had to be it.

Albert first located Bretton and the other agent, who had headed back towards the Ford. They looked clearly disappointed that the hiker whose car they had checked out wasn't their man. As they walked back towards their Chevy Tahoe, Albert headed the other way, towards the nearby Mini. He had gone unnoticed so far.

Reaching into his pocket he pulled out Leah's Israeli army knife. "Now which one was the lock-picking tool?" he wondered frantically. He knew that he couldn't be seen to be fumbling around. But his good memory served him well. He stuck the odd-shaped blade into the driver's side lock cylinder and with one quick turn, he was in.

After he adjusted the seat, his fingers reached under the dash towards the wiring cluster. It all felt familiar to Albert, like his good old MGB. A few deft twists of the wires with the aid of the knife and the engine sprung to life. Albert eased the car out of the lot, being careful to give the Chevy Tahoe a wide berth. He knew that there would be outlier vehicles of the surveillance team in radio contact with the "eye". But they wouldn't be looking for an old Mini.

Unobtrusively as possible, he drove the Mini down onto the main highway leading through the village. Then, without looking back, he set out immediately for Lyon, France, 136 miles away.

XVI

Tuesday, August 7th, 2012, Tehran, Iran, 08:30 GMT +2 ½

General Reza Houshmand was in a foul mood that morning. It had just been confirmed to him that Captain Abbas Sorushian had been killed and that the Israeli agent, Leah Shalev, had escaped unharmed. Nor was there any further word of her whereabouts or that of the American fugitive, with his devastating weapon. All cell phone traffic between them had gone quiet. Now Houshmand had to contemplate the chilling probability that Shalev had completed the deal and that the American and his doomsday weapon was clandestinely in Israeli hands, well out of reach of Iran. Worse yet, he had to report all of this directly to the President, who had demanded to be kept personally informed.

"Hamayoun!", he barked, summoning his orderly into his office. "Have the car brought over. I must go see the President immediately." It would be a very difficult meeting.

Tensions between Israel and Iran had risen to new heights after the Israeli invasion of Lebanon in 2006. Iran had also deeply infiltrated the Shiite south of Iraq, fighting a proxy war there with the beleaguered Coalition forces before they left. The hard-line Islamic state was clearly positioning itself to be the leading regional power. It continued publicly to doubt the Holocaust and displayed a deep, abiding hate for Zionism. It had often repeated its threat to wipe Israel off the map. Batteries of nuclear tipped missiles were aimed at Israel's major population centers, although the Iranians intuitively knew that the Israelis were similarly armed and ready. A devastating nuclear exchange, plunging the entire region into chaos, was always a distinct possibility.

Arriving at the presidential offices, Houshmand was made to wait an uncomfortably long time in an ornate anteroom. Finally he was summoned into the presence of the President.

"Have a seat, General" the short, stocky, bearded president said curtly. "Some tea?"

"Yes thank you, your Excellency." Hot, sweet tea in tall glasses, cradled in silver holders, was delivered to both men.

The President sipped thoughtfully at his tea. Houshmand dreaded the storm that was about to erupt from his angry superior.

"General, where is this doomsday weapon you were told to seize?"

Houshmand squirmed uneasily in his chair. "We don't know, Excellency. The trail has gone completely cold since...."

"Since your incompetent agent, Sorushian, failed in his mission!"

"Yes, your Excellency", Houshmand replied with resignation.

"So the Israelis have it then? So the Zionist dogs have the means to destroy us now?" the President continued in a shrill voice, pacing the room. "The Supreme Leader is holding me responsible for this failure!"

"I am very sorry, your Excellency. You know that we sent our best man. He was well briefed and supported. I don't know how he failed. But we don't really know if the Israelis succeeded either."

"No matter. We must assume that they did. We cannot risk a Zionist attack on our precious oil resources! I have already put the Revolutionary Guards on highest alert. Qods units are guarding all of our major oilfields and pipelines. They are under orders to shoot to kill any suspicious persons. We know what this terrible weapon can do. The British are still reeling from their great loss. If the Zionists strike at us, we will annihilate them once and for all. Tel Aviv, Jerusalem, Haifa, will all be in nuclear ashes! And, if the Great Satan tries to protect them" the President continued, face reddening, "we will deal them a final mortal blow on the killing fields of southern Iraq!"

"Yes, Excellency. Good planning. What can my people do now to help?"

"What can you do to help? Idiot! You must find out *now* what has happened to Shalev and Stern. Where are they? Did she take him to asylum in Israel? What are we up against? Do the Israelis have the weapon? Until we know otherwise, I am assuming the worst. Now go, immediately and do it!"

A chastened Reza Houshmand bid a respectful farewell to the President and headed back to his office in his black Mercedes limousine. He knew that he would quickly have to pick up the thread of events that had been broken, suddenly and unexpectedly, in Geneva.

XVII

Wednesday, August 8th, 2012, Herzliya, Israel, 09:00 GMT +2

Jamal Safir sat in stunned silence in his office. He couldn't believe what he had heard. His best operative was dead. Her critical mission had failed at the very end. The American was still unaccounted for. Had he been killed too? What happened to the priceless weapon? Had it been lost? Or did Stern still have it, ready now to deal with another willing purchaser, perhaps? What of the twenty million dollars that had already been wired to Stern? Attempts to recover it from UBS in Geneva had met with only stone cold silence. There were just too many questions without any satisfactory answers.

At least Safir could find some solace in the fact that the dreaded weapon hadn't fallen into the hands of the Iranians. Shalev had dutifully reported her near fatal encounter with Sorushian in Geneva. Nothing else had happened after that with regard to activities of Iranian Qods operatives. And the Mossad's routine intercepts of electronic diplomatic traffic to and from Iran had gone completely silent on the matter. But there were more serious questions to address on the home front. Safir was due to see the Prime Minister in half an hour.

As soon as Safir arrived the Prime Minister made it plain that he was furious with the Mossad's failure to secure the weapon. Had Stern escaped with it? Would he offer it to another State for an even greater fortune? What did the Iranians know?

"Jamal", the Prime Minister said coldly, "we must assume that the Iranians believe that we have the weapon. Now they will look for any opportunity to strike at us."

"Yes, Prime Minister, it is a very dangerous situation".

"So, we must turn to our great ally for additional protection", the Prime Minister continued.

"But how can we do that now, Prime Minister? They must know all about our contacts with Stern."

"Yes, Jamal, but diplomacy has many different shades of gray", the Prime Minister said, smiling. "We were only trying to help them, correct? Isn't that what any loyal ally would do?"

"How so, Prime Minister?"

"Stern contacted us first, right? We sent an agent to apprehend him. More so, we tried to recover the deadly weapon for its rightful owners, our closest allies. Tragically, we didn't succeed. They inadvertently killed one of our best operatives. They owe us a lot for that", the Prime Minister concluded.

"But they will surely ask why we kept silent for so long. Why we didn't cooperate with them from the outset", Safir objected.

"We didn't need their overt help at Entebbe or in Lebanon, did we? They know very well how we operate. Secrecy and stealth are our international calling cards. But we normally succeed."

"I see, Prime Minister. But we could use their strong backup now, right?"

"Exactly. Time to seek assurances from Big Brother. I'm going to Washington next week for yet another meeting with their president. We'll need some more of his country's Arrow 2 missiles to protect our eastern flank from the Iranians. In the meanwhile, you get in touch immediately with their intelligence director, Baker, in Washington. Tell the Americans everything we know, spinning it, of course, the way we have just discussed. I'm sure they will be very grateful."

XVIII

Thursday, August 9th, 2012, S.Waziristan, Pakistan/Afghanistan Border, 07:00 GMT +4

The gaunt leader sat, unsmiling, on his small prayer rug, pensively sipping a cup of sweet mint tea. His trusted second in command, Ayman, was seated cross-legged next to him, awaiting the leader's words.

"This news is most unfortunate, Ayman. It seems that we have accomplished nothing."

"I know, leader, a thousand pardons! But we have some new information which may finally lead us to our prey".

"How so, Ayman?"

"Our man, Aly, inside the Israeli mission in Geneva, made a new Belgian identity card at the request of one of their Mossad operatives. He thought that the photo looked familiar. A bit thin and haggard, but it was clearly the face of this Jew, Stern. The one who stole the weapon from the Americans. He has had many names since, but we know him now as a Belgian national named Herbert Moran. We can track him down and still secure the prize".

"Excellent! How will we do that?"

" Aly served us very well, leader. All of these identity cards contain a smart chip with the holder's vital statistics encoded in them. They can also be made GPS sensitive. Seeing whom he was dealing with, he made the card traceable by GPS. Only we know that. The Israelis don't. He reported this all to the head of his sleeper cell in Geneva. Our man in the field there, Ahmed Samir, has been fully informed. He can track Stern with a simple, hand-held computer program which will find him, wherever he goes."

"*Inshallah*, Ayman! Have them find him and do the job properly this time. No further unfortunate mistakes. Obtain this mighty weapon from him and then kill him. Have them bring the weapon here to us. We shall then use it most effectively."

"It shall be done right this time, leader, *inshallah*!"

XIX

Friday, August 10th, 2012, Lyon, France, 10:00 GMT +1

Albert had arrived in Lyon, France, several days earlier, but it was only a transitional staging point. He knew that he could not return to Geneva, nor to anywhere else in Switzerland. But there was no reason to go back there anyway. His new fortune was safely out of that country, sitting in his numbered account in the Cayman Islands. He had the Belgian identity card that would allow him safe passage anywhere within the European Community. The stolen car could have been a problem, but he had abandoned it in a large Carrefour supermarket parking lot nearby, as soon as he had arrived. By the time anyone found it, he'd be long gone.

In the meanwhile, Albert had taken a room in a cheap hotel near the central Lyon-Part-Dieu railroad station. He needed to get some rest and to do some deep reflection. After almost 18 hours of sleep, Albert awoke to confront grim reality once again. It didn't take long to bring him back to the present. He picked up an old copy of the local newspaper that had been left in his room by the previous occupant. It was dated Tuesday, August 7th and its front page headline screamed, *"Une Frappe Massive de Terrorisme a Geneve!"*

Albert was astonished. As he read the story, his astonishment turned into a cold chill. Persons unknown had tried to abduct an American businessman named Philip Bloom from one of Geneva's most expensive hotels. The abduction was almost thwarted, but at a critical moment, a remote controlled bomb had been set off in the lobby, killing and maiming dozens of innocent bystanders. In the ensuing chaos, the kidnappers escaped with their victim. Swiss police were extremely puzzled, but they were, nonetheless, sure that the incident had all of the hallmarks of an al-Queda attack.

Albert stared at the newspaper. "Philip Bloom", he thought, "I'm Philip Bloom! They abducted the wrong guy, poor bastard!" Mind racing, Albert started to total up the number of mortal adversaries still pursuing him. There were the Iranians, the Americans, the Brits and now even al-Queda. Clearly the Israelis would want a piece of him too, now that he had taken their $20 million for no return. And he didn't even know about the Russians.

The Viking sands had been a double-edged sword for Albert. As he thought back over the past few tumultuous months, he realized that he had let a monstrous genie out of its bottle. There was certainly no putting it back in, ever. The only question left was what to do now?

In the past few days Albert had thought long and hard about the terrible weapon that he had accidentally discovered. It was clearly not something that would be safe in any country's hands. For anyone to possess it was a sure recipe for world chaos. Already it had driven him to previously unthinkable deeds, like some satanic talisman. It had engendered acts of greed, avarice and pure evil in the actions of seemingly responsible parties. Nations would kill for it. Deceit and betrayal had become the norm for all who were concerned with it. And yet the loss of the weapon was not the end of it by any means. Not yet. There was still another cargo coming soon, of which his countrymen and others were certainly well aware. Would it all ever end? No, Albert realized, not unless he finally made it end.

Albert knew that his only choice was to destroy Viking 4 before it splashed down safely in the Gulf of Mexico. Could he do that, though? At least, he thought, he still had a chance.

Only he and Yoshi Tanaka knew the intricate programs and protocols that controlled Viking 4's navigation and re-entry sequences. Yoshi, he assumed, would be exiting the picture soon as a casualty of NASA's drastic downsizing. He was to have been laid off as soon as Viking 4 made a safe splashdown. Thus the spacecraft was probably still on autopilot, just as Albert had originally programmed it several months ago.

If he could gain access one more time to the NASA network, he could irrevocably alter Viking 4's command programs and send the spacecraft and its lethal cargo careening out of control, to a fitting, flaming and final end. Direct access to NASA's computer network was now completely out of the question, of course, but there were still other ways.

To start with, Albert recalled, he had carefully provided in advance for any possible contingencies. He had secretly created alternative access for himself by way of a "backdoor" password. Not even Yoshi had known about that. Now it was just a question of accessing the NASA network without being immediately detected.

That would take some doing, but Albert had some good experience with hacking tools. NASA had gone out of its way to educate its top technical staff on recognizing and deflecting cyber attacks. Now those remaining would be put to the test, as soon as Albert could find a secure internet connection from which to attempt his covert break in.

But if he succeeded in gaining entry, to where should he redirect Viking 4? He had several scores to settle and a definitive warning that he wanted to send to all concerned.

He was furious with the Israelis. They had treated him as a naive fool. They had sent a *femme fatale* to win his confidence, seduce him and kill him. They would have to pay dearly for that.

Then there were the Iranians. They, too, had sent a death squad to hunt him down. How could he even the score with them both? Perhaps he could let them each do the work for him? Wouldn't it be fitting to have these two sworn adversaries destroy each other as the price for their mutual treachery? The idea had a perverted attraction to it; one that Albert vowed to develop further, once he had computer access again to Viking 4's final descent path.

In the meanwhile, Albert knew that he had to leave Lyon very soon. But where should he go next? "Amsterdam", Albert suddenly thought, "that's where I'll head to."

It would be a perfect temporary destination from which to finish his work. He knew it quite well. During his Cambridge years, it was a favorite amongst him and his friends for long weekend sojourns. It was bustling city, full of both permissiveness and pleasures of every sort. No one ever looked too closely at what one was up to there. Albert knew that he could blend easily into its diverse crowds while he went about his final piece of important business.

Amsterdam was also not far from the Dutch port of Rotterdam, from which Albert planned ultimately to make his final escape from Europe. Albert resolved that early the next morning, he would set out for the Dutch capital city. From Lyon, Albert would book his rail passage to Amsterdam. A TGV departed daily from Lyon to Paris. In Paris, Albert would have to hop a cab from the Gare de Lyon to the Gare de Nord. Then he could board the Thalys inter-city train that would take him directly to Amsterdam. If he made all of the connections, he would be there in about 6 hours.

XX

Friday, August 10th, 2012, CIA Headquarters, Langley, Virginia, 09:00 EDT

Chris Wytham and Brian Bretton had returned from Geneva and Chamonix empty handed. Stern had never been apprehended, but there was still one ace left to play. Viking 4 was no more than a week away from Earth with a cargo of at least half a pound of Viking sands secure within its hold. The US had lost those that

Stern had stolen, but now at least they, and everyone else, knew what they could do. It would now be a top national security priority to focus all attention on assuring a safe splash down and recovery of the second Viking craft, with its priceless cargo.

DOI Baker had asked to see the two agents that morning at 9:00 sharp. There would be a lot to discuss. Baker beckoned them both into his office from behind his imposing mahogany desk. "Have a seat at the conference table gentlemen. I'm going to teleconference in Director Morse as well", he added. An IT staff member busied himself setting up the video link.

"Good morning, Tim, gentlemen." FBI Director Calvin Morse greeted them all from the large LCD screen at the end of the conference table. "So where do we stand now?"

"We're a week away from recovery of Viking 4, Cal. The sands from Viking 3 were lost forever in the French Alps, as you know. We think that Stern was eliminated there too, but we have no definitive proof of that. In any event, it doesn't really matter anymore. It would have been nice to have taken him alive, though. The Brits would have been very grateful to have him - after we were finished with him, of course."

"Clear, Tim. What arrangements are we making to secure the sea lanes around where Viking 4 is scheduled to land?"

"The usual and then some. All shipping will be banned from a fifty mile radius of the projected splashdown area. The Navy will send a cruiser and a destroyer to patrol, along with the Coast Guard. Helicopters will be deployed from the cruiser to reach the re-entry vehicle the minute it splashes down in the Gulf. Then they'll take it by convoy to the Galveston navy base where it will be transferred to an armored vehicle. A convoy of National Guard troops will then escort it up to the Johnson Space Center in Houston.

We'll both be on open lines in case anything untoward should develop. The White House will be on standby as well."

"Sounds very secure to me, Tim. I guess my only regret is that we didn't apprehend Stern and bring him to justice here though. That's what this Agency was tasked to do. His body was never found, huh?"

"No. Only the remains of the Israeli agent, Shalev. At least that's all that the French will tell us. They are still mad as hell about out "accidental" intrusion into their airspace!"

"We had the parking lot in Chamonix thoroughly staked out, in case Stern reappeared" Bretton interjected. "No one ever came to reclaim the Israeli embassy staff car that they used to drive down there."

"But there was still one unexplained development" Wytham added. "While the surveillance team was there, someone stole a car right out of the lot. It was an old Austin Mini, not any of the ones that were being watched. It might just have been a routine theft, but then it turned up abandoned in a public parking lot in Lyon, France, the next day. It looks like someone was quite desperate to flee Chamonix and then to cover his tracks. I have a hunch that it was Stern. But if so, we don't have any idea where he might have gone from there."

"You and Brian should stay on top of that, Chris", Morse ordered.

Baker quickly agreed. "Viking 4 is our main priority, but if Stern is still around, it would be good for the collective reputations of our agencies to nail the bastard once and for all. I doubt that he can do any more damage, but he's done a hell of a lot already!"

XXI

Friday, August 10th, 2012, The Lubyanka, Moscow, Russia, 13:00, GMT +3

Ivan Chestnoy and Mikhail Kutusov watched intently as young Boris Sagadiev sat down at his desktop to initiate the hijacking of Viking 4. There was no need to camouflage his tracks. He would log in to the NASA network as authorized user, Yoshi Tanaka. It was 3:00 AM in the morning in Houston, so it was unlikely that there would be anyone on the network to query his access.

Sagadiev had no trouble entering the NASA network undetected. Scrolling through the various classified programs, he quickly found that of Viking 4. Current data showed that the spacecraft was now only 7 million kilometers away from earth and ready to execute its first retro-burn to begin braking for its re-entry. It was programmed to splash down in the northern sector of the Gulf of Mexico, offshore Galveston, on August 17th, 2012, at about 1:00 PM, Houston time.

"I'm in, Colonel. To where shall I re-direct her?"

"To north central Yakutia, Boris. Here are the coordinates. We want her to make a nice soft landing in the far eastern *taiga*." Chestnoy gave Sagadiev exact coordinates for an isolated landing site, several hundred kilometers west of the *oblast* capital city of Yakutsk.

"62 00' 05" N latitude, 125 53' 17" E longitude, correct, Colonel?"

"*Da*, Boris Ivanovich, that will be perfect!"

Several minutes later, Sagadiev confirmed. "There, Colonel, it is done. It should touch down there in about a week's time".

"*Atlychna*, Borya!" Chestnoy replied, softening his tone to the diminutive. "But will the Americans be able to detect this change?"

"Not likely, Colonel. Not, at least, until it is too late. I've heavily encrypted the change so that only those at the highest access levels would be able to detect it. It showed that there are only three such users of this program. One has already been cancelled and we are using the access code for the second. The third is for general oversight by NASA's Administrator, which is rarely ever used. If our source doesn't log in to it, no one will ever be able to tell what we have done."

"Not to worry, then, Borya. He won't be logging in ever again", Chestnoy said, emphatically.

"But what will we tell the Americans, Vanya? They will ask some very direct questions of our leadership when the spacecraft lands in Siberia", a concerned Kutusov asked.

"Why nothing, of course, Misha! We are not responsible for their navigation errors. Our President shall only tell them how fortunate they were that we didn't mistake this unexpected intrusion into our airspace for a hostile missile attack!"

"But the Americans will still want to recover their spacecraft. They will track it to a soft landing in Yakutia."

"No they won't Misha. Once it begins its re-entry sequence we will use our Kobalt class Kosmos satellites to jam their communications and tracking capabilities. They will assume that it has crashed. We will indignantly confirm this to them at the highest diplomatic levels. The wreckage will be terrible! They will be very fortunate that it fell to Earth in a remote far corner of eastern Siberia. Even we will have difficulty reaching the site. It will take months to recover anything that remains of their errant piece of space junk." Chestnoy smiled with obvious satisfaction.

XXII

Saturday, August 11th, 2012, Amsterdam, The Netherlands, 16:00 GMT +1

Albert arrived at Amsterdam Central Station. From there he walked briskly through the crowded, narrow streets, along the inner circle of canals, until he reached the main Herengracht canal.

He was headed for the Ambassade Hotel, which consisted of 10 originally separated 17th-century buildings, fronting the canal. Not as touristy as the famous Pulitzer Hotel nearby, the quiet little Ambassade would suit his purposes perfectly. He checked in under the name Herbert Moran and requested a room with a clear view down to both the narrow street below and the adjacent canal. Then he headed back out into the late afternoon rush.

On the top of Albert's list was to find a secluded internet café, off the beaten tourist track, where he would have access to a high-speed connection. Albert walked a short way further down the Herengracht and then turned onto a side street that crossed the innermost, Singel, canal. The next street was Spuistraat, where he found exactly what he was looking for. Chocolata was a tiny, unobtrusive hash and internet cafe on two levels.

On the street level was a tiny coffee shop with a few stools in front of the counter. Another four stools were arranged along a shelf in front of the window, providing a view of the passing humanity, for anyone who might be interested. Most patrons were too stoned, however, to care. In the back, a narrow, spiral staircase, surrounded by mirrors, led to a chill-out room with a TV and a few internet terminals, discreetly located in dim, secluded booths. Albert ordered a double espresso and took it up stairs to the internet terminals. It was still early by Amsterdam party standards, so the shop was pretty much deserted. "Fine", he thought, "no one here to bother or observe me."

Settling unnoticed into a corner booth, Albert first opened the internet browser, Mozilla Firefox. Then he typed in the web address for RIPE.net, the Réseaux IP Européens, which is the European Regional Internet Registry, providing internet resource allocations, registration services and co-ordination activities that support the operation of the internet globally. Most importantly, it provided a list of IP addresses in all of the subscribing European countries.

Albert focused first on Poland. Why so? Because Polish IP addresses have only a very low 56 bit encryption, making it quite easy to hack into them. His plan was to computer hop through Poland to elsewhere in Eastern Europe and then, ultimately, into the NASA mainframe in Houston. By doing so he could cover his trail and make it very difficult to track his actual location within a timeframe that could foil his plan.

Selecting several IP addresses in Poland that looked vulnerable, he noted them down and closed the RIPE program. Next he downloaded the Nmap security scanner program from its web site and ran port scans on the IP addresses that he had selected. This program reported to him what ports were open, who owned each process, and which service was typically assigned to the port. Most usefully, it also gave him a remote "fingerprint" of each machine's operating system. It would enable him to take control of each successive remote computer using previously installed, covert rootkits that the scans would detect for him. This way he could hop from computer to computer, leaving a complex trail that would be very hard to follow to its original source.

Quite satisfied with the results so far, Albert repeated the whole process again. This time he acquired additional vulnerable IP addresses in other low encryption Eastern European countries, such as Bulgaria, Romania, Moldova and Serbia. Lastly, he opened the ARIN - American Registry for Internet Numbers - website and looked for a few vulnerable IP addresses within the territorial USA.

At this point Albert stopped to check the time. It was 6:00 PM now in Amsterdam, making it 11:00 AM in Houston. Not a good time to try to access the NASA computer network. No, he would have to wait until early morning Houston time, when their system there would be free of its regular users. That would mean mid-morning, the next day in Amsterdam. So he would have to find something to amuse himself with in the meanwhile.

XXIII

After a very satisfying dinner, Albert headed back towards his hotel. He remembered that a few blocks away from the Ambassade, on the Singel canal, was Amsterdam's most famous and upscale brothel. In his student days, Albert could only dream of its imagined delights. But now he was more than able to afford them. "Why not", he thought, "What better way to spend one of my very few evenings in Amsterdam?" After his experiences with Leah, Albert had rediscovered his once healthy appetite for great sex.

The hotel concierge smiled knowingly. He quickly arranged for the establishment's limousine service to pick Albert up and drive him the several blocks to the stately canal house on the Singel with its trademark green lantern outside. It had begun to rain and Albert preferred a ride in a shiny black Mercedes to a wet walk. As they rode quietly through the dark, damp drizzle,

Albert remembered that he had forgotten to put his identity card and Leah's Beretta into the room safe. But, then, he didn't expect to be frisked entering a brothel.

In only five minutes he arrived. He alighted from the car, walked up the stairs and rang the doorbell. A well-mannered doorman greeted him, showed him in and took his coat. Then the manager welcomed him, discreetly collected the entrance fee, and encouraged Albert to enjoy a drink at the well stocked bar.

"Take your time", he encouraged him. "Chat and dance with any of our lovely hostesses. When you are ready to become more intimate with one – or even two" he said, smiling, "we'll arrange one of our splendid private rooms for you."

The surroundings were opulent baroque, with plush red velvet, leather and silk brocade. There weren't many clients but they were all being fussed over by the generous selection of delectable hostesses. They came in all varieties, to suit any and all tastes. There were classic, tall, blonde Europeans; petite, nicely rounded Asians; and statuesque, dusky Africans. But the one that immediately caught Albert's eye was a sultry Mediterranean enchantress who seemed to have had him in her sights from the moment he had entered the bar. She was small, curvaceous and devastatingly pretty. Her sleek dark curls set off flashing brown eyes. She reminded Albert of Leah. He immediately was mesmerized.

"Hi, I'm Najwa" she purred. "Would you like to share some champagne with me?"

"Sure", Albert replied, a bit awkwardly. But he quickly warmed to her abundant charms and began to relax. "Can we share it together alone?"

Najwa smiled seductively and tossed her pretty curls coyly. "I was hoping that you would pick me. I can arrange it all." She trailed her hand lightly and deliciously down Albert's forearm. "Give me just a moment."

Najwa went to have a word with the manager, who came over to make the necessary further financial arrangements. While Albert busied himself with those details, Najwa slipped away momentarily, opened her razor cellphone and speed-dialed a mobile number. Speaking softly in Arabic, she said, "He's with me now. I can keep him busy for at least the next hour or so."

"Good work, Najwa" Ahmed Samir replied. "Give him some very special treatment, sister. That will give me all the time I need, *inshallah!*"

Najwa slipped the cellphone back into the pocket of her diaphanous evening dress. Then she went over to take a very willing Albert by the hand and lead him upstairs to their private playroom.

XXIV

Samir had easily tracked Albert to Amsterdam on his Blackberry, following the GPS signal from Albert's identity card. He knew that Albert had checked in to the Ambassade Hotel. What Samir had needed was some time to search Albert's room for the Viking sands when he could be sure that Albert would be out for a definite period.

Albert had unwittingly given Samir the opportunity he had sought. As soon as Albert had headed for the brothel, Samir had contacted Najwa. She was part of the large Moroccan immigrant community in Amsterdam that was making even the liberal-minded Dutch increasingly uncomfortable. Many of them had suspected ties to Islamic fundamentalist terror organizations.

Najwa was a good sister-in-arms in one of the proliferating sleeper cells in Amsterdam. She was also a distant cousin of Aly Elbaz, the al-Queda operative in the Israeli embassy in Geneva. Their growing global network was both efficient and tight. All the circumstances had coincided fortuitously to give Samir the opportunity that he had needed to carry out his vital mission in Amsterdam.

Samir had slipped unnoticed into the Ambassade hotel through the rear service entrance. A healthy tip to one of the Tunisian chambermaids, another sister in the network, had secured him the passkey to Albert's room. But almost an hour's meticulous search of the room had turned up nothing of significance. The great weapon was nowhere to be found. "*Ibn charmoota!*" Samir mumbled to himself. "He's hidden it somewhere else. There's nothing left to do but to beat it out of him." This time, Samir vowed, the head that rolled would be the right one.

Samir left the hotel quietly the way he had come in. He positioned himself across the narrow street, against the railings overlooking the canal. Casually he smoked a cigarette. His cell phone vibrated in the silent mode. It was Najwa telling him that Albert had just left by car and would be there shortly. Samir was more than ready.

The black Mercedes pulled up to the front of the Ambassade and Albert got out of the back seat. As the car pulled away, Albert heard a voice nearby call his name.

"Herbert Moran, or is it Albert. Stern?" the voice said softly. Before Albert could turn to identify its source, he became aware of someone directly behind him, poking what felt like the barrel of a revolver deep into the base of his spine.

"Who are you and what do you want?" Albert tried to turn around to face his adversary.

"Don't do that", the middle-eastern accented voice replied, "or I will have to kill you here and now. Just keep walking down the street ahead of me, nice and normally". The rain had let up but the narrow street along the canal was now shrouded in a deep fog. No one was about, nor could anyone really see what was transpiring anyway.

"How did you find me here?"

"Oh, we've been tracking you all along on my Blackberry. We just missed you in Lyon, but we finally caught up to you."

"But how?"

"The same way you American *kilab* track our brave *fedayeen* in Iraq. By GPS. Now enough of your questions. Just keep walking!"

Albert could see faintly through the fog where they were headed. At the far end of the narrow one-way street a small car sat idling, just next to a bridge over the canal. It was about 200 meters away. If these were the same people who had abducted Philip Bloom in Geneva - al-Queda - Albert knew that they'd have no compunction about killing him as soon as they got what they wanted. He desperately needed to buy some time.

"What do you want from me? The Viking sands, I assume?" Albert stopped abruptly under a small, yellow sodium light illuminating the edge of the canal.

"Yes, the great weapon. Where is it? Give it to me and we may spare your life", Samir replied, obviously lying.

Albert knew that Samir would show him no mercy. His only chance was to kill him first. "I have the weapon here with me", Albert bluffed. "It's here in the inner breast pocket of my jacket. It never leaves my person. It's in a small vile. I'll get it out for you." Albert started to reach slowly into his coat.

"Stop!" Samir countered. "Keep your hands in plain view! I'll get it myself."

Samir moved forward to reach roughly into Albert's right breast pocket. As he did so, he momentarily lowered his right hand in which he was holding his Glock 25. That was the opportunity that Albert had hoped for.

In one quick motion Albert reached into his own coat pocket and gripped Leah's Beretta 86F. Two muffled thuds through the silencer and Samir fell back against the canal railings, mortally wounded. As he struggled to stand upright again, his cell phone fell from his pocket on to the wet cobblestones. Before Samir could muster his remaining strength to fire back, Albert pushed him over the low railings, into the dark, turgid canal waters below. The barely perceptible current began to take the now lifeless body slowly away.

As Albert tried to collect himself, he heard the cell phone vibrating on the pavement. He picked it up and listened to an unintelligible, shrill voice in Arabic on the other end. Calmly he said. "Your friend is dead and now I'm coming to get you".

With that he fired another muffled shot in the direction of the waiting car. It ricocheted wildly off the cobblestones and pinged ominously against the car's rear hatch. That was more than enough for Samir's accomplices. With a screech of spinning tires, the car lurched into motion and sped away, across the bridge over the canal.

Still in deep shock, Albert tried again to understand what had just happened. The Viking sands had already caused many deaths, but this was the first time that he had had to kill for them in such a personal manner. It was unsettling for him, but not traumatic. As always before, he felt no real emotion over the death of another person. Only the usual, empty, emotional void.

But there was a real sense of urgency in the moment. Albert's fragile sense of security was badly threatened. How could they have tracked him so easily to Amsterdam by GPS? What could he possibly have on him that had tagged him like some errant house pet? Wracking his brain he could only think of one thing: the Belgian identity card that Leah had given him must have contained a smart chip. One that was GPS activated. The Israelis had to have put it in there. Were they tracking him too? How had al-Queda known about the chip? Did they have an operative inside Israeli intelligence? It was just too much to contemplate all at once. The only thing that was certain to Albert was that he had to get rid of the card immediately. Perhaps he should throw it into the canal as well?

Before Albert could act, however, a bicyclist appeared suddenly out of the fog. He was riding very quickly within the marked red brick bike path along the edge of the narrow road. Albert unwittingly stood right in his path. The urgent jangle of the cyclist's bell was too late to avert a collision.

The rider tumbled heavily off his bike as it glanced off a bewildered Albert and crashed into the metal canal railings. "*Stomme lul!*" the shaken man yelled up at Albert from the wet pavement. He continued on in Dutch in a foul, irritated tone.

"I'm so sorry!" Albert said. "I didn't know about the bike lane. Here, let me help you up." As Albert reached down to help the disheveled and angry rider back up to his feet, he deftly slipped the Belgian identity card into his raincoat pocket. "There", Albert thought to himself, as the angry cyclist sped away, "let them all track him for awhile!"

XXV

Albert arose early after a short and fitful night of intermittent sleep. He was singularly intent on completing his internet work and leaving Amsterdam as soon as possible. He didn't dare return to Chocolata, as he had undoubtedly been tracked to there earlier by GPS. There was certainly no telling who was still out there looking for him with lethal intentions.

No, he needed a new and secure internet café, preferably near the Central Station, from which he would make his ultimate departure from Amsterdam. He had map of Amsterdam *centrum* and noticed several café/coffee shops on nearby Nieuwendijk One of them, Freeworld, looked the most convenient. He would head there immediately, after he checked out of the Ambassade.

"*Goedemorgen, Heer* Moran" the desk clerk said, "checking out so soon?"

"Yes, I'm afraid so. I have some pressing business in Rotter-dam."

"I hope that all of the confusion outside last evening didn't disturb your sleep. There was some dreadful business. The police were about until early morning. It looks like they fished a body out of the canal down by the Raadhuisstraat bridge."

"No, I didn't hear anything", Albert deadpanned. With that he headed out the door and along the narrow streets intersecting the inner canals towards the Freeworld coffee shop, two blocks away from the Central Station.

Freeworld was a decidedly funky place, even for Amsterdam. There was a spaceship on the ceiling and mannequins of aliens everywhere. It featured comfortable padded benches, up-tempo reggae music and a large selection of well-presented cannabis products. Most importantly, however, beyond the usual clouds of hash and weed smoke, there were private internet terminals upstairs. It was early morning, so the place was essentially deserted. Albert bought his morning double espresso, pre-paid several hours of computer time and headed up towards the quiet second floor computer terminals.

It was 8:00 AM on Sunday morning, making it an hour past midnight the same day in Houston. The time was exactly right for Albert to try to execute his daring plan.

Without delay he took out his list of vulnerable Eastern European and US IP addresses. Then he downloaded the Nmap security scanner to re-run port scans on the IP addresses that he had selected. The program quickly confirmed to him that ports were open and accessible on the computers bearing most of his chosen IP addresses.

Pleased, he proceeded to take over, seriatim, each of the vulnerable computers, hopping from several IP addresses in Poland to those he had earlier chosen in Bulgaria, Romania and Moldova. Finally, from a Serbian IP address, Albert moved across the Atlantic to the computer of a vulnerable cable modem user in New Mexico, using a bug in its spam bot drone code that had been secretly installed by a previous hacker. Having covered his tracks well, Albert was finally ready to enter the secure NASA computer network.

The best plan of attack would be first to gain entry to a lower security computer on the edge of the NASA network. To do this he would have to use someone's password to access the NASA Virtual Private Network. That was easy enough, Albert thought.

He could use his secretary, Laura Lincoln's, password, assuming that she was still employed there. She had routine, low-level clearance to the NASA intranet. From there, the final step would be to gain access to the NASA mainframe computer on which all of the classified Viking programs were stored. To do that, however, Albert would need a valid password with the highest of security clearances.

When Albert had originally written the Viking programs, he had put an additional secret entry password in place for him to use as a "backdoor", if ever it became necessary. At the time, there was nothing sinister about his actions. He was merely being extra cautious about always having fail-safe critical access to his most precious project - a "belt and braces" approach, as the English would say. He hadn't even mentioned it to his most trusted assistant, Yoshi Tanaka. Only Albert knew of the backdoor's existence. The time had now come to use it.

Clearly Albert's own password would have long since been embargoed. He presumed that only Yoshi and the Director each still had the highest level of access. So no one should be looking for another, unexpected user.

There was always the risk that NASA's Intrusion Detection System would be triggered by his attack, but not, he hoped, if he had correctly written the backdoor access route into the software. Anyway, Albert would soon find out.

Finally through his circuitous route into NASA'a mainframe, Albert typed in his secret password. Up came an immediate acknowledgement and menu. Scrolling down the menu, Albert clicked on the folder "Viking 3 & 4 Missions to Mars". When that window opened he clicked on "Display Status". A large block of familiar data soon filled the screen. It told Albert all the critical parameters of Viking 4's return journey to Earth.

Everything looked normal as far as current distance to travel; speed; re-entry angle; scheduled retro-rocket burns; and drogue and main chute deployments to slow Viking 4 down, once it had passed through the initial intense heat in the upper reaches of Earth's atmosphere. But one piece of data on display took Albert entirely by surprise. These were the coordinates for the pro-grammed splashdown site. They were completely off target!

"How can this be?" Albert thought, utterly puzzled. He knew the normal splashdown coordinates by heart – 28 00' 00" N, 94 00' 00" W – offshore Galveston, in the Gulf of Mexico. He had programmed them in himself for both Viking 3 and 4. But what he was seeing instead was nowhere near that location. It was half a world away, somewhere in northeastern Asia.

Hastily Albert jotted down the mysterious coordinates on display. Then he minimized the screen and opened the Google Earth program that was already installed on the computer. He had to act very quickly. Typing in the coordinates he had just seen, he came up with a remote location in Siberia, several hundred miles west of Yakutsk.

"My God", he thought, "someone has already been trying to re-direct Viking 4. Its the Russians!" How very cleverly they had done it too. The new landing site coordinates that had been inserted would be visible only to the three highest-level mission personnel. As Albert was already deleted and the new Director would have had no reason yet to look, access could only have come through Yoshi Tanaka.

"Yoshi's sold out" Albert thought. This was not totally unex-pected to Albert, however. Yoshi was to lose his job and promising career at NASA at the end of this month. And wasn't it Yoshi who had first recognized the immense potential value and impact of the Viking sands? So now Albert would have to add the Russians to his growing list of adversaries.

The Russians had set their risky gambit up very well indeed. Just ten months earlier an aging US weather satellite had fallen into a degraded orbit and eventually plunged back to Earth. NASA had been sure that it would burn up in the Earth's upper atmosphere. It had no control over its fiery descent anyway. But some debris nevertheless managed to reach the surface. It fell harmlessly near the Ural mountains, deep in the vast wasteland of western Siberia.

The Russians had protested strenuously at what they considered to be a reckless invasion of both their airspace and territory. It was all a political ploy, but very effective. NASA was embarrassed and the US had to issue a formal apology. Now the Russians could remonstrate even more loudly when Viking 4 "unexpectedly" came crashing down in the eastern Siberian tundra.

Time was precious and Albert hastened to finish his work. He deleted the landing site coordinates that the Russians had entered and typed in a new set of his own. He was very precise about the location – 29 13' 44.63" N; 50 18' 48.01" E – the exact center of a huge crude oil tank farm on a loading terminal island in the Persian Gulf.

For a spacecraft entering Earth's atmosphere to reach the surface successfully, it must do so within a very small range of angles, known as the re-entry corridor. The upper and lower parameters of this narrow corridor were determined primarily by three critical factors: trajectory, rate of deceleration and aerodynamic heating. If the re-entry angle was too high, the craft would decelerate too quickly, disintegrate and burn up. If the angle was too shallow, the craft would skip off the atmosphere and bounce back into space, missing the Earth completely. Within these ranges, there was very little margin for error.

Albert knew all of this very well, as he had both written and installed the Viking missions' software programs. He needed to be extra careful, though, to re-guide Viking 4 along the proper trajectory to survive the extremes of atmospheric re-entry.

With a growing sense of urgency, Albert directed his full attention to the re-entry sequence programs. Viking 4 was approaching Earth at a velocity of 25,000 mph. It would orbit twice to decelerate and then follow a ballistic entry trajectory once it encountered the outer fringes of Earth's atmosphere. The craft would then plunge deeper into the atmosphere and fall through it under the influences of both gravity and drag. The drag force would slow it down so that parachutes could be deployed for a soft touchdown.

The landing point, which Albert had already altered, would be predetermined by conditions when the spacecraft first entered the atmosphere. There would be no control over either its trajectory or landing site once it began its ballistic plunge. Since it would fall almost vertically through the atmosphere, its downrange distance, or ground track, from the point at which it would first enter the atmosphere to its eventual touchdown would be relatively small. Everything would happen very quickly once re-entry commenced. NASA could watch it all happen in growing consternation, but there wouldn't be anything it could do about it.

But Albert didn't want Viking 4 to make a soft landing at its new touchdown site. Rather, he wanted it to hit its target with all deliberate force. The impact would release the Viking sands from deep within its hold into the crude oil storage and pipeline systems. So Albert set about altering the re-entry sequences to make that happen.

First he re-programmed Viking 4 to execute a 180 degree summersault, so that it would begin its approach with its heat shield-clad bottom down. Then he programmed in several retro-burns to slow it down to 17,000 mph as it left orbit and entered the upper reaches of Earth's atmosphere. Lastly, he disabled the drogue and main chute deployment commands so that the spacecraft would plummet down through the atmosphere at terminal velocity.

Albert then proceeded to make all of the changes permanent. He did this by simply deleting both Yoshi and the Administrator as authorized users of the program. Thereafter, they, or anyone posing as them, could still observe the data, but they couldn't change it. Albert didn't have to delete his own account, as NASA had already done so. But he would keep the backdoor access he had created alive, just in case.

Albert then exited the Viking programs and returned momentarily to the NASA intranet screen. There a black-bordered box in the lower right hand corner caught his eye. It contained some shocking news. It read, "NASA is deeply saddened to inform all staff that Dr. Yoshi Tanaka, Deputy Mission Controller of the Viking 3 & 4 programs, died tragically in an automobile accident on I-45 N yesterday evening, August 8, 2008."

As Albert finally exited the NASA network, he intuitively knew that the Viking sands had claimed yet another life.

XXVI

Albert sat on the new, high-speed HSL-Zuid intercity train to Rotterdam watching the dull, flat Dutch countryside whisk by out the window. For the first time in a long time he was strangely at peace. He knew that it was all done now. It had all been played out. The stakes had been high, but he believed that he had prevailed.

He had lots of money, he was very much alive and he still had his cherished freedom. To keep it all, he would have to flee again, but this time for the last time. He would have to go somewhere remote and establish his new life; his last new identity. It would be somewhere inaccessible, where no one would ever find him. But it would also be his paradise; a place with everything he still loved. He knew where that would be, but he still had to get there safely.

From Amsterdam Albert was heading to the nearby Dutch port of Rotterdam. It was no sense even considering air travel, and further rail travel wouldn't get him to where he wanted to go. It would have to be by sea, to a faraway land. To Argentina.

Specifically, to Patagonia. To the wild, open spaces of the remote southern cone of South America. To the Andes and the *massif* of his beloved FitzRoy and Cerro Torre. Eventually to the little town of El Chalten, hard up against the Andean glaciers, the Southern Icecap and the Chilean border. There he was certain that he could finally find the enduring peace and anonymity that he both craved and needed badly.

Albert no longer had the Belgian identity card that Leah had given to him. Ever the chameleon, he would now seek his destiny as one of his former incarnations. It would be a calculated risk, but one which he had no choice but to take.

His destination in Rotterdam would be the Grimaldi Freighter Lines, a freight service that offered a few simple passenger accommodations on most of its long sea voyages. He would book to Buenos Aires and quietly exit Europe forever, by sea. The passage would take up to 34 days, stopping at various European, West African and Brazilian ports *en route*. In the meanwhile, when the final events that he had set into motion would come to pass, he would be nowhere to be found.

At the steamship line's offices in the busy harbor, Albert bought himself a one-way ticket to Buenos Aires on the next departing freighter. He would have to produce a valid travel document, of course, when the time came to board in a few days. Which one to use would be a very difficult decision for him to make.

He still had three passports from which to choose – one American and two British. His real identity as Albert Stern was entirely useless. "Peter Shaw" was an alleged terrorist, still being hotly sought by the British. Only "Philip Bloom", Albert thought, had any chance of escaping Europe undetected. Both the Iranians and al-Queda knew who Philip Bloom really was, but they had been thwarted so far. The Swiss were probably still in confusion as to whether or not the Philip Bloom they sought had been abducted and brutally murdered in Geneva. As far as Albert knew, neither the Brits nor the Americans had made the connection yet, although it was surely only a matter of time. But was there enough time safely to escape from Europe in the next few days? Albert would have to take his chances.

On the morning of Monday, August 13th, 2012, Albert boarded the freighter *Grande Buenos Aires* as "Philip Bloom", a British subject, heading for an indefinite stay in Argentina. In his gut

Albert didn't like having to revive this identity, but, in all fairness, he didn't really had any other choice.

XXVII

Monday, August 13th, 2012, CIA HQ, Langley, VA, 09:00 EDT

Chris Wytham, sat quietly in his office, looking pensively out over the leafy inner courtyard of the Langley campus. It was time to reflect on and to take stock of all that had happened to date in his relentless hunt for Albert Stern. There was much that he already knew, but there was still much for him yet to uncover.

Open before him on his desk was a file that had arrived by diplomatic pouch that morning from Inspector Jean-Christophe Malbec of the Swiss Securite in Geneva. Malbec had continued to be deeply puzzled over the shocking events that had transpired the week before in his normally bucolic city. The explosions and terror were as troubling as they were unexplained. Somewhere, the file showed, there had to be a causal link to the man that both Wytham and the Brits were so desperately seeking – this man of seemingly endless identities.

The Inspector had learned from the Swiss Federal Customs Administration that a 'Peter Shaw' had arrived at Geneva's Cointrin Airport on an Easy Jet flight from Stansted on Friday, July 15th. Swiss Rail then confirmed that the same Peter Shaw had left Geneva shortly thereafter, by train to Chamonix on July 19th. He had purchased a five-day excursion ticket, but he appeared not to have used the return portion. So the terrorist sought by everyone seemed to have passed, unnoticed, quickly through Switzerland.

A further report from the Swiss Customs border post at Bardonnex-Saint-Julien showed that a 'Philip Bloom' had entered Switzerland by rail from Chamonix on Saturday, June 23rd. But he couldn't have been the same 'Philip Bloom' who had been abducted from the Mandarin Oriental Hotel du Rhone on Monday, August 6th. He had just arrived two days earlier from the US. It now appeared that he had been brutally killed for no apparent reason. It had clearly been a tragic case of mistaken identity. Al-Queda had wrought wanton terror on him and on the city in deadly error. Unless, of course, the terrorists had really meant to abduct the first 'Philip Bloom', who might well be another alias for Peter Shaw. That would certainly make a lot more sense. Both Malbec and Wytham agreed on this.

Reading further in the file, Wytham saw that the Swiss Rail ticket number used by Philip Bloom on his return to Geneva was the same as the outgoing one used by Peter Shaw. Suddenly it all became quite clear. Shaw had re-entered Switzerland as Bloom. Bloom, Shaw, or whomever he called himself, was clearly Albert Stern, Wytham's avowed quarry.

But where had Stern gone now? He had been, undetected, right under the very noses of the Swiss authorities for at least a month, living in a rented flat in the Veille Ville, cantonal rental records now revealed. He had quit that flat only a week earlier and gone to Chamonix, where his life may, or may not have finally been terminated. If not, he would certainly surface again soon, perhaps in yet another identity? Neither Shaw nor Bloom was a safe alias anymore, Wytham realized. What would be his next guise?

Malbec had, of course, passed this information on to his direct superiors. He had informed the Americans and the British as well. They both had common cause with the Swiss. Deciding to dig deeper into what the Swiss may have surmised, Wytham asked his secretary to schedule a call to Malbec in Geneva for later in the day.

PART 5
APPROACHING ARMAGEDDON

"Who knows, but the world may end tonight"

I

Tuesday, August 14th, 2012, Dulles International Airport, VA, 06:00 EDT

Jamal Safir was tired after the almost 13 hour El Al flight from Tel Aviv. Special security arrangements had been made for him in First Class to assure him both privacy and anonymity.

Safir was acting on direct instructions from his Prime Minister. He was there expressly to spread soothing oil, like a balm, on potentially troubled waters. It was imperative to defuse any possibility of a rift developing between Israel and its most staunch ally over the years. The situation in the Middle East was growing increasingly dangerous every day and it was no time to alienate Big Brother.

As Safir arrived at Washington Dulles Airport, a van drove up to the plane to disembark him before the rest of the passengers boarded the transporters that would ferry them to Customs and Immigration in the main terminal. He wouldn't pass through there though. He was going directly to a VIP guesthouse in Langley, Virginia. After he had had a short time to freshen up, he was to meet with Director Baker at the CIA at 9:00 that morning.

A staff car arrived punctually to pick Safir up and drive him over to Langley. Once inside the compound it was waved into the VIP parking lot next to the old main campus building. Safir alighted and was ushered into a private elevator up to the Director's office.

"Good morning, Jamal", Director Baker greeted him as he entered. " Thanks for coming over. I hope that you had a chance to rest a bit on the flight?"

"I tried to catch some sleep, Tim." Safir replied, smiling.

"Good, we're happy to see you again. Let me introduce Chris Wytham, the head of our Counter-Terrorism Unit and Special Agent Brian Bretton from the FBI. I think that they can both contribute significantly to our discussions. Anyway, it was you who requested this meeting. So what's on your mind, Jamal?"

Safir started cautiously. "Well, Tim, we had an unfortunate incident in France recently with one of our best Mossad agents. She was killed by your 'friendly fire'. I'm sure you know all the details."

"Yes, of course I do. It was most unfortunate. But what was she doing there anyway?"

"Trying to help you people. She was acting under my direct instructions, which I had received from our Prime Minister."

"I'm afraid that's not what we thought. But please tell us more."

Ready to spin his best ever story, Safir began to recount the facts in his own inimitable fashion. "I sent Leah Shalev to Geneva to find out if this was your fugitive, Albert Stern. If so, she was going to recover your priceless substance from him and then either turn him over to you, or kill him, whichever was more convenient. She was right on the verge of succeeding when your drone shot her dead."

"You know that she wasn't the target, Jamal. Stern was. Your agent was unfortunate collateral damage. We're very sorry about what happened. We know she was highly valued by the Mossad."

"Thank you, Tim. But she would have secured the goods and we would have returned them to you, along with Stern. That was always our intention."

"Well then, why did it take you until now to tell us all of this?"

"Look, Tim, here's exactly what happened. We were first approached in London by a Peter Shaw, who carried a British passport. What he told us seemed like pure fantasy. We dismissed him out of hand as a crank, a madman. Later we were informed through diplomatic channels that you were searching for a US national named Albert Stern, but we didn't fully know why. We couldn't make any immediate connection between the two. Besides, we hadn't heard from anyone called Albert Stern."

"So you decided on that basis not to inform us of that first contact?"

"You know that we tend to do things on our own, but we do them very well. Entebbe, for example. I know that you would have wanted to be informed sooner, but we weren't sure ourselves. As I said, there was no obvious connection. But after the Sterling oilfield disaster, we began to wonder about this Peter Shaw. Would he contact us again? And then he did so, electronically from Geneva. By then we had read all of the intel on the Houston and Sterling oilfield occurrences and we started to put two and two together. Perhaps he was your Albert Stern? The only way we could find out for sure was to engage with him. So we arranged to meet him. We sent our best and most alluring agent to do the job. An unabashed 'honey trap', as you might say.

We were ready to try anything to keep his interest long enough to see what was the truth in all of this."

"And what did you find out then? How fast did you connect all of the dots?"

"When Shalev got to Geneva she managed to *rendez vous* with Shaw. By then he had morphed into a Philip Bloom, also a Brit."

"We know", Wytham interrupted. "The Swiss informed us yesterday of Stern's latest identity. Someone must have thought that the poor bastard who was abducted and murdered in Geneva was Stern."

"And, of course, Jamal, you Israelis wouldn't have been interested in keeping the weapon, right?", Baker continued over the interruption.

"Of course not. It wouldn't have been ours to keep. We just wanted to be sure that it didn't fall in to the hands of our enemies. We would have returned it to our great ally immediately."

"It would certainly have been a potent force in your hands, though" Baker mused.

"You could have marginalized the Iranians, the Saudis and all of your Islamic enemies with it quite easily."

"True, but that's not our way of showing our loyalty", Safir replied, smiling.

"Well it's all water under the bridge now, but thanks for coming over and briefing us, Jamal."

"There is one more thing that you should know", Safir concluded. "To get Stern across the border into France to recover the weapon where he had hidden it, we had to give him yet another false identity. Our mission in Geneva supplied him with a Belgian identity card in the name of 'Herbert Moran'. If he survived the incident in Chamonix, that's whom he is likely to be masquerading as now. Interpol may still be able to track him, if he hasn't ditched that identity already." With that Safir got up to leave. Thanks and handshakes all around and he was gone.

"He's lying through his teeth", Wytham said, after the door had closed behind Safir.

"Well, not completely, Chris" Baker replied. "He's an old spin master. He gave us the version that the Israelis wanted us to believe. They can't afford a rift with us of any kind. But he certainly confirmed a lot of what we already knew." Turning to Bretton, Baker continued, "Brian, get on to Interpol and see if they have any record of this 'Herbert Moran' still being in Europe. You know - border crossings, flight and train records, hotels - however they can trace him. If anything turns up, you and Chris pursue it. We'd really like to get Stern, if he's still alive!"

II

Wednesday, August 15th, 2012, Johnson Space Center, Houston, 08:00 CDT

Acting Mission Controller, Steve Contadino, sat tensely hunched in front of his large screen desktop. His hands were cold and even in the air-conditioned control room, beads of sweat ran continuously down the back of his neck. He knew that if he couldn't solve the riddle of Viking 4's uncooperative behavior, NASA would lose the spacecraft and its priceless cargo forever.

The new NASA Administrator, Richard James, watched intently over Contadino's right shoulder. James had just taken office on July 1st. It hadn't been an easy transition from Don Carter's scorched earth regime. Many of the remaining staff would sit at their computers for the last time on the morrow, expecting to see Viking 4 splash down safely in the Gulf of Mexico.

Viking 4 was less than a day away from the top of the Earth's atmosphere. It appeared to be on a correct trajectory for re-entry. It had originally been programmed to orbit twice, while slowly decelerating. Then it was to have begun a controlled, parachute-assisted, ballistic plunge earthward, to its predetermined splash down point.

The problem was that it didn't seem to be programmed any longer to do all of those things. Neither the orbiting nor the deceleration commands showed up on the computer screen. Despite Contadino's repeated attempts to correct these errors, Viking 4 wasn't responding at all to his commands.

"What's the problem, Steve?", James asked nervously.

"It won't respond, sir. I've tried everything to communicate with it. It looks like someone has been into the program before us and changed all the original re-entry data. Then they somehow managed to lock us out."

"Can we determine where it is headed, though? Still for splash down in the Gulf?"

"No, Sir. Not from what I can see of the coordinates on the screen. They certainly aren't in the Gulf of Mexico. I've tried to correct them several times, but I just can't do it."

"Where then?", James demanded. Now he was getting quite agitated.

"Offshore Iran in the Persian Gulf. It looks like there's an in-habited island out there. It's programmed to land right smack in the middle of it."

"Show me fast." Contadino brought up the GPS satellite image of the newly programmed target area on his screen.

"My God!" James exclaimed, "That could only be Kharg Island, the site of the Iranian crude oil terminal!"

"Who could have gotten into the program, sir?"

"It certainly wasn't me or Tanaka. It could only have been Stern!"

"But he's been deleted. He's no longer an authorized user."

With mounting concern James almost shouted "How did he do it?"

"He had to have put in a backdoor password, which only he knew. He must still have it active."

James sighed deeply. "In fact, that's the least of our problems. This could precipitate a real international crisis! If Viking 4 crashes in Iran, a nuclear holocaust could erupt in the entire Middle East. We have to inform our federal overseer of the danger immediately. I'm going to call the Office of the Vice President right away."

With that, James rushed out to his own office.

III

Wednesday, August 15th, 2012, Eisenhower Executive Office Building, Washington, DC, 10:30 EDT

"Where did you say it's headed?" The Vice President's voice showed irritated amazement.

"Kharg Island, offshore Iran, sir", James replied apprehensively.

"Are you absolutely sure?"

"Yes, sir. We pinpointed the location by GPS."

"Well, damn it, can't you change it? How the hell are you managing this thing, with your head up your ass?" The Vice President was more than his usual irascible self that morning.

"We've tried repeatedly, sir, but it just won't respond. We'll keep on trying...."

"And when the hell will it crash there?" the Vice President continued, interrupting James.

"Well, sir, we don't know yet if it will actually crash. We only know that it will touch down there around 9:00 PM, Houston time tomorrow. That's about 6:30 AM on Friday, August 17th in Iran."

"That's just great. We either hand the Iranians an incredible weapon or we start a nuclear war in the region. Either way, we have a major crisis on our hands. I'll have to tell the President immediately. You keep working on altering its course. I want you to give me hourly updates, understand? Goodbye!"

"Yes, sir", James replied to an already empty line.

The Vice President summoned his secretary into his office. "Gina, put out a highest priority national security alert immediately. I want a Principals Only meeting called for 11:30 this morning in the Situation Room. And get me the President on the line quickly. Where is he this morning?"

"His schedule says that he's at a ceremony in the Rose Garden, hosting the Super Bowl Champion Washington Redskins."

"Well, have them interrupt him. We don't have a lot of time to waste!"

"I'll do it all right away, sir."

IV

Wednesday, August 15th, 2012, The White House, Washington, DC, 11:30 EDT

The President summoned the hastily called meeting to order in the Situation Room. A select group of Principals sat expectantly around the large conference table in the basement of the White House. Along with the Vice President, present were the Secretaries of State, Defense and Homeland Security, the National Security Adviser, Secretaries of the Air Force and Navy, the Chairman of the Joint Chiefs of Staff, the DOI and the Directors of the CIA and FBI. On the wall behind them a battery of LCD TV screen flickered on, ready to videoconference in any additional resources, if necessary.

The Vice President opened the meeting with an up-to-date briefing on the evolving international crisis. "I learned about an hour ago from NASA mission control in Houston that the Viking 4 spacecraft was not responding to any remote commands. It appears to have been re-programmed by a saboteur to land tomorrow in the Persian Gulf, in the heart of the Iranian crude oil export facility on Kharg Island. It would be bad enough if it soft-landed there, but now it looks like it will crash instead."

"Just like the weather satellite which crashed in Russia last year. That caused us a lot of grief", the President observed, perhaps not yet sensing the true danger in the evolving situation.

"But this is much worse," the Vice President continued. "It could cause cataclysmic damage to Iran's oil resources. Worse yet, it could be misinterpreted as a missile attack on them by us or by the Israelis. The Iranians won't wait to find out. They'll retaliate immediately with nuclear force against the Israelis. The Israelis will respond in kind. It could start a devastating regional holocaust."

"My God," the President blurted, "we have to stop it!"

"We can't. We can only try to warn the Iranians immediately."

"But I have no direct line to them on my desk", the President said with alarm. "How can we do that?"

"Through the Swiss, sir" the Secretary of State interjected. "They are our only reliable back channel line through to the Iranians."

"Fine", the President replied. "Contact them immediately and brief them fully. Tell them I would be willing to speak directly with the Iranian President, if they can arrange it. Now how about the Israelis?"

"They know what's going on, Mr. President. We met with the head of their Intelligence Service just a few days ago", the CIA Director volunteered.

"Well, bring them quickly up to date. They should be on full alert for possible Iranian retaliation if we can't stop this event from happening."

"What if we could take this spacecraft out before it crashes?" the Secretary of Defense asked. "Do we have the capability?" He looked down the table towards the Joint Chiefs Chairman.

"We have the newly developed Standard Missile 3, sir," the Chairman of the Joint Chiefs responded. "It would be a long shot, but it's our only chance. It was built to intercept incoming ballistic missiles, but it's still in the advanced testing stage. Two of them are armed and ready right now at the Navy Support Facility on Diego Garcia Island in the Indian Ocean. They were scheduled for a test firing over the Pacific Ocean next week."

"Have them mobilized and ready for firing before day's end!", the President ordered.

"We'll lose the spacecraft's cargo though, Mr. President," the National Security Adviser objected. "It's the weapon that destroyed the Sterling oilfield in Britain. It has immense strategic value for us."

"At what price, though?" the President responded. "We're facing a potential nuclear exchange here. Maybe worse. We'd better raise our terror alert level to red immediately."

Turning to the Vice President and the Secretary of the Air Force the President continued, "Get back to Mission Control in Houston right away and have them coordinate this with the Air Force. I want this thing shot down over the Persian Gulf before it enters Iranian airspace." A visibly shaken President had decided on the final course of action.

On their way out of the Situation Room, the President called CIA Director Baker and FBI Director Morse over to him. Turning first to Baker he asked, "Who did this, Tim? Who's the saboteur?"

"He's a rogue NASA scientist, Mr. President. We've been tracking him for months now", Baker replied.

"Well be damn sure that you get him. Use any means or methods necessary

Put him on the FBI's 10 most wanted list, Cal, and post a reward for him - $50 million. Keep me fully informed." With that, the President strode confidently away.

V

Thursday, August 16th, 2012, NORAD War Room, Cheyenne Mountain, Colorado, 19:30 MDT

The command had come down personally from the President. On his orders, the two operational Standard Missile 3 interceptors were readied for immediate launch from Diego Garcia Island. They would be controlled remotely from NORAD headquarters, deep within its fortified mountain complex in Colorado.

The Standard Missile 3 was designed to detect, target and hit an incoming missile that might be no more than 10 feet long and traveling at up to five times the speed of sound - almost 2 miles a second. The highly sophisticated missile would approach the incoming target at a maximum speed of Mach 9, at a maximum altitude of 165,000 feet. It had the best available technology, but it wasn't always successful. It had registered only 50% 'kills' in recent tests over the Pacific Ocean.

Standard Missile 3s were guided by sophisticated radar that allowed them to get close to their target. They had a computer code and basic maneuvering capability suited to intercept high-speed, incoming ballistic missiles. The target would first be detected by orbiting satellites. Ground-base radar would then lock on to it and track its descent. The missiles would be launched to intercept the incoming target at great altitude, high in the atmosphere. At closest proximity massive charges would be exploded to try to destroy the target with shrapnel. However, nothing was assured.

Brigadier General Lee Weathers would be in command of the operation. He was a decorated Air Force general who had flown bomber support missions over Hanoi in the late 1960s. He had risen solidly through the ranks, specializing in ballistic missile strike capability and its deterrence. He knew the strengths and weaknesses of the new missile system as well as anyone. He wouldn't say it out loud to his staff officers, but he was only cautiously optimistic of it having any success.

VI

Thursday, August 16th, 2012, Johnson Space Center, Houston, 20:30 CDT

Since the meeting of the Principals and their decision on a course of action, no further progress had been made on altering Viking 4's re-entry path. There was no choice left now but to try to shoot it down. Those were the President's orders.

Steve Contadino was back at his computer terminal, still trying in vain to contact Viking 4. Richard James watched intently. Secure video and audio links had been established to both NORAD command in Colorado and to the Office of the Vice President in Washington. All eyes were on NASA Mission Control.

"It's over North Africa now, heading towards the Persian Gulf. It hasn't started to decelerate at all. The drogue and main parachutes were disabled by the intruder. It will crash at terminal velocity in about 30 minutes", Bennington reported.

"Do you have an exact plot on its course?" James asked.

"Yes, sir. I'm relaying it on now to NORAD."

The audio line acknowledged receipt of the data. "We have satellite confirmation of the target's course. Ground radar in Diego Garcia, Kuwait and Turkey are now triangulating its exact trajectory. We're ready to launch the interceptors when it enters the 180,000 foot corridor."

"Got that. It's passed through the atmosphere's outer layer, the thermosphere, and is entering the mesosphere now. Estimated altitude is 200,000 feet".

"Initiating launch sequence now" came the reply. "Bird one away! Readying bird two; fire!"

VII

General Weathers watched the screen intently as the radar display showed two missiles streaking skyward in tandem. His flight controller monitored their course as they rose to meet the incoming spacecraft.

"Interference, sir" the flight controller exclaimed. "Something is jamming our radar."

"Can you identify the source?"

"Negative, sir. It's not ground based. It must be coming from a satellite."

High above, the pre-programmed Russian Kobalt class Kosmos satellite had initiated its radar jamming sequences. In Moscow, both Chestnoy and Kutusov sat glued to their computer monitors, wondering, with absolute consternation, why the Viking 4 spacecraft was plummeting to Earth over the Persian Gulf instead of over Eastern Siberia.

"Can you still control the missiles' flight paths?" Weathers asked frantically.

"No, sir, detonation is only moments away. We can only hope that they still have radar locks on their target."

To add to NORAD's difficulties, the annual Perseid meteor shower peaked each year in mid-August. The current display was particularly vivid. Over 100 meteorites an hour were entering Earth's atmosphere from the remnants of a cloud of cometary debris crossing Earth's orbit. Particles as small as grains of dust and others as big as pebbles were assaulting Earth's upper atmosphere. Traveling at immense speed, they packed a lethal blow for anything that might cross their path. The two missiles were about to do just that.

"We have detonation on one", the NORAD flight controller confirmed. "Now on two as well. Both looked premature. What's your read on the target, Houston?"

Back in Houston, Contadino and James stared at the large computer display before them with complete dismay. Viking 4 was still plummeting to Earth on its lethal course. The mission to eliminate it had clearly failed. There was nothing left now to stop all hell from breaking loose.

VIII

Friday, August 17th, 2012, Kharg Island Crude Oil Terminal, Iran, 06:30 GMT +2½

Kharg Island is a continental island in the Persian Gulf belonging to Iran. It is located 16 miles off the east coast of Iran and 300 miles north of the Straits of Hormuz. It provides a seaport from which more than 90 percent of Iran's crude oil is exported.

The island sits atop the prolific Darius oilfield offshore and is connected by a latticework of pipelines directly to the giant Gachsaran and Ahvaz (Omidieh) oilfields onshore. An intricate web of additional pipelines link the terminal on Kharg Island to most of Iran's abundant petroleum reserves.

Kharg Island contains the world largest crude oil terminal and is the vital heart of Iran's petroleum export facilities to the world. Crude oil is transferred directly from oilfields into the vast oil tanks of the terminal where over 200,000 barrels a day are refined and prepared daily for export in ultra large crude carrying tankers.

Adel Kazemi was up early that morning driving his Samand coupe across the newly completed, long sea causeway that would take him to his job on the island. He was the principal engineering superintendent for the vast crude oil exporting complex. He monitored the carefully controlled flow of crude oil into the giant tank farm that held reserves ready to be pumped into waiting tankers, moored at each of two long loading piers. He and his staff also regulated flow in the spider's web of pipelines leading into the terminal from most of Iran's major oilfields. Hundreds of thousands of barrels of crude oil were in transit daily towards the terminal. Almost the entire volume of Iran's petroleum wealth was under Kazemi's daily scrutiny and control.

The eastern horizon glowed a warm pink from the rays of the soon to rise morning sun. The summer constellations overhead grew dim in the diffuse, pre-dawn light. It looked like it would be another clear and hot summer day in the Gulf.

As the stars began to twinkle out, Kazemi could still see numerous, feint trails of shooting stars tailing down from the seasonal Perseid meteor shower. Amongst them, streaking across the sky from west to east, was an especially big, bold and bright one. It looked like a bolide meteor, one of those rare exploding fireballs that assault Earth's upper atmosphere from time-to-time, with spectacular effects. It appeared to be heading towards the island, right in front of him, but Kazemi knew from experience that it was only an optical illusion. These space visitors never reached the ground. Rather, they exploded far overhead, unleashing a shower of sparkling stardust. Still, it was quite a thrill to see it all.

As Kazemi approached the security post at the near end of the causeway, the meteor still filled the sky, trailing a long, luminous tail behind it, like an errant comet. It appeared closer now. He even thought that he could hear it approaching, with a whistling roar. "This is going to be quite a show!", Kazemi thought.

All of the guards at the security checkpoint seemed transfixed by the sight of the approaching unexpected visitor from space. It was much closer now, and beginning to take on quite a definite shape. Not so much a meteor anymore as a flaming projectile, heading straight towards the center of the tank farm.

"My God", Kazemi thought suddenly, with horror, "we are being attacked! It must be an Israeli missile!" That was all the time he had left, though, to think rationally. Everything else happened with frightening speed.

Viking 4 sped to its final demise in a crescendo of flame. Falling out of the sky at terminal velocity with the accumulated energy of a small nuclear device, it scored a direct hit on the very center of the vast tank farm complex. A resounding explosion rent the still air, followed instantly by a series of billowing fireballs, each fueled by exploding crude oil storage tanks. That was horrific enough for Kazemi to see, but what happened next was completely beyond his ability to comprehend.

As the continuing explosions rocked the center of the complex, they suddenly paled in comparison to the immense bluewhite aura that erupted high into the sky and began to engulf the entire terminal. Crackling with searing heat and static electricity like a monstrous tempest, it rolled out from the center of the complex, directly towards the terrified observers. Preceding it had been an ear-splitting crash and radiating out with it was a massive shock wave that leveled all before it as it went.

Kazemi couldn't have known this in the turmoil, but the path of the unstoppable force traced the web of pipelines leading from the terminal back to their sources in the giant onshore oilfields that fed them. The Viking sands had been loosed from the disintegrated hold of Viking 4 and, after greedily consuming the offshore Darius oilfield, were proceeding methodically down the pipelines towards the very heart of Iran's massive onshore southern oil reserves. In a matter of minutes they would entirely eradicate most of the 132 billion barrels of crude oil reserves that were the central core of both Iran's wealth and power.

The guard post was completely leveled by the shock wave. Kazemi's car was tossed violently like a toy against the concrete retaining wall of the causeway. He was badly battered, bleeding and dazed, and in a complete state of shock. His entire livelihood had been destroyed in a fleeting instant, right before his unbelieving eyes.

Nothing remained now of the terminal but grim, charred wreckage, strewn across the silent waters of the once again placid Gulf. Barely conscious, Kazemi fumbled in his pocket for his cell phone. He at least had to try to notify central operations of what he assumed to be the unspeakable Israeli treachery that had just unfolded in front of him.

IX

Friday, August 17th, 2012, Tehran, Iran, 09:00, GMT +2 1/2

The attack on Kharg Island was immediately attributed to the Israelis by the Iranian President and his Ministers. Now they sat grimly around the table trying to assess the gravity of the situation. The information coming in was still sketchy and incomplete, but despite this, it was evident that the damage was cataclysmic. The Ministers, agitated as they were by the events now unfolding, still quaked in their shoes at their President's seemingly bound-less rage and fury.

"This is a plot by the Great Satan to destroy us, carried out by its Zionist partner!" the President stormed. "It demands immedi-ate retaliation. I've ordered a general mobilization and deploy-ment of our Qods elite forces along our borders with both Iraq and Afghanistan."

In quiet contrast, the Minister of Defense interjected, "Mr. President, the Americans are maintaining that this was a most unfortunate accident. They say that they lost control of their incoming spacecraft."

"That's what they say, but could they really expect us to be-lieve that? The Swiss said that their President wanted to talk with me directly, but I refused. I don't believe for a moment that it was the Americans directly. It had to have been an Israeli missile, guided by American AWACS radar and satellites. We are in ruins from this vicious attack! The time has come to settle all scores with the Zionists!"

Turning to General Reza Houshmand, the President contin-ued his ranting. "So, General, the Israelis had the great weapon after all, and now they've used it to strike our southern oilfields. At least half of our oil wealth has been completely destroyed. Only the Israelis could have done that. The Americans didn't have the weapon, did they?"

"No Mr. President" a chastened Houshmand replied, unhappi-ly. "Of course you are right. It had to have been the Israelis, under the guiding hand of the Great Satan."

"Here are my orders, then", the President continued. "Our Qods units are to cross the border into Iraq and Afghanistan and inflict as many casualties as possible on American and NATO troops and their Sunni allies. Our sleeper agents already in place should rally our Shiite brothers to join in the slaughter. The Israelis must suffer too. First Hezbollah will move against them into northern Israel. Be sure that they are well supplied with tactical missiles, mortars and rockets. They should rain hell and fury down on the Zionist towns and settlements there. When the Zionists move to defend against them, we will unleash our tactical nuclear arsenal on their biggest cities. They will feel our righteous wrath once and for all!"

"But this means all out war, Mr. President", the Minister of State said nervously.

"Indeed. We didn't start it, but we will finish it with a great victory! The Supreme Leader has given us his blessing, Now, all of you, go and put my orders into action!"

X

Saturday, August 18th 2012, The White House Situation Room, 07:00 EDT

The Principals had hastily reassembled early on a Saturday morning, responding to an urgent summons from the White House. The reports coming in from Iraq, Afghanistan and northern Israel were dire. At least 200,000 mechanized Iranian Revolutionary Guard elite units had swarmed across the borders into both Iraq and Afghanistan and were fanning out, south towards Basra, north towards Baghdad and east to towards Herat and Kabul. Innumerable fierce firefights were being reported as the Iranian Qods forces engaged US, Iraqi and Afghan forces in deadly onslaughts.

In northern Israel missiles, rockets and mortars rained down from Hezbollah fortified positions in Lebanon's Bekaa valley onto Israeli territory as far west as Haifa. Not even the Syrians could rein Hezbollah in, if, indeed, they really wanted to do so. It was clearly the start of a definitive all out war in the region.

Spurred on by the Iranians' call for vengeance, huge crowds had assembled in major Middle Eastern capitals, intent on ransacking and burning down Israeli and American embassies. The situation had already gotten far out of control in Cairo, Amman, Damascus, Riyadh, Ankara and Islamabad. The flame of indignation was spreading fast, all throughout the Islamic crescent countries. The enraged Muslim populace was chanting and screaming for all out war on Israel.

The President broke the silence. "I tried to speak with the President of Iran, but he refused to take my call." His voice trembled in fear and horror. "The Swiss assured me that they had made full disclosure to the Iranians, but Iran obviously didn't believe any of it. The whole region is now on the brink of total annihilation."

The Chairman of the Joint Chiefs then confirmed the worst of the reports coming in from Iraq and Afghanistan. "The Iranian Revolutionary Guards are moving in two armored columns against our combined forces. Their only strategic objective seems to be to kill our soldiers. They've thrown everything they have at us with overwhelming force. Our commanders on the ground are holding firm, but the casualties are already horrendous. Insurrectionist Shiite militias have joined the Iranian army forces to fight alongside them in Iraq. We may have no choice, Sir, but to use tactical nuclear weapons against them soon."

Before the President could react the Secretary of the Navy delivered his bad news. "The Iranians have already hit neutral tankers and freighters in the Straits of Hormuz with Russian supplied SS-N-22 anti-ship Sunburn missiles. They've scuttled enough shipping by now partially to block access to the Gulf. Our carriers, Stennis and Nimitz, and their battle support groups, will have to fight their way out to the Arabian Sea. We don't even know if our Aegis radar defense system can deflect these missiles. We've never seen them in action before. Some of the missiles are bound to get through."

The Secretary of the Treasury winced visibly. "This will halt tanker traffic through the Straits for weeks, or even months. Without a regular flow of oil from the Gulf, crude oil prices will skyrocket. The entire global economy will grind to a halt!"

The stunned group of Principals already couldn't believe what they were hearing. But the next piece of news was the worst. A senior aide to the Chairman of the Joint Chiefs had rushed into the room unannounced and passed to him a top priority dispatch from CENTCOM headquarters in Tampa, Florida.

Reports from the region indicated that nuclear tipped Shihab-4 missiles from Iran had been launched against Tel Aviv, Jerusalem and Haifa. There were no confirmations yet as to whether the Israeli batteries of Arrow 2 interceptor missiles had deflected them or not. Israel's major cities could have already been wiped out. There would be no stopping the Israelis now from retaliating with their own deadly nuclear force, if they were still in a position to do so.

XI

Saturday, August 18th, 2012, Security Bunker Complex outside of Tel Aviv, 14:00 GMT +2

The Israeli Cabinet and leaders of the Knesset had been evacuated to a fortified bunker complex outside of the city as soon as the preliminary warning of a possible Iranian strike had been received from the Americans. Now they all sat grim-faced, listening to reports coming in from their major cities.

At least a half dozen Iranian Shahib-4 missiles had been targeted at Israeli population centers. Arrow 2 interceptors had been launched to deflect them before they could wreak havoc. Many had succeeded in taking out the incoming missiles.

Not all, though. Central Tel Aviv and Jerusalem had survived reasonably intact thus far, but both cities had suffered catastrophic damage to their outskirts, to where the errant Iranian warheads had been deflected and detonated. Haifa, however, was another matter altogether. It had taken two direct hits. It was in ruins. Estimated fatalities ran into several hundred thousand from the initial blasts and an unknown number that would subsequently die from radioactive fallout.

The Prime Minister had ordered a full retaliatory strike against the heart of Iran's military and nuclear installations and on its major cities. A much-weakened Israel, already struggling for its very survival, had no choice but to deploy its nuclear arsenal against its attackers and their supporters. Nuclear-tipped Jericho-2 missiles had successfully targeted the major population centers of Tehran, Esfahan, Tabriz and Shiraz. Another battery of missiles had taken out the Iranian nuclear processing facilities at Natanz, Bushehr and Arak.

Israel was reeling badly, but Iran was now totally crippled. In less than two days the Middle East had erupted into complete mayhem.

XII

In the midst of all of the turmoil the Prime Minister turned to a distraught Safir.

"Jamal, I must talk with you. Come with me."

In the far corner of the complex was a private office for the Prime Minister. "Tell me how all this happened", the Prime Minister continued, once the door was closed behind them.

"Clearly the Iranians thought that we had the weapon and that we used it. Even though the Americans tried to explain, they would never have believed them", Safir began.

"But how could the American spacecraft have crashed on Kharg Island?" the Prime Minister demanded.

"It must have been diverted and disabled at the last minute. I can only believe that it was the work of the American fugitive, Albert Stern. He must have survived the incident in Chamonix and found a way to re-program the spacecraft to hit the Iranian oil complex."

"But why?"

"He's obviously a wanton sociopath. Paranoid too, but per-haps justifiably so. If Leah Shalev ever reached the point of carrying out her orders to kill him, he would have seen it as a huge betrayal. And he knew that the Iranians were after him too. So he cold-bloodedly decided to take revenge on us both. I wonder if he really knew what chaos he would wreak? Anyway, it's too late now. It will be all we can do just to survive."

'Of course we will survive. We always do", the Prime Minister replied, as if to reassure himself as well. "But when this is all over, when we have prevailed, I want you to finish the job. Find the bastard once and for all and kill him. Work with the Americans, the Brits, with whomever it takes. He is the number one enemy of the State of Israel."

"Understood, Prime Minister", Safir said, promising himself that the Mossad would not fail the next time.

XIII

Sunday, August 19th, 2012, Aboard Ship Crossing the South Atlantic Ocean

Albert was the only passenger onboard the freighter. He had adapted to its monotonous daily routine, the only highpoints of which were occasionally watching CNN or Sky News on satellite TV, reading trashy paperback novels from the ship's sparse collection and taking his meals with the ship's officers.

At seven bells in the evening, Albert headed down to the captain's dining room for his evening meal. With their usual punctuality, Captain Giuseppe Fanelli and First Officer Maurizzio Luchesi were already seated at the table. They were in the midst of an animated conversation in Italian when Albert entered.

"*Buona sera, signore*" the Captain greeted Albert. "Have you seen the news today on TV? Terrible events are unfolding in the Middle East!"

"Good evening, *signori*. No, I was reading all afternoon. What's happening?"

"What's happening? My God, it looks like World War III has started in the Middle East! How fortunate we are to be way out here at sea!"

"How so?" Albert asked, curiously perplexed.

"Iran and Israel are at each other's throats", the Captain replied. "Turn the television back on, Maurizzio, so that we can all watch CNN while we're having dinner."

The satellite-linked LCD screen in the Captain's dining room flickered to life. Above a red border labeled "Breaking News", a grim faced Wolf Blitzer was recounting the ever changing, chaotic developments in the afflicted region.

"To our viewers worldwide, welcome back. You're in the Situation Room where news is coming in every minute on the unfolding Middle East crisis. We have a fresh report from our correspondent in Baghdad. Let's listen."

"Hello, Wolf, this is Connie Edgewood in the Green Zone, Baghdad. US Central Command just confirmed a startling reversal in the Iranian offensive against our forces in the south and east of Iraq. It seems to have ground to a complete halt. Iranian tank column commanders have stopped their advances and many are displaying white flags of surrender. The same seems to have happened in Afghanistan. We can only speculate that they are leaderless after the massive Israeli nuclear decapitation strike against the Iranian heartland yesterday evening. Iran's major cities have been devastated under a nuclear onslaught. Nothing has been heard from the Iranian leadership since the Israeli counterattack. I don't know about you, Wolf, but I wouldn't want to return to a country covered with raging fires and nuclear fallout."

"Thanks for that, Connie. Keep us up to date, please, and take good care of yourself! Now over to ITN reporter, Lee Hingham, in Cairo. Come in Lee."

"Good evening, Wolf. After massive rioting here yesterday things have quieted down considerably. The Egyptian President has declared martial law. You can see the tanks patrolling the embankment along the Nile behind me. We've just heard that Egypt's President has called an emergency Arab summit meeting for tomorrow morning in Sharm el-Sheikh. It's reported that the US Secretary of State, the EU President and the Russian and Chinese Foreign Ministers have been invited to attend as well. The regional situation still remains chaotic. Riots in Amman, Damascus, Jeddah and Karachi are still raging. Tomorrow's meeting will try to broker a ceasefire between Israel and what, if anything, is left of the Iranian government."

"Many thanks, Lee. Right now I'm getting notice that the President will be addressing the nation at 9:00 PM this evening. Let's hear from our White House correspondent, Alexandra Dartmouth, who's on the scene."

"Hello, Wolf. The President's press secretary has alerted us that all channels will be carrying the President's hastily scheduled address this evening. We've got some preliminary details here of what he is likely to say. It seems that he has been able to contact the surviving Israeli leadership. No one has been able to do the same with the Iranians. There are still skirmishes in northern Israel with Hezbollah, but for the most part, things have gone eerily quiet in the region. The President will reaffirm that we will stand in solidarity with our ally, Israel, and that we will do what we can to help them recover and reconstruct their shattered cities. The US will support Egypt's ceasefire initiative fully. The President will also reaffirm that the US was not directly involved in the initial attack on Iran, but that the destruction of the rogue state was an inescapable consequence of its support for world terrorism."

"Many thanks for the heads-up, Alex. We'll all be watching. Now let's hear from our chief economic analyst, Wolfram Klotz, for the latest report on how the international oil markets are reacting to the ongoing crisis."

"Oil prices have stabilized a bit since yesterday, Wolf, but they are still in uncharted territory. Brent North Sea Blend closed this evening at $356.69/barrel, up just over $16 from yesterday's close. Volumes in oil futures contracts on the commercial exchanges have hit record highs. World oil supplies remain very tight. The closure of the Straits of Hormuz has almost halved the volume of crude reaching world markets. Most countries have imposed severe restrictions on usage and have instituted very strict rationing. Stockpiling of oil reserves for national defense has become a top priority worldwide."

"Thanks, Wolfram. Please keep monitoring the situation closely for us. Meanwhile, here with me in the studio we have Dr. Robert Victor, Chief Meteorologist with NOAA. Dr. Victor, how bad is the nuclear fallout and where is it headed?"

"From what we can tell at least a dozen fission bombs with up to 500 kiloton yields were released by both sides. Most of the column of debris from each device rose way up into the stratosphere where it is being pushed eastward by the prevailing jet stream winds. There are already reports of significant fallout having reached Afghanistan, Pakistan, India and central China. The Korean peninsula, Japan and the Philippines are bracing for a heavy fallout event. I wouldn't doubt that fallout will reach the west coast of the US in a few days. Eventually it will encircle the globe. This is a man made environmental disaster of a scope unprecedented in world history. We could be looking at a world-wide nuclear winter."

"Thanks, Dr. Victor. Chilling news indeed. Now let's get the latest report from London where Prime Minister Cameron will be addressing the British nation shortly....."

At that point Albert had also heard enough. He was stunned by the overwhelming gravity of the news. He excused himself from the table while the Captain and his First Officer remained glued to the newscast, riveted by the unfolding story of destruction and chaos.

While Albert had anticipated dire consequences from the crash of Viking 4, he had never imagined it on such a broad scope and scale. The entire world was being drawn into the abyss. And in the face of it all, the US President was lying to the public again. His spin doctors were managing the facts, as usual. It was the same old story of accountability denial.

Albert new the truth, of course, but he certainly wasn't in any position to tell it. "I'd best get back to my cabin", he thought, "before I get drawn into a discussion." As he walked along the main deck, he looked far off towards the southwest horizon, where the ship was headed. Everything was deceptively calm and serene at sea. Steeling himself, he vowed to keep an even lower profile for the rest of the voyage.

PART **6**
ENDGAME

"The winner will be the one who makes the next-to-last mistake."

I

Friday, September 14th, 2012, Langley, Virginia, CIA Headquarters, 09:00 EDT

Chris Wytham's office phone rang at 9:01 AM sharp. It was a call from the head of the Agency's IT team that had been sent to Houston to analyze the NASA computer records regarding control and navigation of the ill-fated Viking 4 spacecraft.

"Good morning, Chris. I think we finally have an answer for you."

"Good. Let's hear."

"We've traced the actual source of the break in to computer terminal in an internet café in Amsterdam. The hacker was very sophisticated in his approach. He computer-hopped from there through several Eastern European countries before crossing the pond electronically to New Mexico. Then he used someone on NASA staff's password to gain entry to its internal network. It seems that the victim was a 'Laura Lincoln'. Ring any bells?"

"Sure, she was Albert Stern's staff assistant for years. It makes sense that he would still know her password, even though NASA staff is supposed to change theirs regularly. It was more than just a lucky guess."

"Once he got in, the hacker used a backdoor entry into the Viking control and command programs. He was able to bypass NASA's Intrusion Detection System initially because he logged in as a seemingly authorized user. But once the system auto-backtracked to the lower security entry point into the network, it flagged it as an unauthorized intrusion. This all happened in the early morning of Sunday, August 12th, but it either went unnoticed or was ignored. If the hacker had stayed active a bit longer, the IDS would have been able to follow the path of the attack back to its original source. But the intruder was too fast and efficient. He obviously knew very well what he was doing."

"Great work! Thanks a million. I'll deal with it from here." Wytham hung up.

He noted to himself the deep irony that there had still been a brief moment when the whole ensuing world disaster could have been averted. But NASA had been asleep at the switch.

Wytham called Brian Bretton on his direct line. "Brian, Chris here. I just got some interesting news from our IT team in Houston. The intruder into NASA's system was Albert Stern, as we suspected all along. The information places him in Amsterdam on the morning of Sunday, August 12th."

"So your hunch was right. He survived Chamonix after all. But where did he go next? By the way, Interpol didn't find any record of hotel stays by any of Stern's known aliases, but it did turn up a one-night registration at the Ambassade Hotel in Amsterdam by an alleged Belgian businessman named 'Herbert Moran'. Wasn't that the name that Safir mentioned to us when he came to Langley?"

"Exactly. That tracks perfectly. It was Stern, using Amsterdam as a staging point to complete his hijacking of Viking 4. Then he had to flee Europe somehow. Any ideas?"

"Jaap van Noort personally questioned all of the staff at the Ambassade Hotel. The desk clerk who had been on duty the morning of August 12th recognized Stern from one of the series of identisketches that Jaap had with him. So that confirms that Stern had registered under his latest Belgian alias."

"Did van Noort get anything at all from the desk clerk about Stern's travel plans?"

"Only that Stern had cut his stay short, checking out on that Sunday morning.

The clerk seemed to remember Stern saying in passing that he had some pressing business to attend to in Rotterdam later that day."

"Rotterdam, Brian, that's Holland's biggest seaport. Sure, it makes a lot of sense. Stern knew that he couldn't risk flying anywhere internationally. There was an Interpol APB out at all European airports for him and his two known aliases. His only escape route would have to have been by sea."

"Interpol has been checking that too, Chris, but no 'Herbert Moran', or any other Stern alias, booked out of Rotterdam on a commercial ocean liner."

"He's too smart for that. He would have had to use a more unconventional sea escape route. How about other sorts of commercial shipping lines out of that port, Brian? Sometimes they carry passengers."

"Fine, Chris. I'll get back to Jaap to have his people check on that as well. It sounds like a long shot to me, but, then, Stern couldn't have just disappeared!"

II

Monday, September 17th, 2012, Port of Zarate, Argentina,
23:00 GMT -4

The *S/S Grande Buenos Aires* rested at anchor on a moonless night, just outside of the port of Zarate, Argentina. It was the last port of call before Buenos Aires. It lay on the western shore of the Rio Parana , some 90 kms. in distance from the Argentine capital.

The ship was waiting in the river's broad estuary for a pilot to come aboard in the morning to guide it into the bustling port. There it would discharge some cargo and pick up some additional freight before moving on again.

Albert had dined, as usual, with the Captain and First Officer that evening. Then he had returned early to his cabin. Since he had shared the unsettling news of world chaos with them that evening almost a month before, he had tried to keep a very low profile to avoid any possibilities of inadvertent, probing conversation. He was sitting in his bunk thoroughly engrossed in "Enduring Patagonia", Greg Crouch's epic account of climbing in the Patagonian Andes, when he heard some commotion out on deck. "What could that be at this late hour?" he thought. But he was so absorbed in his book that he decided to ignore the noises overhead.

While the Rio Parana was certainly famous for its schools of voracious, carnivorous fish, the top predators on the river were modern day pirates. Not your buccaneers of old, these were highly organized, heavily armed, hi-tech bands of ruthless marauders. Increasingly they had become the scourge of international private shipping, worldwide. Such a band had been watching the freighter intently since it had anchored earlier that evening, about a mile outside of the entry to the seaport.

Moments earlier, First Officer Luchesi had been standing a quiet watch on the bridge.

It was too late by the time he saw a dark black Zodiac boat with a silent electric motor heave to alongside the freighter's stern. Grappling hooks had been catapulted up over the railings and a swarm of pirates were already on deck, heading towards his command compartment. He only had a few seconds to push the alarm bell to warn the captain and crew. Then the intruders were in and upon him.

The man in front was a dark, swarthy Latino holding a Kalichnikov. In broken English he asked if Luchesi was the captain. Before Luchesi could answer, a sleepy but alarmed Captain Fanelli appeared on the bridge from his cabin.

"I am the Captain", he said. "What do you want of us?"

The pirate leader smiled a crooked grin and replied, "Perhaps your cargo, *Senor Capitan*, but perhaps your lives. What are you carrying in the holds?"

"Automobile packs and parts for assembly in Argentina. Not very valuable on the black market, eh?"

"And what's in the ship's safe, *Capitan*?"

"Wages for the crew. Not much, really. These men are all Turks. They earn very little."

"But you and your First Officer are valuable prizes, *Capitan*", the pirate leader replied. "Your company will pay a good ransom for you two. Maybe $250,000 each?"

Into the cabin stepped two henchmen, brandishing guns. The pirate leader signaled to them to bind the Captain and First Officer's hands and to blindfold them. They were, he thought, the most valuable prizes on the ship.

The pirates knew full well that the freighter's owners wouldn't report the incident to the Argentine coast guard if they could quickly negotiate a ransom for the officers. Once they had secured their freedom, the ship could move on again with its scheduled voyage. Piracy was a heinous international crime, punishable by death, but very few incidences of it ever came to justice. It was just another insurable risk that had sadly become reality in the modern era of international commercial shipping.

The crew of ten sailors had been rounded up on deck by the remaining pirates. They stood, terrified along the rail, backs to their captors, facing the sea. Another pirate was scattering life belts and inflatable life jackets down into the water, as if to offer the crew slim hopes of survival, if they cooperated.

"Shall we kill them all?', a pirate asked their leader in Spanish.

"No", he replied, "just make an example of one or two of them. We want the *gringo* ship owners to know that we are serious *hombres*."

With that, the pirate promptly shot the first two sailors in their backs and pushed their corpses overboard. He yelled "Jump!" to the remaining crew, who all dove over the side in frenzied haste.

Still locked in his cabin, Albert had heard the alarm bell ring. He knew that this meant some kind of an emergency had occurred and that he was required to muster on deck immediately with his life jacket. Reluctantly he put his book down and gathered up his few critical belongings. As he exited his cabin he heard two gun shots ring out from the deck above. Caution suddenly replaced his initial irritation. Something serious was going on.

The pirates hadn't bothered to check for passengers. It wasn't usual to have any on a freighter. They didn't know that their most valuable prize was still in his cabin, there for the taking. The Americans, Brits and even the Swiss would have paid handsome rewards to have Albert, dead or alive. But the pirates' oversight gave Albert precious few minutes yet to escape.

No one was in the corridor as he made his way aft, towards the rear deck. As he quietly opened the hatch he could see the drama unfolding below him on the main deck. There were at least eight cutthroats holding the bound and hooded Captain and First Officer as hostages. In the dark waters below, muffled noises told him that the crew had been thrown overboard. Some were swimming, but others were floating, lifeless. Albert knew that he had no choice.

Creeping noiselessly towards the rail, Albert bolted up in one quick instant and vaulted over it, down into the murky waters below. A burst of gunshots whistled by him in the dark, but they were all errant. Shivering in the winter-chilled sea, he managed to grab hold of another inflatable life vest to buoy him up, along with his own. The tide was coming in, pushing all before it towards the rough ledge beach, less than a mile distant. Albert swam as best he could. Fortunately for him, the tide did the rest.

III

Cold, wet and sodden, Albert opened his weary eyes to the first rays of the faint winter sun. He shivered with the morning's chill as he took stock of his situation. He was on a rough shale beach, heavily soiled with oily smudges of ship's bunkers and illegally dumped bilge. He could only barely remember having hauled himself out of the foul smelling waters before he had fallen into a deep sleep.

As if graphically to remind him of the events of the night before, Albert saw a bloated corpse bobbing gently in the lightly breaking surf, just a short way offshore. It was one of the slaughtered crew of the freighter.

Albert shuddered involuntarily and looked out to sea. Sitting quietly but lifelessly at anchor, the *S/S Grande Buenos Aires* was rolling ever so slightly in the early morning swell. The pirates with their ransom prizes were surely long gone. Anyway, it was no longer Albert's concern. Once again, he had narrowly escaped with his life.

Thinking more clearly as the warming sun began to rise higher, Albert realized in a flash that the pirates had actually done him a very great, if unwitting, favor. There he was, already on Argentine soil, not more than 50 miles away from Buenos Aires. Not the best way to have arrived, perhaps, but, equally, he had entered the country completely unnoticed. There would be no awkward moments at Argentine customs and immigration to endure. He had no entry or immigrant's visa, of course, but that he could remedy later. With his newly acquired fortune, he knew that anything could easily be bought in a still developing country. *"Que bueno"* he thought whimsically in Spanish, "finally some good fortune is on my side!"

In his damp wallet Albert had a thick wad of both Euro and Dollar banknotes, more than enough to get him to Buenos Aires by bus or train. There he could refresh, regroup and arrange a sizeable transfer from his Cayman Island bank account to a new account he would establish at a local Argentine bank. He would need to bring considerable capital quickly and confidentially into Argentina to accomplish his ultimate objectives.

IV

Tuesday, September 18th, 2012, Langley, Virginia, CIA Headquarters, 08:00 EDT

"It looks like we finally found him after a long, cold trail, Chris!" Bretton's voice said excitedly on the phone line. "You guessed right again. A British national named 'Philip Bloom' boarded the Grimaldi Lines freighter *S/S Grande Buenos Aires* out of Rotterdam on Monday, August 13th, bound for Buenos Aires. He was the only passenger aboard. It was to have been about a month's sea passage from there. That means that he'd be arriving in the port of BA any day now. What assets do you have down there to meet him when he disembarks?"

"Not an easy scenario, Brian. Our relations with the Argentines have been very tense these last few years. They've continued to drift further into Chavez's leftist orbit. We do have some covert operatives in BA, though. The question is whether we can mobilize them in time, without getting them outed in the process. They are well trained in extraction operations, but a lot would depend on the timing and circumstances of the ship's arrival. We certainly can't count on any help from Argentine law enforcement officers. We don't even want them to know! We don't have an extradition agreement with Argentina either. We'll have to pull off a well-executed extraction, right under their noses."

"It wouldn't be the first time, Chris. Maybe you'd better be there this time. Stern gave us the slip too easily in Chamonix."

"I plan to. I'll get on to our Chief Information Officer at the embassy in BA immediately. When is the ship due to arrive?"

"Our best estimate is this Thursday, September 20th. It was waiting to enter port at Zarate to offload some freight. From there, steaming time to BA would only be half a day. You'd better get on a direct flight tonight. United leaves around 10:00 PM from Dulles."

"Thanks, Brian, I'll arrange it immediately." Wytham was already hastily bringing up the United Airlines flight schedule on his desktop.

V

Wednesday, September 19th, 2012, Buenos Aires, Argentina, 13:00, GMT -4

When Albert walked into the lobby of the upscale Buenos Aires Hilton in the recently rejuvenated old city port district of Puerto Madero, the concierge and the head desk clerk immediately exchanged disapproving glances. In the hotel's opulent front hall, lined with expensive shops, Albert's ragged appearance made him stand out like an unwelcome vagrant. Undaunted, however, he approached the front desk.

"Good afternoon. I need a nice quiet room facing the harbor for a few days, please."

"*Si, Senor*", the obviously disapproving desk clerk replied. "You have a reservation, of course?"

"Unfortunately not, but perhaps this will help?" Albert slid a 50 Euro note across the smooth, black marble desk.

"Ah, I see, *Senor*", the desk clerk replied, quickly pocketing the banknote. "I think that we can help you. Can you fill out this registration card, please? I'll need to see your passport too, *Senor*."

"I'm sorry, but it was lost in an unfortunate incident at sea. I plan to get a replacement tomorrow at my country's embassy.

Kindly register me as Alberto Portillo Lopez, originally of Spanish descent." Albert slid another 50 Euro note across the counter.

"Of course, *Senor*. Is there anything else we can help you with?"

"Yes, what is your best men's shop here in the hotel?"

"We have a branch of Galerias Pacificos here in the lobby, *Senor*."

"Fine, give me an hour to bathe and freshen up and then send a representative to my room, please. I'll need a whole new wardrobe."

"*Excelente, Senor.* I'll see that it is done!", the desk clerk replied enthusiastically.

Six hours later, a showered, shaven, rested and freshly attired Albert strolled leisurely across the hotel lobby and out into the cool, dark evening. He walked across the Macacha Guemas footbridge and turned left along the scenic pedestrian promenade, fronting Dique 3, in the old harbor.

Not far along he came to the Puerto Cristal restaurant on Avenida Alice M. de Justo, which was renowned for its fresh caught fish, fine Mendoza district wines and superb views of the old port. Albert sat down at a table outside, under the heated veranda, from where he could see the 19th century sailing *barque*, the Sarmiento Frigate, moored permanently near the Calatrava Bridge.

From the varied menu he ordered an appetizer of crepes from the sea, with salmon, leeks and cream, followed by the restaurant's signature sea bass "Vizcaya", grilled with lemon, capers and fingerling potatoes. He washed it down with a good demi-liter of Sauvignon Blanc from the Mendoza valley. Lingering over an espresso, Albert selected a Montecristo No. 4 Cuban cigar to go with a snifter of Remy Marten XO cognac.

It was tempting, in that calm, moment, to contemplate staying in the Argentine capital. A nice apartment in upscale Recoleta or Barrio Norte was well within Albert's reach. The lure of the good life in Buenos Aires was obvious, but so too were its dangers.

One could lose oneself comfortably in this ambient metropolis, but not without unnecessary risk. He would be too vulnerable to detection if he chose to live the high life in what is considered by many to be the Paris of South America. He'd be too noticeable as a rich, new émigré. Besides, he'd need a permanent resident visa, which would be far easier to buy from less questioning and more needy provincial officials.

No, a big metropolis wasn't really where Albert's heart was either. Rather, he still longed for the solitude of the vast open grasslands and the rugged granite towers of Patagonia.

VI

Wednesday, September 19th, 2012, Buenos Aires, Argentina, 09:45 GMT -4

United flight 847 touched down at Ministro Pistarino Airport at 9:45 on Wednesday morning, September 19th. A tired but alert Chris Wytham disembarked and made his way through the diplomatic channel at Customs & Immigration. He was traveling under cover of being an adviser to the US Foreign Agricultural Service representation at the embassy. A car was waiting for him outside to take him the 26 kilometers to the embassy compound on Avenida Colombia, in the heart of the city.

At the embassy, he was immediately shown into the office of the Chief Information Officer, Dick Brooks. Wytham had been in touch with him by phone the day before from Langley. In the seclusion of Brooks' office the two old colleagues greeted each other warmly.

"Everything organized, Dick? Are the men briefed and ready?"

"Of course, Chris, but we've had a problem develop overnight, while you were on the flight down here."

"What's the matter?" Wytham was taken by surprise.

"The ship, *S/S Grande Buenos Aires*, was forcibly boarded by pirates just outside of the port of Zarate. We only just found this out this morning. Naturally, the owners weren't too anxious to report the incident to the Argentine Coast Guard. The pirates had taken the Captain and First Officer hostage and were demanding a ransom. It happens much more often these days than anyone ever admits."

"So, what happened then? Is Stern still on board?"

"The Argentine Coast Guard boarded the ship this morning, but there was no sign of anyone left on it. They had earlier found the bullet-riddled bodies of two of the crewmen on a nearby beach. Most of the rest of them must have drowned, but there were a few survivors. Stern wasn't amongst them. When the local police questioned the survivors, they had no recollection of having seen the passenger on deck before they were forced overboard."

"Damn! He's either slipped us again or he's finally dead. How will we ever tell this time?"

"Well there still might be a way, Chris. DOI Baker called at 8:00 this morning. He wanted to talk with you as soon as you arrived. He said he had some new information and a good idea to go along with it. I'll have the call placed immediately."

Moments later the voice of Tim Baker came through on a secure satellite line. "You've had the bad news already. Sorry, Chris. But I may have some good news to offset it. The Israelis have been a lot more forthcoming with us after what we did to avert their total annihilation. Jamal Safir personally told me the rest of the story that he started over a month ago when he visited us. It seems that he had left out an important fact."

"What's that, Tim?" Wytham replied, hoping for any new lead.

"To coax Stern into delivering the Viking sands to their agent, they had to pay him a substantial sum of money as a partial down payment. He wanted wealth, asylum and a new identity from the Israelis. Safir says that they never planned to give it all to him, but they had to pay him some serious earnest money up front."

"Like how much?'

"Twenty million dollars, wired to a numbered account at UBS in Geneva."

"That disappeared then into a black hole, huh, Tim?"

"Normally it would, but not this time. The Swiss are very motivated to be helpful. They want Stern as well for felonies committed in Geneva. It didn't take much to convince them that their banking secrecy laws could be ignored in this case. They told UBS to produce the account records immediately."

"And what did they show?" Wytham sounded a bit more hopeful.

"The money was wired in from The Bank of Israel in Tel Aviv on Monday, August 6th. It was transferred out the same day by wire to a numbered account with Coutts (Cayman) Limited in Georgetown, Grand Cayman. The accompanying notation was "advance on a real estate purchase", whatever that meant."

"Like a real estate purchase somewhere in Argentina, perhaps?" Wytham ventured.

"We don't know, but we do know that the account belongs to a nominee trust which doesn't directly identify Albert Stern. The Cayman's have strict banking secrecy laws as well. But, remember, they are a British Overseas Territory. We're sure the Brits are leaning heavily on Coutts & Co. to open their files. Their parent company is an old, established London bank. We'd like to see the funds in the account frozen, but it may take a court order to do it. Then again, it may just require some good old British persuasion. In any event, remember the old saying about when all else fails, follow the money? That's what I want you to do now. As soon as there's some further movement, you'll get an encrypted email or a call from me. Meanwhile stay there for now, because if Stern is anywhere, that's where he must be."

"Right, Tim. I'll wait to hear further from you." Wytham felt slightly more encouraged as he hung up.

VII

Thursday, September 20th, 2012, Buenos Aires, Argentina, 09:45 GMT -4

The largest commercial bank in Argentina was BNA, Banco de la Nacion Argentina. That was with whom Albert wished to do business. At 9:30 AM on Thursday morning, September 20th, as the bank was just opening, he walked into the Almagro branch on Avenida Corrientes and asked to see the manager.

"*Si, Senor*, concerning what matter, please?" a clerk asked politely.

"I wish to open a new account here", Albert replied.

"*Bueno, Senor*, but we can attend to that for you over at the teller's window".

"No", Albert insisted. "I must see the manager personally. It will be a very large account".

"*Claro, Senor*, let me tell him that you wish an appointment. Your name, please?"

"*Senor* Lopez. Alberto Portillo Lopez".

"*Gracias, Senor* Lopez. One moment, please."

Albert was shown into the branch bank manager's old-fashioned, ornate office.

"*Buenos dias, Senor* Lopez" the manager greeted him, "please be seated. I understand that you require some special banking services?"

"Yes. I want to open confidential accounts with your bank."

"Would you like to explain your specific needs more fully, *Senor*?"

"Certainly. I need a numbered savings account linked to a checking account. I will want to be able freely to transfer money between the two accounts electronically. Periodically, I will replenish the former account, as may be necessary. I will also want to keep at least half of my money in currencies other than Argentine Pesos – US Dollars and Euros, for example. Confidentiality and absolute secrecy are my two most important concerns."

"Most assuredly, *Senor* Lopez, we do have such accounts for our best customers. But they require a rather large initial deposit and the maintenance of a substantial daily balance thereafter."

"And how much would that be?"

"At least 1,000,000 Argentine Pesos, *Senor* Lopez."

"Very good. Can I have the signature cards to fill out, please? Also, I assume that BNA has a branch in El Calafate, in Santa Cruz province?"

"*Si, Senor,* we do. How much were you thinking of funding these two linked accounts with?"

"Two million US Dollars initially. That's well over six million Pesos." Albert replied.

"That will be fine, *Senor*" the manager said with awakening interest. "How will you make the large opening deposit?"

"By bank transfer from my account in the Cayman Islands. I'll need wire transfer instructions, along with my new account number and BNA's Swift code. I can arrange it all for value by noon tomorrow. Everything must be ready by then, as I'm leaving Buenos Aires on a late afternoon flight for El Calafate."

"I assure you that everything will be ready as and when you requested. May I order you a coffee and some *medialunas* while we complete all of the paperwork, *Senor* Lopez? Thank you for choosing to bank with us."

VIII

Friday, September 21st, 2012, US Embassy, Buenos Aires, Argentina, 08:00, GMT -4

Chris Wytham was in early to the embassy that morning. He was hoping to receive further news about any money movements out of the Cayman Islands account. If anything left it for Argentina, he would know that Stern was both alive and on the move again. He got himself a double espresso out of the canteen and logged into his email account. Amidst the many accumulated messages from the last few days was a new one marked "Urgent" and flagged in red script. He opened it and read:

"'*Eyes Only'* Gavin Lorimer, MI6, London, reports electronic money transfer request of US $2 million made to Coutts (Cayman) Limited on presumed Stern account. Request originated in Buenos Aires on Thursday afternoon, September 20th. CCL was instructed to remit sum overnight, partially in Argentine Pesos, to a newly opened, numbered account with Banco de la Nacion, Almagro Branch, 4279 Avenida Corrientes, BA. Under severe pressure from the Brits, CCL identified the beneficiary as "Alberto Portillo Lopez". No further details available due to Argentine Banking Secrecy Law. However, Lorimer was able to learn that a subsidiary account was also opened in BNA branch in El Calafate, Santa Cruz Province, Argentine Patagonia. We have asked the British Treasury not to attempt to block this transfer. We assume that this is Stern and that he is on the move south. If you succeed in extracting him, the Brits will want to prosecute him first, but we can deal with that all later. First, follow the money trail urgently and report back ASAP. Regards, Baker"

"Bingo", Wytham thought, "the penny has dropped! My God, Stern is here. He's somewhere in Buenos Aires right now!"

Wytham almost ran down the corridor to Brooks' office. "Dick" he said, interrupting the CIO's first cup of coffee for the day, "how fast can you reassemble the men?"

"Why? What's up, Chris?" Brooks replied, startled.

"It's him. It's Stern. We think that he's here in BA right now! He set up accounts yesterday with BNA's Almagro Branch over on Avenida Corrientes. Director Baker emailed me all of the details overnight. The money transfer in from the Cayman Islands bank is set for this morning. What time do banks open here?"

"10:00 AM, as usual."

"That gives us time to set up a stakeout and extraction operation. Let's get moving. Do we have a safe house to take him to once we snatch him? Can we arrange military or private transport to get him quickly back to Washington?"

"Hang on, Chris! Let's get the team together and in place first. You can use one of the embassy's Chevy vans as your "eye" vehicle. We can have the stakeout in place just before the bank opens. But what about the country risk for us? What if the Argentine police get involved, even if accidentally?"

"There's always that chance, Dick, but I still think we can pull it off without incident. There's enough street crime here already to keep them busy. They would probably see it as just another kidnapping of a western businessman for ransom. That's really very common here. Anyway, we'll have to take our chances. We're pretty damn good at pulling off these type of operations without incident."

"OK then, I'll get it all organized. Be ready to brief the men in half an hour and then to leave in the van at 9:15, OK?"

"Thanks. By the way, no 'suits', please. I want these guys to look like locals. None of them should arouse any undue suspicion. We'll post one out front and two across the street. I'll tell them to stay in motion, not to loiter. They should be packing concealed side arms just in case, but we want Stern alive. And, oh yeah, change the plates on the van to local ones. We sure as hell don't want to go out there with diplomatic tags."

"Got it all, Chris. I'll see you in 15 minutes in the downstairs briefing room."

IX

Friday, September 21st, 2012, Buenos Aires, Argentina, 09:30, GMT -4

Albert's last morning in the Argentine capital was a busy one. After breakfast he checked out of the Hilton, leaving his bag with the concierge to collect later that morning. The night before he had logged into his Cayman Islands bank account from the hotel's business center. He had given the necessary instructions to make the initial wire transfer to BNA in the name of "Alberto Portillo Lopez". Naturally, the Cayman Islands bank would not ask any questions.

Albert first headed for the main Aerolinas Argentinas office on Avenida Leandro N. Alem to buy a one-way ticket to El Calafate. The flight would leave from the domestic airport, called "Aeroparque" by the locals. It was very conveniently located, just 20 minutes away from the Hilton by taxi.

The flight would depart at 14:48 that afternoon, arriving in El Calafate about 4 hours later. The lines were long at the ticket office and the service was dismal. It took an inordinate amount of time for Albert finally to purchase his ticket.

Looking at his watch as he left, he realized that he couldn't make his planned stop at BNA to pick up his documentation or he would miss his flight. So he made an urgent call to the manager and arranged for an express motorcycle courier to deliver it all to the concierge desk at the Hilton in half an hour.

Satisfied, Albert headed back to the Hilton by cab. The traffic was terrible and it took almost 45 minutes. There he signed for and collected his package from the concierge desk. It contained his checkbook, ATM card and all other documents relating to his new accounts with BNA. The transfer of funds had been success-fully completed and everything was in order. Well satisfied, he recovered his bag from the left luggage room and then asked the doorman to hail him another cab to take him straight to the Aeroparque.

Albert planned to spend the night in El Calafate. The morning after he would seek out real estate agents to inquire about available properties in Santa Cruz province, in the vicinity of El Chalten. He would be looking for an old *estancia* needing new ownership and capital investment. He would then hire a taxi for the scenic, five hour ride to El Chalten, where he had booked into the comfortable Hostelaria el Puma for an indefinite stay.

On the way to the airport, Albert did some thinking about where he stood in his tumultuous life. He could only make some reasonable assumptions.

The Iranians would appear to have lost track of him in Gene-va. Besides, they had since been dealt a deadly blow. They would no longer be dangerous adversaries. He believed that he had escaped the Swiss when he crossed over finally into France. The Americans and Brits knew that he had been in Chamonix as late as early August, but he hoped they believed that he had been killed along with Leah. The Israelis had gone silent since Leah's death, but he had a large sum of their money that they could be doggedly tracing. Thus he had tried hard to cover his tracks by using a number of different banks, multiple transfers and the secrecy of the international financial system.

Some nefarious forces had tracked him to Amsterdam, but he had dealt with them as well. In the event that any of his pursuers would ever find out about his sea voyage to Argentina, the pirates had conveniently converted that into a dead end. In all, then,

Albert liked his chances for establishing his anonymous new life in Patagonia!

X

Friday, September 21st, 2012, US Embassy, Buenos Aires, Argentina, 18:00, GMT -4

A very frustrated Chris Wytham sat at his desk in the embassy's guest office. He and his extraction team had spent most of the day before, unobserved, waiting outside of the Almagro branch of BNA. No one even vaguely resembling any of the many iden-tisketches they had of Albert Stern had either entered or left the bank. It was now obvious to Wytham that Stern had already made arrangements the day before to access the $2 million that was to have been transferred in overnight from his Cayman Islands account.

In front of Wytham on the bare desk was the file he had me-ticulously assembled over five months on Albert Stern. Here was a man with whom Wytham had been in two different cities. But he still had never seen him. Stern was either very skillful, very lucky, or a bit of both. He was a real chameleon, with his ever-changing identities. Wytham's *forte* was personality profiling. He had been right many times so far about Stern's likely motives and moves. But could he get it right just one more time, he wondered?

Why Argentina, Wytham thought? What thread in Stern's past would draw him here? Obviously neither Europe nor North America would any longer be safe havens for him. And with nuclear fallout settling on Asia, that would have been both a poor and ironic choice. So South America made sense. But, still, why Argentina in particular?

Wytham knew that Stern's only real recreational pastime was mountaineering. He had been an ardent and accomplished climber in his youth, especially while he was at Cambridge. Wasn't it an old Cambridge climbing buddy that he had contacted when he was first in difficulty in London? Hadn't he chosen to hide the Viking sands in one of his old climbing haunts, Chamonix? And then he had escaped the deadly drone like a deft mountain *chamois*. Instinct told Wytham that Stern would be heading for a mountain stronghold somewhere.

The Andes stretched the full western length of South America. Some of their most prominent peaks were in Argentina. Wytham poured over a map of the high Andean *cordilla*. El Calafate was the tourist center of Santa Cruz province in Argentine Patagonia. Stern had chosen to open a subsidiary BNA account there. Clearly he was headed in that direction. Where to exactly?

The detailed map revealed a small town set hard against the high walls of the Andean *massif*, just east of the Chilean border. Around it, in an impressive *cirque,* were some of the most famous granite spires of Patagonia. It rested just below the massive Southern Icecap. Bounded by behemoth glaciers, swift running rivers and deep glacial lakes, it was a Patagonian climber's heaven. The isolated little town was called El Chalten.

The name jogged something in Wytham's memory. In the file there was a note about how the Cambridge University Mountaineering Club had sent an exploratory expedition there in1993. It had done reconnaissance of possible new climbing routes on some of the granite pinnacles that formed subsidiary peaks to the mighty Mt. Fitzroy. The President of the Club then had been Albert Stern. He had organized and led his colleagues to El

Chalten for a two week climbing sojourn at Christmas break. So Stern knew the little town already. Given his predilections, it would probably be drawing him back now like a magnet.

Wytham both hoped and expected that Stern's complex and sometimes contradictory personality ultimately would give him away. He was both secretive and cautious, but, equally, sometimes vain and reckless. For the most part he had managed to keep a very low profile while, occasionally, doing outrageous things. He obviously had little regard for human life, having already been responsible for innumerable deaths.

But Wytham knew a good deal about this sort of person. Stern was not a deliberate or premeditative killer. Rather, he seemed neither to know nor care about the consequences of his actions. He was solely focused on self-preservation and achieving his desired ends. His personality was heavily sociopathic and paranoid. So he would be cautious and secretive, but inclined to make an occasional careless slip in pursuit of his monomaniacal objectives. All Wytham needed was for Stern to make one more such slip for the seasoned hunter to snare his prey.

Stern was also quite wealthy now. He had a bundle of money from the Israelis. He had hidden it carefully, but he had already tipped his hand that he would use a significant amount of it in Argentina. It was to be at least $2 million to start.

"What would he do with such a large sum in a little hamlet like El Chalten?", Wytham wondered. He could buy the whole town if he wished! But he was too smart to make a big, overt splash. No, he would be cautious, but very self-serving. *Senor Alberto Portillo Lopez* would want to live clandestinely, but well. He would buy himself a nice property, well out of the town center. In Los Glaciares National Park, for example. An old *estancia*, perhaps? Someplace where he could monitor and control his perimeters. Surely there were a number of such places readily available, suitable for renovation and modernization. Stern would then be an unnoticed but substantial presence in the area that he loved.

Wytham's instructions from Baker had been clear enough. Get Stern at all costs. Stay there as long as it took. Expect no help from the Argentines, but probably no hindrances either. While there was no extradition treaty in place with Argentina, it was tacitly understood at the highest levels of government that if Stern were truly to be found there, the Argentine authorities would look the other way if he were to meet with an unfortunate accident. That was exactly what Wytham had in mind for him.

Finally ready to wrap up after a long and fruitless day, Wytham resolved that he would take the next morning's flight to El Calafate. There he would outfit himself as a climber and head on to El Chalten.

It was a hunch, of course, but one he believed was well thought out. He would make discreet inquiries about any new arrivals in this small, tight community. Mingling in the bars and hostels amongst the climbing brotherhood, he would keep a very open ear for local gossip. It might take considerable time, but he believed that his years of experience would guide him eventually to his quarry. If Stern were indeed there, he would patiently hunt him down and then quietly kill him. Those were Wytham's orders, originating from the President himself.

After all of the devastation and misery Stern had caused, he could never ever be allowed to get away completely free. Wytham knew that he owed it to himself and to the world to close this account forever.

EPILOGUE

"The supreme irony of life is that no one ever gets out of it alive."

I

Monday & Tuesday, October 22nd and 23rd , 2012, El Chalten, Patagonia, Argentina

This haphazard little town of about 1,000 hearty souls living at the foot of the imposing, granite *massifs* of Mt. FitzRoy and Cerro Torre was abuzz with rumors. In the few bars and *asadors* lining the unpaved, rutted, muddy main street, locals mingled with foreign climbers over liters of iced Quilmes beer, gossiping about the still unconfirmed news.

If it was true, it would be a big development in the otherwise quiet life of this small, remote community, nestled in a deep glacial valley at the foot of the Andes. There had been persistent talk of the arrival of a mysterious new inhabitant who had bought the vast, old, run-down *Estancia Huemul*, on the far bank of the Rio de las Vueltas, for cash. Some said that he was a wealthy Chilean; others thought that he might be an Iberian European. No one had actually seen him, though, and the absentee former owners of the *estancia* were certainly not talking.

Life in this remote corner of Argentine Patagonia was hard. The summer was short and the winter was cold and cruel. But the natural setting was incomparable. Any communications with the outside world were sparse. The nearest airport was 214 kilometers away in the town of El Calafate. Roads in to El Chalten were unpaved stretches of dust and fine glacial stone, leading straight as dies across the empty vastness of Patagonia. During the long winter they were often impassible. It was a perfect place permanently to escape from the world's prying eyes.

The locals knew the group of regular climbers well. They were a predictable corps of mountaineering daredevils who returned each climbing season to challenge the airy granite heights of the Fitzroy *massif*. So they all noticed a new face amongst them, frequenting the bars and restaurants where the polyglot climbing brotherhood mixed and mingled in the evenings.

He had booked into a local hostel, popular with the international climbing community. The stranger was tall, muscularly wiry and well outfitted in the latest technical climbing apparel. He asked knowledgeable questions about local climbing conditions and routes. But most of all, he seemed to be full of questions about the new *patron* of *Estancia Huemul*. There was nothing much that anyone could tell him, though, on that topic. The *patron* had been mostly invisible so far.

The stranger asked frequently if anyone had ever seen the *patron* of *Estancia Huemul*. "No", most answered, but he was reputed to be a climber of some note. Rumor was that he was about to attempt a daring, early-season ascent of the treacherous Compressor Route on Cerro Torre with a local guide from *Expediciones Exupery*. It was thought that they would set out in the next few days, if the ever-changeable Patagonian weather held up.

This seemed noticeably to peak the interest of the inquisitive stranger. Could this be the one slip by Stern that Wytham needed? But no one could confirm the plans for sure. The *patron* was a very secretive man.

II

At the main house of the rambling, old *estancia* a lone gaucho tended the roaring fire of *lenga* wood in the great room. It was early morning and the new *patron* was just awakening in the master bedroom.

"He's an odd one", the old gaucho thought, "very secretive and private." He was paranoid about who might come to his *estancia*. He demanded that the gauchos give him plenty of warning if any strangers approached. Yet he seemed a confident *hombre*, well in control.

"Carlos", a voice called from the master suite, "has Cristian come? We must set out very early today!"

"No, *Senor* Alberto, no sign of him yet. But it's only 6:00 AM."

The plan was for the *patron* to hike 15 kilometers with his guide to Thorwood Camp, just below Lago Torre and the Torre Glacier. Early the next morning they would set out to tackle the challenging Compressor Route up the treacherous granite and ice tower called Cerro Torre.

By 7:00 Cristian and Albert were underway. As Albert walked along through the high Patagonian desert scrub, he was smugly content. He had prevailed, he thought, fully and completely! All of his troubles were now behind him. It had been very tough, but he had handled it masterfully. He was safe, secure and comfortably rich. No one would ever find him in this remote corner of the world, which he loved so dearly.

The night at Thorwood Camp was clear and cold. There was a coat of hoar frost on the tent and Albert's warm breath created rime ice patterns inside. He was warmly snuggled inside his fleece-lined down sleeping bag when Cristian came to wake him, just before dawn, for their early start up the glacier.

Albert was still groggy but quite excited. This was a climb of which he had dreamed of all his life! He dressed quickly in his technical climbing gear and walked out into the crystal clear Patagonian pre-dawn. It was very early spring in the southern hemisphere and the usually crowded, sprawling campsite was essentially deserted. Just a few other tents scattered randomly throughout the *lenga* forest. Albert was unaware that in one of them, a determined assassin waited patiently.

Cristian Rodrigues was a hardy young guide whom Albert had had hired from *Expediciones Exupery* in El Chalten. He didn't know him at all, but he had come well recommended. Wiry and strong, he was somewhat of a loner. But he knew the route up the perilous mountain wall quite well.

Albert felt strangely akin to this taciturn young man, but he couldn't quite put his finger on why. There were clearly some undefined commonalities shared between them. "We will make a good rope together", Albert thought.

In the bitter early morning chill they set out together across the Torre Glacier, crampons crunching into the thin snow crust coating the ancient blue ice below. At the foot of the airy rock wall they roped up and proceeded at first through easy ground, towards the Col of Hope. There the almost vertical Compressor Route began. Not far behind, hidden in the fading gloom, Chris Wytham doggedly shadowed them.

Reaching the Col, Cristian took the lead up the crenulated, rock wall, towering 5,000 vertical feet above them. Good solid granite, full of cracks into which to place protection for the dizzying climb ahead.

Several 60-foot rope lengths acrobatically up and they were well onto the wall, just beginning to feel the first warming rays of the sun as it rose through a translucent haze on the far eastern horizon.

Well-concealed in a gully below the Col, Chris Wytham took his M24 US Army sniper rifle out of his backpack and began to assemble it. He slotted the kevlar and graphite stock into the stainless steel barrel and snapped the 10X Leupold-Stewens M3 telescopic sight securely on its top. The M3's range was 1000 meters. It was a deadly accurate killing instrument. "The time has finally come to settle all scores", Wytham thought, as he carefully calibrated the rifle's sights for both windage and bullet drop.

He had been told by the Company to do the job quickly and discreetly. The Argentine authorities wouldn't extradite Albert, but they wouldn't raise any serious inquiries either in the event of any untoward "accident".

Holding the butt firmly against his shoulder, Wytham looked through the sight, targeting the juncture of the climbing rope and the piton securing it to the rock face. The heavy 7.62 mm slug would tear into the belay point, shattering its hold and sending Albert crashing down to his death on the glacier below. The guide would never hear the bullet strike, as the wind blasting the exposed wall would obliterate all other sounds. But as Wytham prepared to squeeze the trigger, he saw an unexpected drama unfolding high on the sheer rock cliffs above him.

Well up on the vertical wall, with Cristian leading the pitch, the rope had fouled on an erosion-sharpened, overhanging granite flake. Cristian had tapped a piton in place for protection when he had gained a stance on a precipitously narrow ledge. He had already signaled Albert to move up on his only lifeline, the taught rope.

It was too late now to try to free it with a pendulum motion from above. Cristian couldn't see Albert yet below, but he could feel the tension on the rope increase as Albert put all his weight on it to jumar up. The 60 feet of strong, nylon rope stretched under the stress, but failed to budge off the jagged flake. As the rope stretched and swayed, it repeatedly rubbed against the sharp edge, scraping relentlessly. In seconds the taught rope began to fray into severed strands at its critical stress point.

All of a sudden it was *déjà vu* for Albert. But this time he was the one in the unexpected race against certain death. Inevitably, but almost predictably, the tenuous piton belay above Cristian was torqued loose from its crack with a tremendous, destabilizing tug. The full weight of Albert was now in Cristian's hands. Could he hold Albert? Would he?

Looking up, Albert could now make out the strangely impassive face of his guide. Cristian was all that was holding him from the abyss.

Intuitively, Albert knew full well the likely outcome. Looking deeply into Cristian's dark eyes, he saw an emotionally empty well. They were unmistakably the eyes of a sociopath. They were his own eyes, he thought, devoid of any feelings whatsoever. He had unwittingly but fatalistically picked a clone of himself to guide him!

The precariousness of Cristian's own position would spur him into cold, calculated action, just as it had Albert, many years ago in Chamonix. To save himself, Cristian would have to let go of the rope. Remorselessly, he did so, at the exact same moment that it snapped in two at the frayed stress point.

As Albert fell 3,000 feet to his death on the glacier below, the remnants of the rope tumbled to Cristian's feet on the narrow ledge. He picked it up and put it into his rucksack. There would be many questions to answer in El Chalten later, but the tragic death of Cristian's client had clearly been an unfortunate climbing accident.

Printed in Great Britain
by Amazon

37816255R00148